ONLY THE LIVING ARE LOST

Also by Simon Strantzas

COLLECTIONS:
Beneath the Surface
Cold to the Touch
Nightingale Songs
Burnt Black Suns
Nothing Is Everything

CHAPBOOKS:
These Last Embers
Black Bequeathments

AS EDITOR:
Shadows Edge
Aickman's Heirs
Year's Best Weird Fiction, Volume 3 (with Michael Kelly)

ONLY THE LIVING ARE LOST

Simon Strantzas

Hippocampus Press

New York

Publication history: See p. 244.

Published by Hippocampus Press
P.O. Box 641, New York, NY 10156.
www.hippocampuspress.com

Hippocampus Press logo designed by Anastasia Damianakos.

First Edition
1 3 5 7 9 8 6 4 2

ISBN 978-1-61498-421-4 (paperback)
ISBN 978-1-61498-422-1 (ebook)

Contents

For my mother and father

The King of Stones

Judith regretted letting Rose talk her into the car trip. It was a huge mistake; she knew as soon as she agreed to it, but there was no snatching the words back. Not without causing a rift between them. So she swallowed her regret and assured herself it would be fine. How wrong could it go? Two days later she knew, silently fuming behind the wheel, stuck in a line of traffic with no visible end. And there were still four more days of vacation left ahead of them.

The worst part was Rose appeared unfazed. She sat in the passenger seat, feet on the dashboard so Judith couldn't help but be confronted by those gnarled, twisted toes as she looked through the windshield. Rose whistled and hummed as though the two of them were strolling through a park. As though it were a bright, lazy Sunday morning at home, and there were no troubles anywhere in the world.

Judith wanted to hit something. Instead, she sighed deeply.

Rose looked up from under her sun hat.

"Don't let it stress you out, love. This is part of the adventure. Just try to relax."

Judith took another deep breath. Held it. But was overwhelmed by how much longer they'd be stuck.

"Screw this," she said. "I'm getting off the highway."

"But we're in the middle of traffic. How—"

"Just watch me."

She signaled, more out of habit than courtesy, and forced her way to the farthest lane amid a chorus of honks and curses. There, she took the car onto the shoulder and put the pedal down. Rose pressed herself flat in terror while Judith navigated the slalom between concrete walls and other cars, inches of leeway on either side. If Rose said something, Judith couldn't hear it. Not within her haze of anger. And it wasn't until they reached the exit and left the traffic snarl behind that either of them could relax enough to speak.

"That was . . . dangerous."

"It all worked out. Nobody was hurt."

Rose's calm was slow to return.

"Do you even know where we are?"

Judith didn't. She hadn't made note of the exit, nor did she see any street signs that might help them find the exit on a map. But she had a quick plan.

"All we need to do is drive around the traffic. If we follow the highway using side streets and roads, eventually we'll get to a place where whatever caused the tangle is gone, and we can get back on. Meanwhile, we get to see some more small towns and scenery. And should we end up loving a place, we'll just stay over for a night. That's the whole point of this trip, isn't it? To explore?"

"Yes," Rose hedged. "Though I was hoping we'd reach Murtaugh before we stopped. This will put us behind schedule." She took a moment to ponder the idea. "Ah, who cares? Let's just go and see what happens!"

How had they ended up together? Judith was still amazed. They experienced the world so differently. Rose with her hippie skirts and positive thinking, Judith in her black Slits T-shirt and blurry tattoos; they didn't look as if they lived in the same universe, let alone knew each other. And yet when her ex-girlfriend Kim introduced them at a Bikini Kill show twenty years ago—back when Judith was writing music reviews for Idaho's second-most popular alt newspaper and Rose was irregularly publishing her photocopied zine—Judith was blinded by a light that pierced right through her darkness. Even if she didn't always appreciate Rose, part of her knew how much she needed her. It was impossible to put into words how much.

They drove along wooded streets and past untended fields, trying to keep the highway in view as regularly as possible. When it looked to be going north, they drove north. When it appeared to veer west, they too veered west. Sometimes they saw it snake through the woods for a stretch of a few miles, always backed up with red lights—sometimes not for a long while. And eventually they stopped seeing it altogether.

"Maybe the road curved without us realizing it?"

"It's okay, love," Rose said in the supportive voice that made Judith feel like an infant. "Should we stop and ask somebody for directions?"

"Who are we going to ask?"

Rose was optimistic they'd find someone, but Judith knew they hadn't seen a single person since exiting the highway. At first it was satisfying: not to be caught in the grinding traffic, driving freely without anyone in the way, made Judith feel liberated. Even stoplights seemed foreign. But after a time it grew uncomfortable. Nobody walked along the side of the road. No one passed them, driving in the opposite direction. Nobody at all.

Even stranger, there were no houses along the streets. No postboxes or signs. There was the road and nothing else, not even a place to refuel if needed.

It wasn't until half an hour passed that they saw proof they weren't alone. Rose was the one who spotted it because of course she was. She grew immediately excited, dancing in her seat, and urged Judith to pull over without explaining why. Judith did so, but only because the aimless driving was starting to affect her mood for the worse. Getting out of the car, if only for a moment to stretch her legs, might fill Judith's reserves for another hour.

But Rose had seen more. As soon as the car stopped, she leaped out and jogged to the edge of the road, beyond which the ground gently sloped away. She stood there, yellow sundress rippling in the breeze, and put her hand to the brim of her enormous hat.

"I knew it," she said, pointing into the distance. "Those are peach trees!"

*

They left the car behind as they walked downslope toward the orchard. There were almost two dozen trees, arranged in three rows, surrounded by thinning woods. Rose had grabbed her camera from the trunk, so Judith did her best to tolerate the occasional pauses for photographs of drifting pink blossoms and petals. The day was nearing its warmest and brightest, and Judith was starting to burn beneath her black T-shirt. She regretted not bringing a better pair of shoes for walking through grass and dirt, as she'd expected to spend most of the trip on sidewalks and pavement. Her military boots were too cumbersome, and the extra weight she'd put on since she and Rose had met wasn't helping. Besides, if Rose could handle the trek in a pair of open-toed sandals, then surely she could.

When they reached the peach trees, Rose laughed effervescently and held out her hands as though the petals were snowflakes. All Judith noticed were the fallen peaches littering the ground. Every footstep was precariously close to rot, and she wondered if that was supposed to mean something more than it did.

At the far end of the plot they made an unexpected discovery. Hidden from the road was one more peach tree. It had been felled at some point in the past, though it wasn't clear by what. It was much larger than the others, yet they remained upright while it lay on its side, not just toppled but uprooted as well.

"This thing is huge," Rose said. "I can't even tell how tall it was."

She paused, taking the sight in, before excitedly adding, "Get a photo of me with it!"

Judith accepted the camera begrudgingly. Waved her onward.

"I guess go to the uprooted end. It will probably be more interesting."

"But you won't see how tall the tree is," Rose said, pouting from beneath her wide brim.

Judith choked down her lack of interest.

"Maybe, but you'll see how thick it is. You can count the rings. Isn't that almost as good?"

For Rose, it was.

They took measured steps around the fallen tree, careful to avoid the crown's dried branches that jutted like spears toward them. Judith reached for the massive trunk for balance and was repulsed; it was like putting her hand on a decaying wet sponge. When the two of them reached the foot of the tree, the sight was astonishing. The roots pulled from the ground were splayed like dozens of fingers, twisted and woven into gnarled knots and patterns. Untold years of weather had stripped away any loose dirt, leaving plenty of room for the spiders and insects to build permanent homes.

"What is that?" Rose asked. Judith peered around the tangled roots.

It was a small cast-iron pot, worn and weathered, sitting knee-high on a slice of tree stump. Around it the ground had been trodden down to the dirt, and there were two larger indentations that couldn't have been footprints. Judith thought they might have been made by someone's knees.

The pot appeared to be filled with black peach stones, each wrinkled and hard. Judith imagined whoever harvested the peaches would eat one on occasion, but it was baffling why they would bother saving the stones.

"Whoa . . ." Rose said, staring into the fallen tree's roots.

Judith turned and was equally dumbstruck.

The roots had clearly grown randomly and naturally, but nevertheless they'd miraculously woven into an illusion that could be seen only when standing directly in front of the pot. The way they bent and twisted created the illusion of a man seated with eyes closed, his beard twisted into tendrils. The image was rough and gnarled, but there was no mistaking what it was. Judith stepped closer, the better to examine how the trick worked, but as she did so the figure returned to being a shapeless collection of roots. A step back allowed the illusion to regain its shape.

"That's the most incredible thing I've ever seen," Rose said. Even Judith had to agree. "Take the photo so I can show everybody when we get home. No one's going to believe it!"

She bounded in front of the trunk, then straightened her sundress and adjusted her hat so her face found the light.

Rose's hair caught the sun and wouldn't let it go, a corona enveloping her like a halo. Judith was breathless when she saw it—a deep and sudden remembrance of how much she truly loved her. Despite the irritations and minor disagreements, she was lucky to be with her. Judith was so overwhelmed she nearly forgot to raise the camera, and when she did the lens captured the waves emanating from Rose like something by Vermeer. What the camera didn't capture, however, was the illusion of the rooted man. Even when Judith knelt down beside the pot or tried different angles, the results were the same. The camera saw Rose, but could not see him.

"Photos flatten everything," Rose eventually said, as though the words were meant to comfort Judith, not mollify her. But it didn't help; Judith's inability to capture the illusion was too frustrating. "It's probably better this way. More special. You and I will remember this moment even if we don't have any pictures."

"I'm sure we will," Judith said, deciding she no longer cared. "We should probably go now. Find the highway before we lose more of the day."

"Okay," Rose said. "Just let me do one thing."

While Judith waited, Rose kicked at the rotten peaches in the dirt, looking through their scattered remains. When she found a suitably dark stone, she picked it up and rubbed it between her hands to flay any remaining flesh, then walked to the pot, knelt down in the worn spots, and laced her fingers together as if in prayer, the stone between her palms. She whispered something into her hands before dropping the stone into the pot. She then stood and let her dress fall back to her feet.

"For luck," she said.

Judith rolled her eyes.

*

The return journey to the car was worse because they walked uphill into the sun. Rose still had boundless energy, taking more photographs of the peach trees and their blossoms, while Judith trudged behind wishing they'd never left the house. She couldn't help but wonder where they'd be now if they hadn't taken that off-ramp. Probably already in Murtaugh, sipping a drink on a patio.

"Hey, someone else has pulled over," Rose said, and Judith looked up to see a small truck parked next to theirs. It was old, a pale shade of blue, and two silhouetted people stood on the edge of the road looking out over it. Judith couldn't get a clear look at the pair with the sun at their backs, but she suspected they were an older couple by the shape of their shadows.

"I bet they saw the peach trees and stopped, too," Rose said. "Those blossoms really are beautiful. Where do you think they're headed?"

"Does it matter?" Judith said. "It's not like we're going to see them again anyway."

Rose stopped, slumped her shoulders, and turned to face Judith. The look on her face was unexpectedly halting.

"Why do you have to be like that?"

"Like what?"

"Like—like you are. Always so negative about everything. Don't you care about me?"

"What? Of course I do."

"It affects me, you know. I try to not let it. I try to be cheerful for the both of us. I try to keep us happy. But you make it so hard sometimes. It's like you're trying to ruin things. I feel like—like—like you're emitting bad vibes or something. All this negative energy radiating from you that I constantly absorb, and I don't know how much longer I can do it. Do you get what I'm saying? I don't know how much more I can take on."

Judith didn't know what to say. The shock of Rose's confession was disorienting, and her first instinct was to question what she'd done wrong. But she hadn't done anything. She wasn't at fault.

"I don't know what you're talking about. I'm not being negative. I'm just being me. This is who I've always been. You used to tell me you liked that about me. That I wasn't fake."

"It's not about being real or fake. It's about not treating me like your emotional punching bag."

"I really think you're blowing this out of proportion."

That was too much. Rose sputtered, threw up her hands, and stormed off toward the car. Judith felt irritated; the couple on the road probably saw the whole exchange and was judging them.

She let Rose get a minute or two ahead before following. A short break would help, she thought. Let Rose cool off and regain some perspective. When Rose got nearer the car, Judith watched her wave at the couple who were standing there, though Judith wasn't sure if they returned the gesture.

*

Judith woke in the dark, not sure where she was. Opening her eyes made her head hurt, an ache that spread from the base of her neck forward, and when she tried to reach up to feel what happened she discovered she couldn't; her hands had been bound. But that made no sense. And why was it so hard to think?

Her last memory was of sweating through her shirt by the time she reached the road. Rose had been speaking to the strange couple, two women somewhere in their forties or fifties, dressed in ill-fitting clothes and looking slumped and miserable. She babbled, not giving them the chance to talk, while Judith continued to the car, having no interest in meeting strangers, not when she was already upset. Why had they chosen to crowd her and Rose instead of driving an extra few minutes up the road? The orchard had to be visible from elsewhere. Or if not, there was probably another. Orchards aren't planted in isolation. Judith had popped open the trunk and forcefully pushed aside Rose's bags to get to her own. There was another shirt in there, an extra she brought in case of emergency. The last thing she remembered was turning her back on Rose and the nameless couple to find it.

Where was she? Indoors, in a room that was dark, but not without some light coming through a window. Each blink was painful, but she forced herself to ignore it. Judging by the color of light, it had to be late afternoon, which meant she'd lost a few hours. She tried again to pull her arms free, but they were tied behind her back. Maybe with coarse rope, like something used on a farm. The air had that kind of smell, too. Earthy, mixed with dust and manure. And peaches. She smelled peaches. The chair she was seated on was hardbacked, and in the gloom she made out shelves around her. On the other side of the room was a steel sink beside a stack of crates. It was some sort of storage room.

Where was Rose?

If they hurt Rose . . .

She couldn't let herself think about it. Focus on the immediate. Her hands were tied, but her legs weren't. Could she somehow stand? Maybe get to a shelf and find something to cut herself free? She tried kicking out, but the chair wouldn't budge. She tried planting her feet on the floor and leaning, but the ropes were too tight; she couldn't get enough leverage. Fits of struggling didn't loosen anything. They just tired her out.

The door opened before she could do more. Two middle-aged women walked in, stooped with dark scarves wrapped around their heads. Judith couldn't tell if they were the women from the road. She couldn't remember what those women looked like.

"Where am I? What's going on? Where's Rose?"

Her own voice was so loud it made her head throb. But the women didn't respond. The one with a lower lip that extended in a permanent pout filled a bucket in the sink while the other, round-faced with gray wisps of hair protruding from under her scarf, took hold of Judith's face and inspected it from different angles. Judith considered trying to bite the woman or just spit at her, but with her hands tied she feared how vulnerable she was.

Once satisfied, the woman shuffled back to the door and opened it for a third woman to enter. This one was stern and lean, her hair tied up and as close to silver as Judith had ever seen. The new woman approached Judith and said nothing. Instead, she bent close, nostrils flared, and inhaled deeply. She ran her finger along the side of Judith's face and scowled. Shook her head. Stood up. The round-faced woman reappeared, accompanied by the pouting woman who was carrying the bucket. The silver-haired woman pointed at Judith, then left the room.

"Please, tell me what's going on," Judith implored, but there was no suggestion of understanding. Rather than answer her, the pouting woman set down the bucket and lifted out a sopping rag. She twisted out the water. The round-faced woman's arms dropped on Judith's shoulders, pinning her down. Judith screamed, but they disregarded her as they scrubbed her clean.

*

They led her outside, still bound by coarse ropes. The sun had already ducked behind the horizon, but there was still enough light for Judith to see where she was. A small village formed by no more than a dozen hand-built ramshackle houses. The inhabitants of those houses stood in their mismatched clothes, witnessing Judith's march into the on-coming night. The pair of haggard women had cleaned her and re-moved her T-shirt, her jeans and boots, dressing her instead in a long yellowed gown that felt gritty against her bare skin. They did not give her shoes.

She didn't know where they were taking her. No one would an-swer her pleas. The realization that she'd been trapped and would not survive didn't escape her, but she struggled to keep from thinking about it. That ended, however, once she was in open air, being stared at by dozens of scrutinizing eyes. The fear took hold faster than she could contain it.

"Rose!" she screamed. "Where are you, Rose? Rose!"

The villagers looked at one another, aghast. But Judith couldn't stop screaming. It went on and on and did not cease until her pouting captor struck her hard across the face. Judith shut up immediately from shock. The woman appeared shaken, too, unsteady, while her partner stared with wide eyes. The rest of the villagers looked shocked as well, some of them mouthing their confusion. Some of those looks then shifted toward anger.

The grunts and chirps from the villagers drowned out Judith's cries. They ran toward her, a wave of unwashed people dressed in patched clothes, and she struggled to escape. But when the villagers descended, it wasn't on her but on the pouting woman.

The woman didn't try to run or protect herself. She stood stoically as they arrived, unmoved by fear or regret. When their punches and kicks landed, she said nothing. There was no sound except of meat pounded and bones broken. The villagers tore at the woman in silence while Judith, unable to watch without wanting to scream, was led away by the round-faced woman and another, taller woman with graying black hair and pinched eyes.

Behind Judith the bloodthirsty attack did not slow or stop. When they loaded her into a rusty and puttering truck filled with crates of peaches, she could not bring herself to look back. If that was what happened to one of their own, what might happen to her? To Rose? It was too painful to contemplate.

No one spoke to her in the truck. No one answered her questions. She struggled against the hands that pinned down her arms, but couldn't shake them free. And if she could, so what? There would be nothing she could do. Nowhere she could go. She had no option but to sit there and tolerate the stench of sickeningly sweet peaches while she conserved her strength in hopes an opportunity would present itself. Were she younger, were it the days before she met Rose, when she attended rallies and raves, the anger and aggression would have carried her through. When she was all wired muscle and attitude. But she'd grown older, less interested in changing the world, and become too soft and weak, too unobservant. And because of that, she'd lost both herself and Rose.

The truck pulled over to the side of the road. The sky was an impenetrable black: devoid of stars, devoid of light. Judith didn't even see the reflection of the taillights ahead until she was dragged from the truck. They looked familiar, but it took a moment to realize why. They belonged to her car. Hers and Rose's. Its trunk was open.

In the distance a group of torches burned. The round-faced woman and her tall partner yanked Judith again, directing her down the slope and toward the distant flames made smaller still by the vast darkness.

Upturned roots and branches, fallen brambles and pebbles, dug into and scratched her bare feet. This would be her end. She knew it. So much time fighting, so many things done wrong. And for what? To lead her to this moment? She'd carried so much hate and anger for so long, but it amounted to nothing in the end. It made no difference. It made nothing better.

The air stank sour of rotten fruit, and Judith couldn't keep from stumbling over the uneven ground. But the two women would not be slowed; each time Judith tripped, they lifted her and pushed her forward. Even when she hesitated, even when she fell, scraping her face on something she couldn't see, they pressed her on toward the flames.

And when she was finally pushed through the penumbrae and into the light, the crowd of villagers was revealed. Some were dressed in gowns similar to hers, both women and men, shoeless, hands together in supplication. Others were dressed as they'd been in the village, in old worn clothes, unwashed and unrepaired. She saw a man with a graying beard wearing a shirt that looked familiar, like one of hers. It had been rolled up in her suitcase, left in the trunk of the car. Judith knew what that meant and wanted to scream.

But didn't. Instead, she stopped, powerless to speak. The crowd of villagers had parted. And in their parting Rose was revealed, feet torn and bloodied, face bruised and reddened from her own hard scrubbing.

Judith let out a throaty chirp when she tried to call Rose's name. Yet Rose heard it, and her eyes alighted with hope and love and terror. Judith struggled to run to her but was held in place. The distance between them insurmountable.

Judith lashed out, but couldn't connect with anyone. The cast-iron pot waited before the fallen tree; the stump she'd seen earlier was gone, replaced by a circle of misshapen bricks and a fire. The pot hung above it from a metal tripod, the stones inside dulled by the heat.

"What do you want?" Judith demanded. "Why are you doing this to us?" And still there was no answer.

But some faces turned to her. Some opened their mouths and made a horrible wet clucking. And Judith understood with horror why the villagers had been so silent. Behind their cracked lips, behind their decaying teeth, their tongues were gone. Cut out. Only stumps of dark flesh that rolled and convulsed in the firelight.

"Judith!" Rose yelled as she struggled to escape. "I love you, Judith," she said, and began to weep.

"Let her go!" Judith screamed. "Let her go! Oh my god, Rose. I love you! I love you so much! Let her go! Let her go right now!" She fought against the hands holding her. "I'm going to kill you! I'm going to kill you all! Let her the fuck go!"

Judith screamed and screamed, but no one cared.

They dragged Rose forward to the burning pot and forced her to her knees. She sobbed uncontrollably, tears and mucus streaming down her face, her speech unintelligible. Her captors took care to position her in the worn grooves as more villagers approached, grabbing hold of her arms, her legs, her shoulders. She cried out in pain, cried out for help. But Judith couldn't give it to her, no matter how much she struggled and cursed. The villagers continued, slipping a cracked wooden yoke around Rose's neck, twisting the oiled bolts tighter until her head couldn't move. Rose's tear-strewn face was pointed toward the splayed roots of the fallen tree, and she stared directly at the illusion she and Judith had discovered an impossible few hours earlier.

"What's going on?" she blubbered, the yoke forcing her jaw shut. "What are you doing?"

"Let her go!" was all Judith could say in her manic state. Over and over again.

The silver-haired woman appeared from the crowd, dressed in a long brown patchwork skirt that just covered her bare feet. Her long tresses had been let down, her eyes glistened, and in her mottled hands she held a long pair of metal tongs. She pointed at Rose with an unsteady hand and the villagers pulled back Rose's hair, away from her face.

Judith screamed, no longer capable of forming words, becoming a primal force of rage and terror. She felt it embody her, overwhelm her, become her; an enveloping and transforming red mist of pain. With her newfound power she wrenched with all her strength and tore an arm free from her captor. And, before anyone could stop her, she drove her elbow into the tall woman's face, breaking something, and tried to claw out the shorter woman's eyes. Villagers appeared suddenly, piling onto her, trapping her arm before it could do further damage. She roared with rage but couldn't prevent what was happening. Couldn't prevent herself from being subdued.

All the while, the woman standing over Rose wasn't distracted. She lifted the heavy tongs and placed them in the cast-iron pot. By the time Judith was immobilized, everyone had stopped to watch the silver-haired woman with reverence. Everyone except Rose, who continued to sob endlessly.

The stones shifted and popped until the woman removed the tongs, holding a smoldering black stone in their grip. The villagers uttered a sound in unison—an indescribable low-pitched drone as though they were attempting to sing—and the silver-haired woman placed the burning stone on Rose's forehead.

Rose's scream nearly shattered the world.

Judith screamed, too. Anger flowing as she watched the villagers push down on Rose, steadying her so the old woman could add another burning stone, then another. One by one the stones were placed in a circle around Rose's head while Judith cursed and sobbed impotently. Rose no longer cried, no longer moved as the stones embedded themselves in her melted flesh. Blood streamed down her unconscious face, soaking her gown as Judith continued to rage.

She screamed until she couldn't hold a breath any longer, screamed until her throat was raw and her limbs were weak. Until she could no longer fight against the villagers bearing down on her. Then, depleted, she collapsed in the grip of her captors. All strength and rage burned away. An empty shell.

But the villagers would not allow her to fall. They held her up, striking the sides of her face until her eyes opened, and made her watch as they lifted the unconscious Rose from where she knelt and brought her to the felled peach tree. They hoisted her into the tangle of roots, her arms spread wide, her legs crossed at the ankle. Blood soaked the top of her gown black.

They pitched Judith forward, dragged her to the cast-iron pot, forced her to kneel. Hanging before her was Rose, caught in the roots of the tree, the mirage of the bearded man behind her. It was too much to bear. Judith wished she could close her eyes, but couldn't. They were locked on Rose's drooping face.

The silver-haired woman approached, her arms spattered to the elbow with Rose's blood, dragging the long tongs behind her. She stood between the pot and the tree and looked at what remained of Judith. She cocked her head, then put her hand on the side of Judith's face. Judith recoiled, tried to pull away as the vestiges of herself fled. The woman waited until they were gone before stroking Judith's face.

When she was done, she stood and inserted the tongs again into the burning pot. Judith did not move, but the villagers pinned her down nonetheless. Pinned her as the woman removed another wrinkled black stone. Judith's body tremored, but she was unaware of it.

And the woman dropped the stone onto the ground.

She held out her hand. A villager rushed to her side and handed her a full waterskin. She uncorked it and spilled the contents over the black stone. It sizzled under the stream, and when it stopped the women bent and fished the stone from the mud. She stood and, without brushing away the dirt and debris, placed it in her mouth.

There was a moment of silence before the first tremor traveled across her body. Then there was a second, forewarning the seizure that quickly followed. The woman made a choking sound, like something being pulled from the muck, and pointed toward Rose's limp body. Blood poured out of the silver-haired woman's open mouth and over her chin, followed by the squirm of a shriveled black tongue. It danced across her lips as the woman croaked a single word.

"Watch."

And Judith watched, too beaten and numb to resist. She watched Rose hanging there, her body limp, her chest heaving with troubled breaths. And as she watched she thought of nothing. Not of why this was happening. Not of the last thing she'd said to Rose. Not of all the times she'd been irritated, impatient, or angry with her. Not of all the times she wished she were somewhere else. She thought of nothing. Nothing but of Rose and how she'd failed her.

Judith wanted to speak, but there were no words.

Suddenly, Rose's unconscious body jerked. The villagers dropped to their knees. Bowed their heads.

But not Judith. She was transfixed.

Rose jerked again, and every limb went rigid at once. They stretched out from beneath her filthy gown like sticks. Her eyes opened wide. So wide. So very, very wide. As though she were trying to see everything at once.

"Oh my god!" she screamed. "Oh my god!

"I can—all of—oh my god!

"All the secrets. All the secrets and the pains. Oh my god, I can feel them. I can see them. Oh my god.

"They're in me. Under my skin. I'm overflowing. I'm transforming.

"Oh my god. Look at me!

"Look at me now!"

She convulsed, limbs flailing, eyes rolling white. And the roots of the dead tree began to tremble, to creak. To move. They curled toward the hanging Rose, reached across and wrapped around her, one at a time. Over and over, constricting until they enveloped her, pulled her in. Took her and her crown of thorns away from this world.

"The King needs his Queen," the silver-haired woman croaked as she stood, one tired leg after the other. "And she is a vessel primed."

The woman bent down and placed something on the ground in front of Judith. Then stood and touched the kneeling woman's face.

"From their union might sweet fruit spill."

With that, the woman spit the bloodied stone back into the pot.

*

Judith knelt in front of the fire and whispered. No one held her down any longer. No one had to. There was nowhere for her to go. With Rose gone there was nothing left. Just Judith and her memories of all she'd done wrong, of all the trouble she'd caused. She knelt where Rose had, a stream of words falling from her underbreath while the villagers stood in a circle, silent and patient.

It was her fault. She'd prepared Rose. Had been preparing her since the moment they met at that show, so many years before. Primed her to suffer, to take on what wasn't hers, until it bore her out, opened a hole that needed to be filled. Judith had prepared her unknowingly for this moment. To suffer their sins, to carry them away. To be taken below as some ancient payment, some ritualistic bargain. It was Judith's fault it happened. Judith's, and Judith's alone.

The knife the silver-haired woman left lay in front of her. Its handle carved from old wood, its blade curved and thin. It did not gleam in the dying firelight. It did nothing but wait for Judith as she whispered and moaned and tried to expel everything she'd seen, everything she'd done.

But she couldn't. She couldn't relieve herself of the burden. It weighed down on her, heavier and heavier. She couldn't breathe. Couldn't do anything but be crushed by it. She was going to die there, alone amid the peach trees. Alone in the dark of nowhere. And her anger would plant itself like a poisonous seed in the soil. Grow outward. Corrupt everything until there was nothing left to corrupt. Until it was all destroyed.

Unless she unburdened herself.

She rattled off her mistakes, listed her crimes, her sins; spoke each, one after the other, until her tongue carried them all.

Then she snatched up the knife.

The blade was sharp and quick and when she was done she took the writhing length of flesh that bore what she no longer could and dropped it into the black iron pot to cook and shrivel, harden and blacken. Become a stone condensed to pure sorrow. Another piece, another rune, to summon the twin bounties of harvest and forgiveness.

But forgiveness had a price. And sometimes that price demanded forgiveness of its own. Forgiveness no one else could grant. Not the King. Not his courtier. Not even his new Queen, the gift of a village to one so much older, adorned with the purest of crowns. Forgiveness that could only come from within.

Forgiveness like that required an impossible amount of strength.

Strength Judith did not have.

So instead of forgiveness, she gave away the only things she had left to give. Gave away her burdens and her pains. Offered them up to the King as so many had before, and as many would again. The act of letting them go filled her with relief impossible to express.

She no longer had the words.

In the Event of Death

I

There were more paperback books in my mother's house than I realized. Pocket-sized, well-thumbed, all with yellowed covers of swashbuckling men and bodiced damsels, they were lurid reminders of a habit that dated back forever. I knew they took up a single shelf, but not boxes beneath her stairs, or shelves in her garage, or crates in her attic. The house overflowed with them, spilling from every corner and nook. So many books, so intricate a reflection of her life, and her own struggles to escape.

"What are you going to do with them?" Wanda asked as I filled another box.

"I have no idea," I said.

"Do you think you'll sell them?"

I shook my head. "I don't know if I could."

The answer seemed to satisfy her, though I wondered if she understood what I meant. Then I wondered the same about myself.

It had been fewer than two days since my mother's death, but I had not yet had a chance to grieve. There were too many things that needed to be done, too many arrangements to be made, and only me to do them. Wanda helped as much as time allowed, but her job at the hospital was the only thing supporting us as I worked on my novel, and we couldn't afford her missing a single shift, not if we were to afford the funeral. I'd managed to put the bulk of the arrangements into place, but I needed to choose a dress for my mother to wear and I didn't feel strong enough alone.

I hadn't taken Wanda to the house before, afraid of letting her see where I'd grown up in case it altered the way she felt about me. I knew it made no sense, but there were so many complicated emotions stored within those walls that I failed to see how she could avoid being changed by it all. The house practically vibrated as we stood there.

Wanda walked from room to room, my mother's death transforming the place from house to museum, picking up and inspecting items as she did. Along the mantle was a series of photographs. Wanda studied them, then looked at me.

"Where's your father?"

I shrugged. It was a question I'd asked in different ways my entire life. My father died of some illness shortly before I was born, and my mother had nothing more to say about it. She had no photographs of him, never spoke his name or acknowledged he had existed, and yet it was clear that she had loved him dearly. I had once asked my Aunt Renee what had happened, but my question caused her to cross herself vehemently and scold me for not minding my own business. My mother had always been overly protective—her worry when I had terrible nightmares as a child only made them worse, and as a teenager I had to rebel before I could escape her smothering arms—so for years I believed there was some deep secret to his absence and her silence. As I grew older I quietly realized that sometimes there are wounds that never heal, and pressing only inflames them. I decided if it was easier for my mother to forget, I wasn't going to keep reminding her.

Wanda and I went through her closets slowly, looking for the right item. Had it been up to me I would have picked the first thing I found, but Wanda was more careful. She knew better what my mother liked, what she thought she looked her best in. I didn't argue, happy to have one burden lifted from me, though all the same worried that one less distraction meant my grief was one step closer.

As my wife pulled down a shoebox from the closet's top shelf, an envelope came loose and fluttered to the ground. She bent down and retrieved it. Reading the front, she frowned.

"It's addressed to you."

The envelope felt lifelessly thin, and printed beneath my name in my mother's hand was: TO BE OPENED IN THE EVENT OF MY

DEATH. In my mind's eye I traveled to the past to watch her carefully scripting those words, and the vision was too much to bear. It took a few minutes and my wife's arms around my neck before I was able to break the seal.

I don't know what I'd hoped to find. The letter was prefaced by a few painful words urging me not to cry or miss her, followed by a list of instructions letting me know where she kept her banking information, and how best to access matters of her estate. None of this surprised me: my mother had been a practical woman and remained so until the end. It was reassuring, in its own way. She concluded the list with two requests. The first was that her entire collection of paperbacks be delivered to Aunt Renee, who, despite how I might have felt about her, had been her closest friend since childhood; the second was that I never read the diary she kept in her nightstand drawer. To be certain, she wanted it buried with her.

Despite my hopes, there was nothing in the letter revealing the mystery of my father's death.

Behind me was the infamous nightstand. I had memories of tracing the patterns carved in its legs with my finger while my mother folded laundry or read one of her novels. It was a piece of furniture I knew very well, yet never once did I realize it had a drawer until I took a closer look. History makes us blind. History, and time.

I gently rocked the handle and slid the small drawer out. Inside was yet another paperback novel, *Lord Vanity,* bookmark halfway between its rich covers of scarlet and gold, and lying beneath it a small diary with a brown faux leather cover. Its pages secured with a flimsy lock.

"You aren't going to read it, are you?" Wanda asked me. The horror she felt was folded into her face.

"Of course not," I said, though I could not deny my curiosity. If my mother had written at all about my father, wouldn't it have been there? Part of me wanted to scour its pages, but the rest was terrified. I had spent so many years blanketed by her worry that I couldn't disobey her final wish, even if it meant forsaking the answers to all my questions.

Assuming they were answers I wouldn't be too frightened to read.

II

I pulled myself out of bed the next morning, the funeral still a day away, and drove an hour to Maple to see Aunt Renee. I went alone, Wanda deciding she'd rather nurse her unhappiness in front of a piano than endure another painful visit. Instead, boxes of old paperbacks kept me company, filling the car with a musty tangy odor. It smelled of the past.

I had other motives for the trip beyond delivering the boxes, most of them centering on the revelation of my mother's diary. It raised questions I hoped my aunt could answer.

It took time for Aunt Renee to answer her door, and when she did her face was puffed and tear-streaked. She didn't smile.

"Oh, it's you," she said, and wandered off. I took that as invitation to follow.

My aunt's house was larger than both my mother's and my own, and yet felt cramped with all the items shelved along the walls and piled in the corners. I had never liked the place as a child: it was dark and oppressing, its strange atmosphere repellent. She rarely seemed to open her blinds, and the giant shrine to her savior that dominated the wall in the front room left me uneasy.

"This is it?" she asked, staring in the box of paperbacks I carried.

"The rest are in the car. She wanted you to have them."

She rummaged through the box.

"You didn't have to bring them today."

"No, I suppose not. But I thought I might as well. It gave me an excuse to come see how you were doing."

She snickered. "How do you *think* I am? How are *you?* Just peachy, I'd guess?"

I smiled as gently as I could.

"It's tough, but I'm doing a little better than I thought I'd be."

She made a disapproving noise but said nothing. Instead, she pulled books out of the box one at a time and set each on the table.

"Are you still writing your satanic stories?"

I looked down at my hands. The back of one carried tiny indentations, as though fingernails had been pressed into the soft flesh. The pale color slowly gave way to red; I tried rubbing away the discoloration with my thumb.

"They're only stories, Aunt Renee. They don't mean anything. Most of them aren't even trying to be scary. They're just about how people feel."

She looked up from the half-empty box and squinted.

"That's how the demons start. They make you think it's nothing at first, and maybe it is, but once they get their talons in you they sink and sink." Her hands were up, fingers curled in shriveled claws and pressed against her chest. "Before you know it, you're doing demons' work on God's Earth for all eternity." She stopped and looked back into the box.

"Where's the diary?" she said.

I was glad for the change in topic.

"I was going to ask you about that. I didn't even know she had a diary until her note said so. But she asked me not to read it. Just to put it with her in the coffin. But what if it mentions my father? All I know about him was that he was sick, but not what he had or what he was like. I need answers, Aunt Renee, and this might be my only chance. Yet the note . . ."

"What's this about a note?" My aunt held out her free hand. "Let me see it."

"I—I don't have it with me," I stammered. "Why would you need to see it?"

"I should ask you the same thing. You don't need to see anything. Especially that diary. Bring it to me as well."

"Why? What are you going to do with it?"

"I'm going to burn it."

"What?"

I was horrified. Then her face transformed into a cauldron of hate and she seethed, "That diary—it's evil and must not be allowed to exist. I would have done it years ago if your mother told me she still had it."

"It's her diary," I said. "There's nothing evil about it."

"You're a fool. You can't possibly be so ignorant. Not when you are already doing *his* bidding. You need to wise up and take the Lord into your heart. He'll help you vanquish the evil."

I didn't know how to respond.

"Aunt Renee, I don't want to disrespect your beliefs, but—"

"You being here, in my house, disrespects them. You're family, and your mother has just passed, so I'm making an exception. But don't misunderstand—" Her voice became intensely quiet; I could feel it crawling up my spine. "—your mother may not have seen it in time but I do. You're your father's son. And I pray every night an angel will come and deliver you. It's been the angel of death twice before. Maybe you'll get lucky. The Lord works in mysterious ways."

Her words hung in the air. What she said, what she implied—I wanted to give her the benefit of the doubt, but as the seconds passed I realized she was right. I was being a fool.

"I'll leave the rest of the boxes, Aunt Renee, then I'm going. After the funeral, you won't have to worry about seeing me again."

My aunt's eyes betrayed her anger as she watched me unload the rest of the boxes from the trunk of my car and drop them in her front hallway. I did so silently, waiting for an apology even though I knew none would come. And she did not disappoint me. In fact, it wasn't until I was done and made the mistake of looking at her that she finally spoke.

"Get out," she said. "Don't you ever bring your demons back here."

"Gladly," I said, storming toward the door. As I pulled my car out of her driveway I saw her on the porch. She looked withered under the bleached light.

"I'd pray for you," she called out after me. "But you don't deserve it."

III

My tongue was sour as I drove, a nauseating shiver of adrenaline bubbling beneath my skin. When I arrived home, my poor wife had to listen to my hatred erupt for nearly an hour, the red heat of it spewing out, and no matter how much I said or for how long it never seemed to end. It was unquenchable, and only my eventual exhaustion slowed me enough for her to interrupt.

"I found something," Wanda said. "While you were—while you were out. I found something in the boxes we brought back from you mother's. Though I'm not sure if this is the best time to show you."

"Show me," I said. "It couldn't make my day any worse."

"I don't know if *worse* is quite the word for it," she said, then opened up a dresser drawer and produced a stack of paper fastened with a blue elastic band. "I thought you'd want to see these, especially in light of your afternoon."

I took the pile from her and without removing the elastic flipped through the first few pages. When I realized what she'd found, I looked up. She nodded.

"They're poems. Look, they're dated. They were written sometime before you were born."

"Why didn't I know any of this? Why did she hide it from me?"

"I don't know, but Dan—"

"Do you think—" Everything rushed through my head; I couldn't keep my thoughts straight. "Was she embarrassed? Did my aunt say something to dissuade her? I bet—"

"Dan!"

She startled me and I stopped talking.

"Dan, before you do anything you should read some of them. Some of the poems."

"Why? What's wrong?"

"Nothing," she said, then paused. "Nothing's wrong. I just think you should read them."

I skimmed the first poem in the pile.

The word that came to mind was *nightmarish,* but in its truest sense. Reading her poetry was like reading a nightmare—an actual nightmare, transcribed. It lacked any discernible narrative, rather inundating me with corrupted images, flashes of that which lurked deep within my subconscious. Men in tailcoats and creatures with long tails slithered over one another. Words mixed and intertwined on the page in uncomfortable juxtaposition. It was unlike anything I'd ever seen, worse than the strangest weird fiction I'd ever encountered, and afterward it was unclear if what I remembered was real or a fevered dream. A dozen stories sprung to life in my inspired mind.

"What do you make of them?" Wanda asked. "Are they your mother's?"

"They have to be," I said, wiping my dry mouth. "I recognize her handwriting. But I don't understand why her poetry was such a secret."

Wanda was surprised.

"I think it's pretty obvious why she didn't show them to you or to anyone else. They're vile."

"What do you mean?"

"I saw your face. You know exactly what I mean."

I touched the ink on the page. Even it was beautiful.

"But what was wrong with them? Nothing vulgar or crass. Nothing profane, as far as I can see. I don't remember much beyond a few images, but they seemed like science fiction. Was there something about aliens? And maybe a name—Varshni, or something? I remember an old clock . . ."

Wanda wrapped her arms around herself.

"I don't like them, Dan. It's as simple as that. Get rid of them."

"But they're my mother's," I said, stunned I had to even say the words aloud. "I can't just—I mean won't just—"

She put up her hand.

"Just keep them in your office, then. Away from me."

That much I could promise.

IV

I stood by the door for an hour the next morning, dressed in my finest pinstriped suit, holding my mother's tiny diary. Behind me, my wife moved from room to room, dressing for the funeral. She was only a few feet away, while I was unmoored and untethered, drifting into the aether and away from the world I knew. Wherever I was going, nothing would be the same for me. And I wanted to cry over what I had lost, and because I was afraid of what was to come.

Wanda and I arrived at the funeral home early to say our goodbyes. My mother lay in her casket, but I only recognized her by fragments—the actual person I knew was gone; a wax stranger lay in her place. Wanda stood to the side while I whispered my final words, then touched the diary waiting in my jacket pocket. It wasn't much comfort.

I dried my damp eyes and turned to my wife, but found my aunt instead, standing in the middle of the room, her eyes bulging, her lips quivering. I didn't know if she was crying, laughing, or barely containing her disgust, and I didn't care. I knew only my own fury.

"What are you doing here?" I said.

"I've come to prevent you from making a serious mistake."

"What are you talking about?"

"The diary. What have you done with her diary?"

"It's none of your business."

She stalked toward me. She was smaller and frailer, yet descended like a fuming giant.

"I'm trying to help you, don't you see? I'm trying to save your soul."

"My soul doesn't need any saving. My soul is doing quite fine on its own."

She stopped and glared at me. Then noticed my wife.

"What's it like," she asked her, "being married to an idiot?"

"Hey!" I shouted. "You talk to me. Stay the hell away from her."

My aunt laughed.

"You have no idea what that book is, do you?" She shook her head. "I'd hoped you'd burned it and its sin from the world. I'd hoped you'd burned it and scattered the ashes. But I knew you were no different from him. I knew it as soon as I laid eyes on you. Your mother didn't listen, but I knew, and I protected her. Your father at least had malevolence behind his eyes. You? You've always had nothing. Maybe those evil secrets will fill you, but if we are all lucky it will be your funeral soon enough."

With that, she wrapped her black silk scarf around her neck and stormed out of the funeral home. She did not once turn to acknowledge me or my mother, the woman who had once called her sister. It was as if she were a stranger, and that was perhaps the most hateful thing she did on that day. She denied my mother one last goodbye before she left this plane. I'd had enough of my aunt and her zealotry and antics, and swore I would never intentionally set eyes on her again.

If I only had the strength.

V

The funeral had been more difficult that I'd anticipated, and the various pains offered me a clarity I could have happily done without. When Wanda and I arrived home, all I wanted was to take off my suit, pour myself the strongest drink we had, and sink into the couch. I needed to clear the thoughts that gathered in my head like storm clouds. Even with Wanda near, I was bereft, and in my distraction I realized the jacket I was trying to hang was too heavy. Something was in its pocket, something that was not my wallet, and as I freed it I felt my heart seize.

My mother's diary. In the commotion of my aunt's entrance and accusations, I'd forgotten that it was still in my pocket, that I hadn't put it in her casket, even as we dropped flowers onto her vault. Everything had been wiped from my mind as I was consumed by sadness and anger, but what I had done was unforgivable. My mistake was irreparable.

The guilt broke me. I became a recluse. For weeks I was unable to function without dwelling on my failure, on what it meant for my mother's journey beyond the veil. Wanda did her best to help me, but I rejected everything she said. I was inconsolable. When eventually she had to return to work, I was left alone to wallow in my private darkness. I knew intellectually she had no choice, but an irrational part of me could not forgive her abandonment. I treated her poorly when she came home at night, which over time caused her to return later and later in the evening.

If only I still had my writing, my one escape from life's torments, but it too evaporated in the shadow of my guilt. As days became weeks became more, my head filled with chaotic imagery—swirling star-studded vistas and cosmic turbulence—and those few sentences I managed to scribble down were senseless. My mind raced too fast and in too many directions to capture it all, and what was left were fragments strung illogically together, wholly indecipherable as soon as I set them down. Without writing, without my wife, without any anchor at all, I slipped further beneath the surface.

As time passed and I became less frequently sober, the voices that pushed in from the edges of my thoughts worked themselves deeper into my psyche. I could not forget my failure to bury the diary, but neither could I spend the rest of my life staring at it—not if I wanted to resist falling irrevocably into insanity. The idea crossed my mind to burn it, but I couldn't. I would be doing my aunt's bidding, and it would be like burning the last piece of my mother, and perhaps my only link to my father. I spent my time daydreaming what might be contained within the diary's pages, what secrets my mother had wanted to keep hidden. My aunt knew something, and it was so vile she could not contain herself around me. Who was my father? What had he done? I wanted so desperately to know.

It was only a matter of time before I could no longer resist the temptation. Between bouts of drinking I found myself holding the diary, running my hands over its worn covers, convincing myself I could feel heat radiating from it. When I finally broke the seal and cracked it open, when I finally saw my mother's name in her large schoolgirl hand, I felt vomitus—my body revolting over what I was about to do. I could have put the diary down easily, forgotten about it, left it behind and restarted and repaired my life. But instead I leafed through pages so well thumbed they were linen, looking for mention of my father.

Quickly I forgot my purpose and became lost in my mother's life. I had known her only as overly worried and overprotective, but I soon came to realize she had once been anything but. She had thrived on ill-considered risk in her youth, and was often joined by my equally adventurous Aunt Renee, not yet quite as angry or as fervorous as she would become. The revelations in the diary were so bizarre and unlikely I could barely believe them. Were they not in my mother's handwriting, likely I wouldn't have.

She was introduced to my father at a holiday picnic. By then she was bordering thirty and still not looking terribly hard for someone, yet he emerged nevertheless from what she called "a sea of Coke bottle glasses." She did not think much of him at the time—he was a quiet, aloof, attractive only in an inoffensive and average way, and was the opposite of every man or boy she'd ever dated. Even his speech was peculiar, as though he'd only read books from a hundred years earlier or more and yet had no idea how to pronounce most of the words. Strangely, instead of repelling her, she found it oddly charming and began seeing him despite Aunt Renee's jealous disapproval.

The honeymoon period of my parents' affair did not last long. Soon after they started spending time together my mother was subjected to a string of intense nightmares. She didn't elaborate, hinting only rarely about what they entailed. What was more concerning were the headaches and nosebleeds they caused. Her suffering was genuine, and the only balm was to start recording those terrifying visions. I recognized a lot of the exorcised images in the poems Wanda had found. As the frequency and intensity of my mother's nightmares grew, the sleepless nights and terrible thoughts ate away at her waking life.

Whatever their cause, my aunt took her seriously. She too had noticed peculiarities about the man, things that were not quite right. Like the way he seemed to forget how to use his hands, or stuttered when he spoke as though warming up an unused instrument. He did not recognize simple things such as streetlights, but his memory for what he encountered was eidetic. And yet he was only interested or aware of his surroundings when he stared into the night sky.

My aunt did not understand my mother's infatuation with him, and for the first time we agreed. My father sounded wholly undeserving of my mother's affection, and yet he remained in her life, despite how poor its quality had become. My mother fell ill and remained so for a very long time, the constant morass of nightmares destroying her sleep, preventing her from doing anything but shambling through the new house she and my father bought together. Then, without incitement, without reason, my mother admitted she'd become suspicious of who my father was. I skipped forward and back, trying to understand what she meant, but she did not mention it again. "He is not who he says," was the entirety of what she wrote, and even that she tried to scribble out.

With the next entry, her journal became consumed with poetry, foregoing the recording and documentation of her life. The poems were as strange and confusing as anything I'd read, made more so by their inchoate nature. They were prototypical pieces without sense of timeframe or inspiration. They simply existed in that no-man's-land of the past, the churning blood of her unconscious. But even jumbled and fragmented, when I read closer I was struck with a kind of terrified confusion. My mother clearly didn't realize what she was doing as she wrote those poems, but I knew. I knew because they were the same images I saw every time I sat in front of my keyboard. I was dreaming my mother's horrors, sharing her mindscape. And instinctively I knew we were not the only ones. Someone else haunted our mutual dreams. Someone else for whom they were not dreams at all.

VI

I found nothing more in my mother's diary. As abruptly as her poetry began, it stopped, and in its wake all she entered were the most perfunctory details of her life. My father became a ghost in the pages, never mentioned, though his presence was felt among the accounts of my mother's activities. His illness was fleetingly suggested during an account of my mother being at the hospital, no doubt near the time her pregnancy was discovered. Shortly thereafter an oblique apology was made about my aunt, but what had caused the falling out was unclear. Whatever it was, words were not needed to communicate its seriousness. Yet it didn't stop my aunt from visiting, as a short entry about going to tea soon followed. Even the date of my father's death was unclear. No mention of it was made before I reached the unexpected end of the diary, and on reviewing the preceding entries to see what I'd missed, I found only more questions. With my mother gone and her diary unresolved, there remained only one person who knew my father at all, one person who might answer those questions my mother did not want me to ask. As loath as I was to see Aunt Renee, I knew I had no other choice.

Sometime in the midst of my breakdown I'd received word from a distant cousin that my aunt was ill. She was confined to a bed in a hospital a few minutes from her house in Maple. After what happened at the funeral, I understood why she never reached out to let me know she was sick: no doubt she expected me to be glad, as though there were some divine justice to it all. She would have been right, but part of me understood that it was a horrible thing to feel. I telephoned Wanda with the news, but regretted it as soon as I heard the distance in her voice. Still, she urged me to go see my aunt.

"Dan, you have to. You'll regret it if you don't. She's family."

"Is she? I don't even know anymore."

"She's related enough. You need to put everything behind you and go. Maybe it's the fresh start you need."

I knew she was right. I needed to see Aunt Renee because she was not long for the world, and when she went the truth about my heritage, about the strange revelations in my mother's diary, would go with her. But I was also terrified about what she might say. I wasn't certain I could bear to hear it. But what choice was there? Wanda was right: I would never be able to move on until I spoke to her, and time was running out. I sobered up enough to drive to the hospital and park on the fifth floor of the garage. Then stayed in the car for thirty minutes, preparing myself.

The hospital had been built within the last decade, so unlike where my mother had suffered through her final days, it was clean and full of sunlight. My aunt's room was private, and flowers filled the window sill—as did crucifixes of various sizes, and a single image of Jesus in a golden frame. My aunt was asleep, snoring gently, her glasses askew on her head. On the tray table beside her sat a covered lunch, waiting for her to wake and eat. I pushed it aside then gently called her name.

"Aunt Renee, it's me. It's Daniel."

One eye creaked open, then the other. There was the wheeze of oxygen pumped into her nose. She carefully licked her lips.

"What are you doing here? You stink."

Her voice was little more than a slurred croak. I tried not to be reminded of my dying mother.

"I need to talk to you. I need to tell me about my father."

She closed her eyes and laughed—one hitch of her shoulders, her breath rattling. She winced immediately, but the smile didn't completely fade.

"You can't be saved. Get out. Go away."

"Aunt Renee, I read my mother's diary. I read it all."

To this, her rheumy eyes opened wider.

"What did you learn? Nothing. You didn't learn a thing."

"I need you to tell me who he was. What happened to him? Why were my mother's dreams so strange?"

I was desperate for answers, growing more desperate when I heard how difficult it was for her to breathe. I did not know how much longer she had.

"Give me some water. That nurse, she's trying to kill me. What's the opposite of drowning? She's trying to dry me out. She wants my jewelry."

I was confused for a moment—my aunt was wearing no jewelry—but when I saw her crippled hands adjusting a clasp that wasn't there, I realized she was hallucinating.

"Do you know where you are right now?" I asked. She gave me a sidelong glance as though that didn't deserve an answer. "Do you know who I am, Aunt Renee?"

She shook her head. She didn't want to say.

"Aunt Renee, who am I?"

"I don't know."

"Who am I, Aunt Renee? Tell me who I am."

Suddenly her hatred exploded, filling her with vigor. Her eyes bore into me.

"You're a blasphemy. You're a thing. You're like *him.* Like your father."

"I'm—what?"

"Your mother told me what he was, what he said he was, so we took care of it. But I never believed. I knew he was lying. Satan's kind always lies. He was a foul-blooded thing sent to test and torment us."

"What did she say?" I pleaded. "What did my mother say?"

"It wasn't in your precious diary?" she spat. I shook my head, and she laughed, then she slumped and I watched the energy dissipate from her like leaking air. She closed her eyes to rest.

"What did she say, Aunt Renee? Please tell me."

My aunt spoke, but it was a mumbled whisper. Her last reserves depleted. One of the machines she was hooked up to buzzed every few seconds. The sound was deafening.

"What did she say?" I repeated, leaning close, my ear to her mouth. Outside, in the hall, there was some commotion.

"She said he was lost. She said he didn't belong then, that he wanted to go back. She said he hated the meat most of all, that it wasn't big enough to contain him. She said in his sleep he would make sounds like he was talking, but the words were so old they made her cry. She said he was not who he said he was, and when she found out he wouldn't let her go. He was a monster."

"What did he do?"

"Do?" she asked, her eyelids cracking apart, revealing a sliver of white. "He made you. Wasn't that enough?"

My aunt fell asleep, then, and try as I might I could not revive her. When I left, the nurses were making her as comfortable as they could.

VII

I'm left with more questions than answers.

Aunt Renee never regained consciousness, and it wasn't long before she was buried, too, in Mount Pleasant Cemetery, not far from my mother. I never found out what she was talking about, and little of what I did know made any sense. I tried going through my mother's diary again more than once, traveling back in time to look for hints about what my father was, about what my aunt discovered that was so vile she turned into a religious zealot, about what my mother had done that caused her to hide from the world. But there was nothing, no stone left to turn. All I had were impressions and my mother's frightening poetry. And my unbearable dreams.

I find it impossible to write now. Every image that appears to me is suspect: I wonder if they are of my own conjuring or strange visions from my father, trying to communicate with me from wherever he is. I'm sure he's somewhere, alive, as out of my reach as I am of his. He still communicates to me through my dreams, and they continue to degrade and become unbearable, as though my inability to lance them through writing is only building up the pressure. And I wonder, if that's true, how long will it be until I explode, and what will happen then? But I can't—I just can't bring myself to write another word, so instead I drink and sit in the dark and wait for whatever truth is coming to finally reveal itself. Wanda has not given up on me yet, but it's only a matter of time. I have nothing left inside that she would want—it has been carved away by death and unearthed secrets. What remains is a shell, a living, breathing shell of meat and blood, existing in the present. The sort of thing an ancient god might want to inhabit, should it somehow be skipping through time and space in search of a vessel. That's the sort crazy idea that occurs to me now, the sort I can no longer exorcize through writing. It is like something that might occur to one trapped deep in the horror of a nightmare. Trapped without any prayer for escape.

First Miranda

Burning summer windstorms. Sand rattling car windows. Wheels roaring on the road. Chinking gravel. Jules searched desperately for something to say.

"How long has it been?" His voice sounded strange after hours of the highway's roar. Miranda didn't turn.

"I haven't been back in a lifetime. It all still looks the same."

"It's the middle of nowhere. Weird to think you grew up this far from everything."

She looked at him; she was still there beneath the folds and creases. That face that he'd fallen in love with years earlier. Time had treated her better than most—she hardly looked different from when they'd met—so why was it so hard to accept what she'd become? Why had he made such a mess of things?

"My sisters and I were happy. I never thought I'd ever want anything else. None of us did, back then. But time creeps up and soon you're scattered like seeds on the wind."

"Well, I'm glad your seed landed near me." Jules moved his hand from the wheel and put it on hers. The rumble of the road traveled upward. Miranda turned to the window, limp hand remaining behind like a fallen comrade. Minutes passed before she rescued it.

The road to the cottage was a flash on the highway; one exit and it was gone, no way to turn back for thirty minutes. Jules was careful to watch for the signs, but its sudden appearance startled him, and he barely had time to stop. Half-covered by hanging branches, improved and narrow, it seemed less a road and more something from a dream. But Miranda was proof it was real and led somewhere.

Jules was lucky to have her back. After he admitted what he'd done she had walked out with a warning not to follow. It wasn't the first time she had disappeared when their fights became too much, but even at her most erratic she was never gone more than a few hours. Then again, he had never done something so horrible before. As days and weeks passed with no contact at all, he grew terrified something tragic had happened. He couldn't help himself—the ideas bred and multiplied and overwhelmed him. Brown liquor and pills could not smother the distant thoughts that chittered beneath his fuzzy blanket of inebriation. But when all seemed lost and his darkest times bottomless, he cracked open his eyes at the sound of keys at the door, and in the streaming light stood Miranda, again and perhaps for the first time. She looked different, her skin rougher, but it was her—he recognized the look of disappointment on her face.

Miranda's childhood home was small. A single story, flat roof, and peeling white paint, but the front door was secure and the windows were clean. If he hadn't known the house was empty most of the year, he would have suspected someone was there regularly to keep it up.

"Why don't you go inside? I'll get the bags down and bring them in." It was well past lunch and Jules's stomach twisted, but he didn't dare speak. The therapist told him to ensure Miranda's needs were the first in his mind—as though they hadn't been since the day the two of them met. He, on an early morning walk home along the boardwalk; she, sitting on that same boardwalk, watching the ocean, having stopped during her own morning stroll. It was something out of a movie, and had been perfect. Perfect, until it wasn't.

The cottage was bright—in every direction there was more window than wall—and he understood for once how living so far from the world might be tolerable, especially with such a view of the lake. Jules rested the bags and walked to the glass separating house from shore. Gazing out at the water, he imagined Miranda as a girl, playing in the narrow patches of sand, swimming in the summer water. Laughing with sisters he'd never been allowed to meet.

So many things moved—the waves, the branches, the soaring birds—that he didn't notice anything at first. A blur, a tiny mar on the day, and when Jules clenched his fists and focused he realized it was moving. Swaying side to side, it poked from the water. A pale arm, trying to pull itself free.

"Do you see that?"

Miranda glanced without interest.

"It's nothing. It's the water."

"No, there's someone out there. Don't you see her?"

Miranda squinted again, held her position longer, but still came back shaking her head.

And when Jules looked back, it had gone.

*

"I think I might take the boat out, see what's around. Why don't you come along?"

Miranda sat in the front room, sunlight falling across her back and the side of her face. She looked up from her book, her inscrutable expression framed by stray hairs.

"Come on, Miranda. It will be fun. We haven't done anything like a mini-adventure in a while."

She appeared to consider it, and he imagined sitting beside her as he circled the boat over its own wake, bouncing the two of them on a short thrill ride. They would laugh as they used to, long before he'd made his mistakes. Long before Miranda had walked out.

"It's okay," she said. "You go on. Have fun. I'm going to catch up on my reading."

"Miranda . . ." he started, but didn't have the energy to fight. He missed the old Miranda, yet there was no one he could blame.

The boat's rusty outboard motor needed to be primed, but once it coughed it kept on coughing. Blue fumes drifted up, a smog that coated the rickety dock and hung in the air long after he'd eased the motor into reverse and backed the boat away from its mooring. Once clear, he gunned it and waited as the boat sputtered worryingly and inched forward. Then a clunk, a long wheeze, a cough, and the boat accelerated. Jules grinned.

The boat skipped over the waves, its prow pointing into the air as it tried to leap free. Relief from the oppressive house, his unreadable wife, all his mistakes, came immediately. It was behind him, a distant memory as he motored toward the tree-lined horizon. Clouds slipped off the sun in response to his rising joy, bathing him in light. He wanted to live in that moment forever. Everything else faded as he pushed the rattling motor faster.

A small island rose from the lake a few minutes from the coast. Jules turned the boat toward it out of curiosity. As he approached the island's narrow shore, the outboard motor grumbled, and he downshifted it to let it cool. The island passed on his right as he circled, row after row of trees with trunks like straight arrows stuck in the ground. Something moved among them, a shadow taking refuge in the thick forest, but his unease lessened when he realized it was simply a refraction of light.

Motor sufficiently rested, he pulled the rudder and aimed the boat back at where he'd come from. The cottage was farther away than he thought—so far he could barely make it out or its drab dock. Without warning clouds drew over the sun.

The thought of returning to Miranda evoked a deep sorrow. The empty seat beside him was filled with an afternoon of unrealized possibilities, but Jules knew there was no way they could have left their problems on the shore. And the lake was not deep enough to drown them all.

The waving from the water caught his eye. The arm, long and lithe, moved dreamily, its mate wrapped around a bobbing orange buoy. It hardly seemed real, like the fragment of a dream. He rubbed his eyes, but it didn't disappear. Worry stirred. Was someone stuck too far from shore? He pulled the steer, angling the boat toward the buoy.

The boat sputtered as he approached. The arm filled his vision, and in its motion he detected desperation and panic. He raced through the possible scenarios, worried he might be too late, and when that arm vanished before his eyes, that worry grew worse. He eased back on the throttle and scanned the lake's surface for movement. His eye found Miranda, watching from the distant shore with shielding hand on her brow.

"Do you mind?"

The disembodied voice startled him.

"Hey! What's your problem?"

He peered over the edge of the boat. Three heads bobbed in the water: a young girl in her late teens, flanked by two boys. Her hair was wet, her face round.

"What are you? Some kind of creep?" she asked.

"What? No. I'm just—" He tried to focus on her face, but her pale shoulders glowing under the water distracted him. Was it *her* arm he'd seen?

"Get out of here," one of her olive boyfriends demanded. "Screw off, loser."

"But I was just— Where did you—?"

"But I was just. Where did you," they mocked.

So much young flesh. He stammered, awkward, unable to think.

Defeated, he revved the outboard motor and slowly backed away from the laughter. He was both humiliated and aroused, and remained so until he glanced at the shore and saw Miranda retreating into the house.

Whatever she thought she'd seen wasn't right. Nothing had happened or was going to, but she wouldn't believe that. Despite all the love he offered, she couldn't look past one small mistake made when things were at their worst. He tried and continued to try, but she made it difficult. Maybe it would have been better to give up and go their separate ways.

The boat reached the dock choking on its last fumes. He glided it across the water and threw a line around each cleat before pulling himself onto the dock. He wrestled with what he'd say to Miranda as he walked the narrow path to the cottage; but when he entered through the sliding glass door, she squeezed past him on her way outside, dressed in her yellow one-piece suit and carrying a towel in her hand.

"I didn't do anything!" The words sounded so tiny and foolish aloud. They trailed her back down to the dock. "Miranda, will you stop and talk to me?" She wouldn't respond. At the dock's farthest edge she sat and dipped her feet in one at a time before pushing herself forward. He heard the splash, and saw her hazy yellow figure swim off beneath the waves.

His fists clenched. Jules turned and went inside, as though that small spiteful action would communicate his hurt, maybe force Miranda to realize she still loved him. He would unpack his suitcase and prepare for the coming nights. With luck, she would remember why they were there and work with him to fix their marriage, not crack it further.

It took no more than a few minutes, but it gave his anger time to dissipate. He had to try harder, be better, if he wanted to reach her. It shouldn't surprise him her solution to conflict was to disappear—she had lived most of her life on the lake's edge, isolated from the world. It wasn't a reflection on him.

Jules watched from the window as Miranda swam in the dark water with graceful ease. The buoys were visible in the distance, orange markers in the afternoon light. They bobbed as the waves pushed them back and forth, and Jules found himself searching for the girl and her two boyfriends. His heart's rhythm increased and his mouth dried as he imagined what they might be doing, what their young arms would feel like wrapped around him. A shiver ran through his spine, and he shook to interrupt the aggregating thoughts. There couldn't be any more mistakes, no proving Miranda right. Still, when he saw the lithe arm rise from the water again, closer to shore, his heart resumed its flutter.

But it looked different from how it had earlier. He squinted, leaned forward, and tried to understand why the sight terrified him so. The realization turned him cold.

"Miranda!"

He ran to the dock and leapt without hesitation. Miranda struggled to keep afloat, arms thrashing wildly, gasping for air in the scant seconds she spent above the surface. Jules's legs pumped, propelling him as his hands clawed the water. When he reached Miranda she aggressively fought his rescue attempt; it was all he could do to keep hold of her as he dragged her to shore. Miranda crawled from the surf and hugged the land as though she'd never been there before. Jules staggered out and to her side. Hands on his knees, struggling for breath, he forced the words out.

"Miranda, what happened?"

Wet hair plastered to her forehead, eyes wide and searching, she appeared unfathomably lost. Her skin was pale and lips colorless as she shivered in the orange sunlight. A few feet away her towel lay on the shore, and Jules stepped away to retrieve it. When he turned back, she was running toward the cottage, and he was left alone and confused, holding the towel in his trembling hands.

He followed her back to the cottage, worried about what had happened. Miranda had nearly drowned, and yet still seemed to be harboring misplaced anger. He didn't know what more he could do to earn back her trust. All he wanted was to hold her and make sure she was safe, but when he reached the bedroom door he found it locked.

"Miranda, can you let me in?"

He jiggled the knob. There was quiet rustling, and a murmur as though she were talking to herself, but the door remained shut.

"Are you okay in there? I'm getting worried."

He waited, then pounded on the door. It still didn't open.

Frustrated, Jules sniffed the reek of fish and algae wafting from his clothes. He wanted desperately to change them, but everything he'd brought was locked behind the door with Miranda.

"I'm going to take a shower," he shouted. "Maybe when I'm done you can tell me what happened."

The odor lingered as he stepped into the bathroom and stripped off his sopping clothes. There was no shower, so he ran the tiny faucets in the tub until the water turned clear and used a hand towel to sponge himself. By the time he stepped back into the front room, Miranda's beach towel wrapped around his waist, the sun had set and the cabin was dark. He lit a lamp and tried the bedroom door again. Miranda was still locked behind it, nursing whatever anger or embarrassment had driven her away. He pressed his face against the door.

"I don't know what you think you saw out there today, but it was nothing. I was just talking to those kids," he said. "I wasn't saying or doing anything you need to worry about. Miranda, I told you before: I love you. I'm here for you. I want things to go back to how they were." He waited, tried the knob again. His frustration mounted.

"Goddamn it, Miranda, open the door!"

He banged the flat of his hand against it.

Anger would not solve the problem. He repeated it to himself. She needed space, and he had to give it to her. Jules forced himself to breathe until he was in control again.

"Miranda, I'm sorry. Take all the time you need. I'll be here, waiting."

Jules sat on the couch, naked except for the towel he pushed beneath him. Miranda couldn't keep him out of the room forever; eventually she'd have to emerge, and when she did he would sit her down and calmly discuss what had happened. The therapist told him talk was the only way to heal the rift. The small television was poor company while he waited—it barely received any channels, and the electronic fuzz across them heightened his disconnection. He turned it off and stared at the bedroom door. Miranda may have been in the other room, but she felt farther away.

He drifted off listening to the crickets outside. When he woke, it was in darkness. Faint moonlight dribbled through the bare windows, enough to illuminate traces of the cabin around him. He shivered, a chill crossing his naked shoulders and arms. Something had roused him, and when he heard the rattle come from the kitchen a jolt traveled along his nerves. He looked up at the long pale specter that approached. Breath caught in his throat.

It was Miranda. She was naked.

Bare footsteps on the wooden floor; eyes drilling into his. Lips full, eyes devouring, she closed the gap. Something stirred beneath his towel.

"Miranda, what are you doing?"

She didn't speak. Instead she pressed her fiery hand against his chest and pushed him down. He reached to embrace her, but she brushed his hands away, then parted her legs and sat atop him. She leaned back and unknotted the towel while he ran his hands over her wet skin. She was soaking, and the steam that rose off her as she slid him inside filled his head with musky confusion. He didn't understand what was happening, only that Miranda was as she hadn't been in years. Eyes closed, wrinkled brow furrowed in concentration, she rocked her hips, grinding herself against him, as short high-pitched noises slipped from her pursed lips. Jules's thoughts were washed away, replaced with a warm tide that moved his body autonomously. Back and forth she rocked, Jules's hips jutting in rhythm to hers, and when every muscle in his body tightened, when the intensifying pressure was about to consume him, he gripped the sides of the couch and tried to hold on. But everything slipped away in an explosion of liquid heat. He gasped and fell backwards into his head, plummeting into an ecstatic obliviousness, waves pulsing along his body. It was some time before he was able to open his eyes, and by then Miranda had gone, retreated into the locked bedroom. She left only the impression of her burning hands on his cooling skin, and the unspoken promise of leaving their past behind.

He drifted into unconsciousness, warmed by the memory of her flesh, and didn't wake until hours later when the sound of Miranda's screams propelled him to his feet, wobbling and disoriented, the towel sliding to the floor. She stood where he'd first seen her during the night, but in the morning sun she was clothed and unleashing her fury.

"What are you doing here? Get the hell out, Jules. I don't want you around anymore. Can't you get the goddamn picture?"

He didn't know how to respond. The smell of her midnight sweat lingered.

"Miranda, what's—?"

"Spare me your oblivious routine. You know damn well what you've done to this marriage. You shit. You stupid, dumb shit. I want you out!"

"Miranda, calm down. I—"

"Oh, shut up for once, you idiot. You good-for-nothing, can't-do-a-goddamn-thing-right idiot. Do you know how ridiculous you are? You're a joke. A big fucking joke. The only reason I'm not laughing is because I was too stupid to realize it in time, and I let you screw up my life. You ruined everything, you selfish prick. You ruined it all. Every goddamn thing and now I'm stuck here in this horrible life with you and I want to die. Honestly and truthfully, Jules. You make me want to die."

"Miranda, I—"

"How many times do I have to tell you? Stay the hell away from me!"

She snatched a vase from the mantel and hurled it. It caught Jules's temple with a hollow sound, and he crumpled, head filling with stars. The front door slammed as he tried to push beyond the pain and follow. He staggered into the harsh sunlight, but Miranda had vanished.

Frustration and anger burned in him. Miranda wasn't the only one wronged. What about Jules, and all he'd had to suffer married to her? The reverence she held for her past—a life with her sisters that was clearly better than any he could provide. Was it any wonder a wedge had been driven between them? As much love as he held for her, even that had its limits, and she'd tested every one, pushed him into straying from her. Miranda ran from the cottage because her first instinct was always to run when things were tough. It was the only solution she knew—to disappear, to return to the lake and the cottage where she'd started life. If there was any surprise, it was that she'd brought him to her sanctum. How it must have bothered her, once her anger flared, that her refuge had been invaded and that she had nowhere to go.

Jules strode inside. The bedroom door finally unlocked and open, he retrieved some clothes from the closet and dressed again, sitting on the edge of the sagging bed to pull on his socks. The sheets were twisted together behind him, curled like a desiccated body, and he realized that after all his work trying to get in, he didn't want to be in that room any longer than necessary. It reeked of her hatred.

Jules paced the front room, bothered by Miranda's cavalier dismissal of the work he'd done to build a life for the two of them. Maybe the mistake was his. Maybe he shouldn't have been working to fix their marriage, but destroy it as Miranda clearly wanted—her every action screamed that was the case. And as much as his previous indiscretions were a mistake, they proved he would have no trouble filling the void in his bed. All he had to do was concede that his life with Miranda was over.

*

Jules's anger ebbed and his sense returned as he awaited Miranda. It was foolish to think there might be anyone else he'd want or love as he did her. She had always been his anchor when the world went mad. Had it not been for Miranda, he would never have made it through the disciplinary hearings and investigations—she had stood by him even when she could hardly keep from crying. Miranda was too important to lose.

Photographs of landscapes on the mantel, unlabeled pencil marks on the wall. Indiscriminate scratches along the wooden floor. The cottage held Miranda's secret history, but Jules could not break its code. There was a vacation photograph of Miranda as a beautiful teenager, seated on a wooden bench and smiling, her hair straight and well past her shoulders. There was another of her at the summit of a small hill, turned toward the camera, skinny child arms raised in triumph, while a pair of girls who were no doubt her sisters continued climbing to greet her. All he saw were the backs of their heads, but the resemblance was uncanny. There were so many sisters Jules wondered how she'd kept them hidden from him for so long. Then he wondered how so many of them fit in the cottage when there was only one bedroom for the family to share.

Stars lit the sky as the sun set, and Jules found himself on the edge of the dock, staring into the dark water, running his dried tongue over his lips as he tried to recognize the familiar shape submerged beneath it. His concern grew the longer Miranda was gone. In the city, he would have known where to look for her, but he was lost at the cottage. He waited by the window as the afternoon passed, ignoring the creeping suspicion something was wrong. Miranda had spent the first half of her life on the lake's shore, and despite her earlier near-drowning he couldn't believe the water had her. But there was no denying it held a secret, one Miranda knew but wouldn't share. Like all Miranda's secrets, it was sunk deep inside her, resistant to his efforts to dredge it loose.

A flash of light pierced his haze. It was small, barely noticeable, but Jules knew it was Miranda—it had to be, waiting past the line of orange buoys on the tree-filled island. Her faint voice called to him over the water. He didn't know how she'd got there—the motorboat was still moored and unfueled beside him, but whoever had taken her had left her abandoned. He didn't care about the reason, he only cared about how long it would take to get the spare fuel can from the trunk of his car.

The motor's roar echoed off the calm water as gulls pushed themselves into the sky. The cottage faded the farther he got from shore, until he wasn't certain he knew where he had launched from. Confusion and fear addled his mind, but he pushed them away. Miranda was why he was there. Miranda. He aimed for the orange glow of the sun and the dark island trees outlined against it.

He slowed the boat as he approached and scanned the shoreline for his wife. In the murk of dusk all shadows appeared the same—a legion gathering among the thick of trees and rock crevices as he motored around the small island. He called out for her, hoping she'd hear him over the motor's din, and searched in vain for another flash of light. When he completed his circle, the sky had grown darker still, and those shadows more numbered. But he continued searching.

A dark mass lay on the edge of the shore. Jules squinted. It was shaped differently from the other shadows.

"Miranda?"

The mass did not move.

"Miranda!"

He revved the outboard motor and headed straight for the blackened heap.

Jules ran the boat on to the sandy shore, but before it stopped he leapt out and stumbled across the shore to Miranda. She lay still, waves lapping around her, torso exposed while the rest remained submerged under water. And when Jules reached her he dropped to his knees and grabbed her shoulders, fighting against the panic threatening to overtake him.

"Wake up, Miranda. Please wake up. I'm sorry. I'm so sorry. Please wake up."

But she didn't move, and the sand that clung to her cold face in the falling darkness only made her appear less human.

So much time was lost—time he would have used to fix his mistakes. It was all gone. Miranda had left him finally and forever. He lifted her too-heavy body from the surf to hold against him—one last memory of her skin pressed against his own. It was penance for what he'd allowed to happen.

But even in the dark something looked wrong. What emerged as he pulled her body from the surf were not the pale heavy legs he remembered. Her body was instead blackened like night solidified, and her slippery dark flesh uncoiled in an undulating corpulent mass that tapered to a point. Pairs of thick short stalks dotted her abdomen, a small slit in each like a puckered mouth that hissed as it opened, quiet screams mirroring those behind his horrified stare. What Jules thought was that his Miranda was instead something half-formed, something born from the dark lake water, and when he felt the first spasm of its muscles against his chest, saw an eye flicker open, then another, he ceased to think straight. Feet barely in line beneath him, he fled to the boat.

And behind him, the tree-line shook.

Jules shoved the boat into deeper water and struggled to leap inside despite the water grabbing his legs. The thing on the shore, the half-Miranda, was moving as other shadows peeked from between the ancient trees. He landed in the boat on his side, but didn't take the time to right himself before gripping the outboard motor's pull and yanking. It coughed to life, and he swung the boat around and aimed for the shore where he hoped the cottage waited. He resisted the temptation to look back at the island; he didn't want to see a series of indescribable shapes, waterlogged and dark, watching him escape. If he didn't turn around, they couldn't reach him. If he didn't turn around, they couldn't really be there.

The motor screamed across the flat unmoving water like a man who had lost everything. He squinted through the fog of tiny insects at the distant light of the cottage. Wind passed his ears too quickly to let in more than a roar, and yet he couldn't move fast enough to outrun the sense he was being pursued.

Jules was unprepared when the dock reared up from the edge of the lake. He narrowly avoided hitting it, but drove the boat straight into the ground, the sudden stop pitching him over the prow. Everything spun, the shadow of something crossed behind him, and the ground met his face as all light went out.

*

Waking was unpleasant. A voice softly cooed as familiar hands stroked his head. His eyes cracked open, but they were swollen and puffy and wouldn't part more than a sliver. It was enough, though, to reveal he was back in the cottage. Back in the loving, comforting arms of his wife. So much time had passed since she last held him that he spoke without thinking.

"Am I dead?"

The caresses stopped.

"Why would you ask that?"

He tried to roll over, but it was too painful.

"I feel dead."

His chest was the worst of it—a stitch cut into him with each breath he took. A stinging ghost of anguish left on his face. Miranda cooed.

"Hush. You're all right now. Safe and sound. Everything is going to be okay."

He closed his eyes as fingers raked through his hair. The pain's urgency dulled. Miranda's breath was warm as it whispered in his ear.

"There's nothing to worry about. I'm here."

"Where were you?" he mumbled. "I went looking—"

"I know, love. I know. I'm here now, though. I just walked into town. There's nothing to worry about."

"But I looked everywhere. The island—I even went to the island."

A pause.

"You shouldn't have gone there."

"I went," he said, though the words were getting harder to speak. "I went and I think I saw you. Only you weren't you. You were on the shore, but something was wrong. I thought—I thought you were dead."

Her body shook. Had she laughed?

"Hush now, Jules. Don't worry about that. Everything is fine."

Hands passed over his body, touching the flesh of his leg, the bald spot on his pate. Arms hugged him, pulled him close, warmed him until he forgot himself in the swell of affection. But as Miranda caressed him, something wasn't right. Perhaps it was the smell of the lake rolling into the cottage or wafting off her clothes; perhaps her skin, rougher and more wrinkled than he remembered. Something peculiar he couldn't make sense of, but knew innately was trouble. Her hands held him close, but they held other things. Too many other things. When he opened his eyes again he found those hands were holding him down, pinning him into place.

"Miranda?"

She shushed him.

"It's time."

The front door rattled, the knob jittered, and the door swung open. Cold night air rolled in, the tang of lake mist with it, and before he could speak another Miranda stepped into view.

Jules sputtered, bewildered.

Was he in a dream? If Miranda stood in the doorway, who was holding him?

"Hello, Jules," the second Miranda said.

He didn't speak. He couldn't. She wore the green sweater he loved so much, the one he'd bought for her birthday, the one he was certain she'd lost long ago. Fingers continued to stroke his hair while, behind the Miranda in the doorway, a third Miranda appeared—hair and clothes disheveled.

All his thoughts drowned in a flood of panic.

He emitted a litany of guttural sounds in place of words. Despite what his senses told him, it had to be some sort of trick. None of them could be Miranda, yet they all looked like her. Each carried herself like her. It was impossible. Impossible. Even more so when the glass door slid open and three more were revealed. Jules screamed.

Miranda's hand—some Miranda's hand—stroked his face as calming whispers floated around him. He struggled to make sense of what was happening. The women couldn't be sisters, couldn't be anything but his wife, but it was impossible. And yet he was surrounded, each wearing a duplicate of Miranda's face.

"Murderer!" one Miranda screamed, boiling with rage and hatred.

"What is this?" he cried. "Who are you? Which of you is the real Miranda?"

They laughed in unison.

"Miranda is gone." He couldn't tell who was speaking. All their voices were the same. "Miranda tried so hard, but you're not worth the effort. If only Miranda had seen it earlier."

"What are you talking about?" He scrutinized each. They had the same face—the same expression. "Where is she?"

"You know."

"How would I know? What have you done with her? Why won't you let me see her?"

"Miranda was a good wife. But you were not a good husband, Jules. You failed."

"How dare you. How goddamn dare you. Miranda and I had problems, but they were *our* problems, not yours. We were working them out—we *are* working them out. Now where is she?"

"Look outside."

"What?"

"Look outside. What do you see?"

He looked out the large window at the side of the cottage. There was nothing—no figures, no movement. Nothing but moonlight, and beneath it—

"I see the water," he said.

"Do you know what comes from the water?"

"What are you talking about? Where's my wife?"

"Everything does," Miranda answered. "Have you ever seen a school of fish? One steers the whole school. Without that one, what do you think happens?"

Jules's impatience turned to anger.

"You better tell me where Miranda is or—"

The closest Miranda struck him hard across the mouth. He tasted blood.

"Without that one, what happens?"

"Nothing," he said, swallowing. "Nothing. Another fish takes its place or something. Nothing changes."

"Wrong," Miranda said. "Everything changes. One dead piece and the whole school rots."

"I don't know what the hell you're talking about. Where's my wife?"

"You know where she is. You put her there."

He put her where? The memory of standing on the edge of dock surfaced. He remembered staring into the dark water. He remembered the familiar shape submerged beneath it. He remembered.

And he staggered.

"No."

"A piece from Miranda was lost because of you, Jules. Miranda brought you here to reclaim it."

"It's time," the Miranda holding him said.

"What do you mean?"

But he knew. His day of reckoning had come. He'd been lying to himself about his betrayal and what he'd done to Miranda. She was never the same and finally he understood why. She was gone. He'd extinguished the last piece of her that loved him. It was his fault. There was no forgiveness left.

The Mirandas converged, a dozen identical hands grabbing his arms, his legs, his head. He kicked and thrashed but couldn't break their grip. The air was heavy and damp, and it grew worse as the Mirandas' fingers clawed into his face, pushed into his nose and eyes, pried open his mouth. Those fingers pulled as he struggled, threatened to tear him apart, and beneath the pain and the screams, those fingers found his tongue and held it down.

The Mirandas hoisted him onto their shoulders and ushered him, hand to hand, body to body, through the cottage in which they had all lived a lifetime. They carried him to the edge of the dock where the world met the water, where everything both began and ended, and with little effort they heaved him into the air. He sailed over the churning lake below.

From above he saw the silhouette of the tree-lined island, larger and closer than he remembered, in relief against the moon.

He saw the line of orange buoys, dancing on the dark waves, marking the limit beyond which no one was safe.

And he saw the dark shadows of gulls circling overhead, carrion eyes glistening in the night like stars.

Jules saw these things before he saw what lay under the churning waters below. Beneath the tumultuous waves dark oily shadows moved, hundreds of them, stretched as far as his spinning mind could see. They were formless, and yet from each black mass a single pale limb rose, one after the other until a sea of arms reached toward the sky. He saw their long recognizable fingers—fingers he had felt touch his face, stroke his hair—and watched them as they clawed the air madly, thousands of hands hungering. Jules's flailing arms and legs could not stop what was to come.

Vertices

Nori's grandmother has a heart attack while changing a lightbulb and is already cold by the time her husband realizes she's missing. Less than a week later he's also gone. Nori asks her father about the suspicious timing, since her mother won't talk to her, but he has no answers. Her sister, Kayla, says the grief killed their grandfather. Nori thinks he killed himself because of the grief. It doesn't matter; once the two were gone, Nori's mother crumbled.

Nori hopes she and Kayla will never again have to go to their grandparents' small, overstuffed house. Instead, they go more often while their father prepares it for sale. Their mother doesn't help. Either she disappears for hours somewhere in the house or sits in a wooden chair like a bag half-filled with bricks and watches them.

It makes Nori feel strange. Both sad and uncomfortable. But she and Kayla wait until they're outside their mother's earshot before they say anything.

"Dad, how much longer is this going to take? I have to get ready."

"Girls, there's a lot of work to do, and I can't do it alone."

"But why do we have to do it all the time? The house isn't going anywhere."

"I don't even know why we're selling it. We should keep it. Granny and Grandpa would want us to."

"I'm sure they'd understand. We can't keep it, hon. We can't afford two houses."

"But it's a free house."

"Not really. We still have to pay the taxes and heat. We'd be spending money for no reason—especially when we could sell it and put some aside for your college funds."

Despite everything, Nori's heart skips at the mention of college. Kayla remains unconvinced.

"But Mom doesn't want to sell, does she? She grew up here."

"Your mom wants to get rid of it most of all."

Nori doesn't know if that's true. Since the funeral, her mother hasn't spoken a word to Nori or Kayla, and whenever Nori tries to talk to her about going away to school, her mother gets a strained look, as though rocks were being added to the weight on top of her. Eventually, Nori learns to stop trying.

But she doesn't let it dull her excitement. Nori dreams of the future. She dreams of college. She has been planning for as long as she can remember. There is a new world opening for her in the fall, and it's so close she can feel its charge. The skin on her arms prickles in anticipation.

But before she can get there, she must finish here. She must finish packing away the vestiges of what remains.

*

Her grandparents were a strange combination of pleasant and indifferent. They cared enough to ask how Nori and Kayla were doing, but never seemed interested in the response. The minutiae of their retired days seemed boring and off-putting to the sisters, and holding their aging attention became tiring. Eventually they gave up, much to no one's disappointment. No one except Nori's mother.

Sometimes, after a visit, Kayla and Nori would hear their mother in the front seat, quietly weeping. Their dad would be uncomfortably silent, fidgeting, and the air would be so full and heavy Nori wouldn't want to speak. Her mother would gather herself to ask, "Why didn't you talk more to your granny and grandpa?" Except it wasn't really a question. And there was no answer, at least not one Nori could supply (and Kayla refused to give). It was easier to look out the window and pretend as though she weren't there.

*

After both grandparents are gone, Nori's mother stops asking questions. She moves in a haze from room to room, eyes swollen, nose raw and shiny, in a perpetual state of near collapse. Nori hates seeing her in the midst of despair. But she's also frustrated and desperate to leave for better things, and she feels ashamed of that desperation. That shame is why, when they reach the house, she doesn't complain about her ruined weekend, her lost time. Why she accepts whatever job her father assigns.

It isn't long before Kayla finds her and tells her to follow. At the other end of the hall their mother shuffles past. It's clear she doesn't see them.

Kayla leads her though the house's rooms and hallways, carefully outside their father's attention, to a surprising bedroom door. Surprising, because Nori has never noticed it before. Kayla points to the frame and there, more an impression in the wood than faded ink, is written her mother's name. Confusion replaces Nori's moping.

"What are you showing me?"

Kayla opens her mouth, but her breath catches. Her eyes narrow as she considers how to answer.

"I don't know. That's the problem. I think this was Mom's bedroom when she was little, but something's weird."

Nori notices it, too. A thrum broadcast from the room. It does something to her head.

"What do you think it is?" Kayla asks.

"Did you already go inside?"

"No," she says. "It doesn't feel right."

Nori reaches to test the lock and current jumps to her fingers. Her body vibrates for a moment. She doesn't know why. The thrum continues.

"There must be something in there," Nori mumbles and knows immediately she's going in. She doesn't want to, but it feels beyond her control.

From above herself, she watches her hand twist the knob. Watches her body slip past the door.

Immediately everything is a blur. It's as though she's looking into a blinding light, except there is no light. Just the pain from it, so strong her eyes tear. Twirling fractal patterns like broken beams through a prism fill her vision, a rainbow corona around translucent, mirrored rods. The room shimmers—static like a snowstorm. Nori holds up her hands to shield her face from the intense non-light, and they crumble. No, not her hands. Everything else. Her tongue dries, goes numb. Words echo against the walls—multiply—amplify. A feedback loop. She squeezes shut her eyelids and puts her decaying hands over her ears, but it does no good. Something brushes past. She is too afraid to see what.

The collar of her shirt tightens against her throat. She's choking. She's yanked back. Everything spins and flips and blackens, and when she regains her senses she's on her hands and knees, coughing and nearly throwing up on her grandparents' hallway floor. There's muffled shouting, but her head spins too fast to focus. Nori wipes her tears away and sees her father's confused face. Her sister's disgusted grimace. Her mother looms like a thunder cloud above.

"What happened?" Nori croaks.

"Why did you go in the bedroom?" her mother says. Her voice angry on the verge of panic. Nori is stunned by her animation. Her father stays silent, eyes wide.

"I don't know," she says. More a plea than an answer. She glances to the bewildered Kayla.

"Stay out of there, Nori. Never go in there," her mother says.

Her mother's building fury is terrifying in Nori's heightened state. She shrinks.

"Let's take it easy," her father says. "It was an accident. She didn't mean anything."

"Accident? Didn't mean anything?" her mother shrieks, then grabs hold of Nori's arms, hard, digging her fingers deep. Nori cries as she's shaken. "You never go in there, Nori! Never!"

Her father leaps to pry them apart. Nori continues crying as she scrambles back on her hands, terrified of what her mother might do.

Her mother's face is tarnished, red and cracked, and she seems unable to control herself. Kayla wraps her arms tight around Nori, and Nori buries her face in her younger sister's shoulder, unable to bear her mother's transformation.

She doesn't know how long she sobs, but when she finally reaches the end Nori discovers bleary-eyed it's her father who now holds her, strokes her hair. Kayla stands behind him, arms crossed, jaw set, and brow furrowed. Further away her mother sits crumpled against a wall. Her hair is disheveled and her eyes red, and her blotched face has a worn, placid look, like a field after a heavy storm. She's smaller than Nori remembers.

"I think we got enough done, today," her father says. "Let's go home."

*

Nori's father waits for her mother to slouch to bed before he sits her and her sister down in the kitchen. Nori feels sick from nervous energy and desperately wants the day to be over, but she's too anxious to sleep. She watches her father at the sink, looking thin and tired, as he distractedly rifles through the drawers.

"You mother wants to apologize for what happened today."

Nori touches her throat.

"If she wants to, then why doesn't she?"

He sighs. Stops pulling things out of the drawers. Half shrugs.

"You know what your mother's been going through. It's been hard on her. Harder than usual. And you disturbing her in her old bedroom didn't help."

"But I didn't do anything! I just—"

He holds up his hand. Reluctantly, Nori stops talking.

"I get it, Nori. But you must understand where your mom's coming from. Imagine what it's like for her right now. To lose her parents so close together while her daughter is about to leave for college. It hurts no matter who you are. It's even worse for someone like your mother. She just needs a safe place she can go to process everything."

"But, Dad, there's something in that room."

"That's enough, Nori."

"It's true! I felt it, and Kayla felt it."

"What did you feel?"

She turns to Kayla, unable to articulate her feelings. Kayla is a million miles away; she can't or won't help.

"I don't know," Nori says. "Like something in there was coming for me."

He looks at her quizzically, then glances at Kayla.

"There's nothing in there, Nori. It's empty."

"What do you mean? How can it be empty?"

He shrugs.

"I had to go in there when I packed the house. It's an empty bedroom. The only thing still there is the wooden chair your mom sits on. She won't let me take it away just yet."

"No." She refuses to believe him.

"The house won't be around much longer anyway," their father says, shutting the cutlery drawer. "Soon we'll never have to see it again. Then everything will go back to normal."

The thought of never returning to that house is a relief and gives her hope. But how will selling the house quiet the thrum she still hears? How? She closes her eyes and reminds herself that she'll be at college in a few months. A few months until everything gets better.

*

Later, when the two girls are in their room, facing each other from their beds, they talk about the future, about Nori's excitement and hopes for when she goes away, about what it will be like when Kayla follows a year later. The conversation helps to take Nori's mind off everything that's happened, but it lasts only until Kayla asks how she's doing.

"I already told you. I'm fine."

"You haven't been fine since Granny and Grandpa's house."

"There's nothing to worry about."

"You didn't have to see it. Mom was screaming as she threw you into the hallway. She looked crazy—gigantic eyes, hair standing out, practically howling like a rabid animal. I was terrified she was going to attack me before Dad showed up."

"I don't remember any of that."

"That's what worries me."

They lie quietly for a moment. Then Kayla asks:

"Nori, what did you see in Mom's old bedroom?"

The thrum grows louder. Nori sits up, pulls her knees to her chin and clings to her folded legs.

"I—I didn't see Mom," she eventually says. "Instead, there was some kind of giant shape. Like a triangle. Like an upside-down glass triangle. And light bent through it, but it wasn't light. I don't know how to explain it. It was like—like you know how when you look through a drinking glass everything gets warped? That, except flipped. It was everything *outside* the triangle that was warped. Everything around it. Only the triangle part was clear, and it was like a mirror. And the weirdest part was the triangle didn't have sides or a bottom. It was flat, but no matter how I looked at it, it was the same size and shape. And it just hung in the air, not falling."

Nori thought she might feel better admitting what she'd experienced. But she doesn't. Nori knows right away. What she feels is worse, because her confusion is now compounded by unfathomable guilt. She's told Kayla something she can never untell, something Kayla will never not know. Nori did to her what that triangle did to the world around it: took everything and irreparably bent it.

Nori suddenly cries. Over what she's done, over what has happened, or for some other reason neither she nor Kayla understands. Nevertheless, Kayla gets into bed with her and hugs her. Nori can't help but notice how stiff her sister feels.

When the crying is done, Nori wipes her face on her arm.

"We can't tell Dad or Mom. Especially Mom," she says.

"Obviously," Kayla replies.

"There's something in that house. In that room. And it still feels like it's coming for me."

She looks directly at Kayla.

"I'm never going back there. I don't care what anyone says. I need you to back me up if Dad tries to make me. I need you to promise me you won't let him."

Kayla thinks a moment.

"I promise," she says.

*

Nori can't sleep. There are too many things running through her head, including that distant thrum. It makes shadows darker, sounds louder. Kayla's light snore becomes the earth tearing open and her wheeze a windstorm through dry leafless trees. They are hammers on Nori's already tightened nerves, each strike delivering a jolt that keeps her awake. She tries to muffle them with pillows over her head, but it becomes too much, and she has to escape.

Nori carries a blanket downstairs. The house is so quiet there isn't a creak as she pads down the hall. It's the opposite of soothing. A noise, any noise, would be normal, as though she were still in the world she knows. The complete absence of sound is so unfamiliar that she questions if she isn't somewhere else. It's only the moon that convinces her otherwise, reflecting its light through the windows, casting elongated rectangles across the floor. If she can make it to the living room couch, she'll be okay. She doesn't know why, but it seems the safest place for her. Perhaps the only safe place.

But when she reaches it, her mother is there. The shock stifles her scream.

"Sit with me," her mother says. Nori can't tell if her voice sounds okay.

"Mom, it's the middle of the night."

"Is it?"

Nori wraps the blanket around her. Sits. She doesn't know what else to do. Nevertheless, she keeps out of arm's reach.

"What are you doing down here, Mom?"

"It was too dark upstairs. I couldn't sleep."

Nori doesn't know what that means. She glances back at those rectangles of light.

"Should I wake Dad?"

"No, let him sleep," she says. "I need to tell you something. What happened at the house? It shouldn't have happened."

Nori rubs her throat. Shakes her head in the dark.

"The truth is," her mother continues, "you should never have been in that room."

"What? Are you saying it was my fault?"

"No, but you need to be more careful."

"Careful of what?"

Her mother sits quiet for a moment. When she speaks, her voice rings flat.

"My mother wasn't the same with me as she was with you and Kayla. With you she was more . . . even. She could hold a thought in her head. And she could love the two of you, even if she couldn't really show it."

Nori hears the thrum again. Her fingers are icicles.

"You wouldn't understand what your grandmother was like before. When I was growing up, she was unpredictable. She was moody and got angry or irritated over the smallest things. And sometimes she was too distracted or aggressive to notice I was alive. She went up and down like that for so long that after she went on her medication, I didn't recognize her. She didn't even look the same. I thought it was some sort of trick. The only place I felt safe from her was my bedroom. When she was at her worst, I thought I could hide there. I didn't realize there was no hiding. Hiding only made it worse."

Her mother pauses again. Nori purses her lips, wonders what she's expected to say.

"Since she and your grandfather died, I've felt a profound emptiness. And I'm worried about what's going to fill it."

As her mother speaks, the thrum in Nori's head grows louder, and the dark around them becomes thicker, more opaque. Thousands of millions of geometric shapes, rotating and overlapping—a kaleidoscope of shadows and night, riding on concentric waves that emanate from where her mother sits. Nori wonders if any of this is happening or if she's stuck in some half-awake state. Maybe she never left her mother's old bedroom at all. A formless panic seeps to the surface.

"Mom, what's in your old bedroom?"

"Nori, I don't think I can keep going." Her mother's voice is so tiny and distant.

"Mom, you don't have to go anymore. Dad and Kayla and I will finish."

Her mother hushes her.

"Do you hear that?"

There is a noise. Faint, lost in the blackness flowing around them. Nori concentrates, searches for something more, but can't find it.

Her mother exhales. The sound of defeat. Of lost hope.

"Maybe you're right," her mother says. "I should go back to bed. You should, too, Nori. It's late, and Kayla needs you. She's really going to miss you when you're gone."

"But Mom . . ."

"Everything will be fine. Go on. Back to bed. I'll be right behind you."

Nori stands and waits, but her mother's shadow doesn't move. It's no different from that inverted triangle: a flat, unknowable specter hanging before her. The chill in Nori's hands spreads, the blackened shapes in the air fold in on themselves, and that foreign thrum drones louder. Her head aches. Nori waits until she can't bear it any longer, then abandons her mother.

She bounds across the rectangles and up the stairs. When Nori reaches the bedroom, she closes the door and leans against it, breathless. The drone ebbs from her thoughts, the air becomes less dense. She sits on the edge of her bed and watches Kayla asleep in hers. Kayla snores blissfully, her arm stretched out in slumber. Nori reaches over and touches her hand, careful not to wake her. Nori doesn't know what's coming, but she's frightened.

*

She doesn't want to face her mother the next morning, but when she goes downstairs she doesn't find what she expects. Her mother is seated at the kitchen table, flanked by her father and sister, laughing with them as she hasn't in months.

"Nori!"

"Mom?"

Her mother eagerly beckons her to sit while her father stands to prepare another plate of breakfast. Kayla is already in the middle of her own, trying to eat while staring at their mother, as though afraid it will all end if she blinks. Nori's afraid, too.

"Mom, how are you feeling?"

"I'm great. How are you?"

Her mother rests her head on a folded hand, waiting for an answer. Her hair is dry and face puffy, and in front of her is an untouched mug of coffee. Nori worries she's dreaming.

"Okay, I guess," she says.

"It's hard to believe soon you'll be off at college. Are you excited?"

Nori doesn't know how to answer that. Everything is a blur.

"I'm a little scared."

"There's nothing to be scared about. You're going to have fun, and you're going to achieve so much. Your dad and sister will miss you a lot, though."

"It's true," her father says, laughing. "We will."

They look at Kayla, who sits quietly, doing her best to butter her toast with the bottom of a spoon.

"Kayla," her mother says, "why don't you use a knife for that?"

"I couldn't find any," she says.

Her father interrupts.

"Girls, we have good news for you." He looks at Nori's mother, and she smiles. It's a strange sight. "After breakfast, we're going back to the house. But this will be the last time."

Nori's mother claps, and Kayla perks up. Everyone is excited. Everyone but Nori.

"I can't go back there."

Nori's father stops and looks at her. He's straining under the pressure of holding the family together.

"Nori—" her mother starts.

"I told you. There something waiting for me there," Nori says. "It's too dangerous."

"Nothing's going to happen," her father says.

"Why doesn't anyone believe me?"

Her voice quivers. She's on the verge of tears.

Her father makes a noise. She knows it well. It's of finality.

"You and your sister are coming. We need you there."

"Mom," Nori pleads. Her mother squeezes her hand. Smiles.

"It will be okay. You'll see. After this we'll never go again."

"Kayla? Kayla, you promised."

But Kayla won't look up from her cold toast.

It's a mistake. Nori knows it is but can't do anything about it. No one will help her.

A sensation like thick, churning oil in her stomach. The inverted triangle reaching out for her.

And she is coming.

*

Her grandparents' house looks shrunken and contracted, huddled in on itself like a wounded animal. Even from the driveway Nori senses the steady thrum, now infused with a faint electrical charge she feels like pins. The inverted triangle flashes through her head, and Nori pushes down her revulsion only to have it spread into her fingers. They turn cold, numb; her mouth, stone dry. Nori is as bottomless and sick as she was outside that door. She shouldn't be there. Nothing could be clearer. But her father won't listen, and her sister won't help her.

And her mother only trembles in the front seat.

Nori helps Kayla cart supplies into the house while her father leads her mother inside. "I'm glad this is such a beautiful day," her mother says, pulling close to her husband. "We're really lucky." Nori's father looks less anxious, and his smile is almost enough to wipe away the scars of his exhaustion. Nori is happy to see it and happy her mother is becoming herself again, but she still can't stifle her metastasizing fear.

When they are all inside the house, Nori's father issues her and Kayla each a dry mop while her mother watches.

"This is the final clean-up," he says. "We'll meet back in an hour."

"Girls, before you go," her mother says, "I want you to come here."

Nori and Kayla approach, and their mother awkwardly embraces them.

"I want you both to know how much I love you, and I always will. I don't want you to ever forget it."

She kisses them on their heads as though they're children. Nori hates it. Hates what she's being forced to confront.

"Mom, can we just get this over with? I want to leave."

"Sure," she says, but doesn't let go. Not immediately. And when she does, it's reluctantly. "Just remember what I said."

"Yes, Mom," they reply unintentionally in unison and go their separate ways.

Nori keeps her distance from the old bedroom. She isn't drawn to it. If anything, she's repelled. The thrum's pressure in her head worsens, crossing the threshold into painfulness. Nori does what cleaning she can, leaving the rest for Kayla. It's hardly enough of a punishment, but it's a start.

It's just after noon when Kayla and Nori help their father carry the last of the boxes to the trunk of the car. They drop them where instructed, and the three watch as the lid is closed. Then their father turns around, looking satisfied and weary.

"That's it, girls. We're done."

"We're done? As in, we aren't coming back?"

"Yup. That's it. The realtor will take care of the rest. Your weekends are yours again."

It seems impossible.

"Girls, thank you again for all your help. It's been hard on all of us, your mother most of all, but you two stepped up, and we couldn't be prouder."

Nori wants to scream with joy. She's going to leave the house and never return. She's going to escape the triangle and what's been waiting for her.

Then Kayla looks back at the house and asks, "Is Mom still inside?"

Nori's relief curdles.

"Your mother needed some time to say goodbye. She'll be out in a minute."

He suggests they wait in the car. Nori and Kayla climb into the back seat while he sits behind the steering wheel. He puts his arm on the back of the passenger's seat and looks over his shoulder at them, asks Kayla about her field hockey team.

All the while, Nori's heart races and body shakes. Something is imminent.

She must bite down to keep from screaming. Her thoughts race with fear and terrible inevitability. That sickening thrum will never fade. There is something coming for her, and there is nothing she can do. She knows she must enter that room and face it.

Her father pauses and mutters, "Your mother should have been out by now." He looks at the front door, this time from under a furrowed brow. "Maybe I should go in and check on her. Make sure she's okay."

"No, Dad," Nori blurts, then stammers, "I mean, I'll go get her."

He thinks for a moment.

"Okay," he says, still uncertain. "But take your sister with you."

"Dad!" Kayla complains, but Nori is already ahead of her.

"Kayla should stay here with you," she says. "It won't be long."

She leaps from the car before he can stop her. And before she can change her mind. Nori wants to say something more but can't. That's how tiny and deflated her lungs have become. She knows where her mother is, and it won't be safe for anyone to come with her. Nori looks back at her father's eyes watching her from the front seat, Kayla's eyes from the back, and she forces a smile and half a wave. Her legs don't want to go, but she makes them.

It's been fewer than thirty minutes since they left the house, but stepping back inside, she hardly recognizes it. Walls seem misshapen and bowed outward. The entranceway stretches into the distance, lined with unfamiliar doorways turned dark.

"Mom?" Nori's voice is barely above a whisper. She hopes her mother won't be in the old bedroom. She hopes that she is already on her way out so they can leave the house behind together.

But her mother is not waiting for her inside. Nori finds nothing but the thrum that grows more painful the further in she staggers.

The bedroom door is locked when Nori reaches it. The noise from within nearly screaming, and she screams too as she reaches to take the knob. Everything shakes, everything jitters. The world rings.

"Mom!" She pounds. "Mom, are you in there?"

Just swirling chaos, deafening thrum.

Nori tries to get in. Can't.

Something inside is waiting for her. It has been patient, but now that she's so close its patience has strained. If she opens the door, it might overwhelm her.

But she must keep going.

"Mom!"

The lock won't budge, so she throws herself at the door. Over and over. She keeps calling out, each scream punctuated by her body's impact. The frame begins to crack. First slowly, then all at once. And when the door gives way Nori tumbles forward, crashing to the ground hard enough to stun her.

Disoriented, she pushes herself to her knees. She looks up.

And sees it hanging in front of her.

The inverted triangle has grown so tall it obscures the ceiling, intense waves of distortion emanating outward. That shimmer, those long rods shifting through a flurry of colors. She feels it in her chest. And in the middle of that horrible shape is a reflection the distortion does not touch. A mirror bounded by three equal sides. Nori sees in it a reflection of the room she's in, the thin hardwood floors stained shades of caramel and coffee, the out-of-date radiator beneath the single paned window. And she sees herself, kneeling where she's landed.

Except she doesn't. The person in the mirror wears her clothes and is shaped like her, but the reflection's hair is messier, streaked, and its face has dark, jagged lines running across it. Her eyes are more deeply set. The other Nori mimics her movements exactly, but she isn't her, really. It's as if she'd been worn down and defeated.

Nori's reflection and she both look at the pulsing triangle hanging above them. In its presence, the thrum is unrelenting, and it affects Nori, siphoning her. She frantically struggles against it. But it's useless. She is pinned like an insect and drained.

The thrum passes through her. The vibrating rods sway. Nori remains on her hurting knees, lost, until she realizes she is no longer afraid. The discovery doesn't startle her. It doesn't do anything because she is no longer anything. She just is. Is just there. Existing in the moment. Whatever the triangle is doing, beneath its glower, its omnipresent thrum, inside her there is nothing. No pain, no fear, no love. Her body, but only her body is alive.

Then the thrum's frequency changes. The incessant drone begins to sound like something new. It sounds like words. Nori concentrates, trying to parse them. Until she realizes she already knows what they're telling her.

They're telling her nothing. Because that's all there is.

The triangle swells, colored rods projecting like an exploding nova. In the reflection, the not-Nori stares at the ceiling. Nori looks up too, her face burning, and sees the triangle move.

It unmoors itself from the ceiling, begins to descend. The gurgling noise, the half-understood words, is deafening as it falls. Nori's reflection doesn't look at her. The other her's gaze is stuck on what the triangle has been obscuring. On what its descent reveals. Nori can't read the look on her reflection's face. She's too distracted by the triangle, slowly dropping, inching closer.

Nori is kneeling on the floor, looking up. The triangle is a flat object against the ceiling. Its shape doesn't change. Doesn't angle, doesn't slide from view. Nevertheless, somehow, impossibly, it moves toward her. The reflection in its middle shows the not-Nori similarly kneeling, watching above. But as the triangle approaches, as the lowest of its three vertices nears, the reflection flickers, the waves of colored rods shudder, and everything turns inward. The triangle turns black. Solid black.

Then the triangle pierces her skull.

Nori's body does not react. Her body accepts the horrible, inverted triangle, accepts the blinding pain and empty void. As each inch presses into her, another inch of her dies. Her hope withers. Her will fades. Until there is nothing but the triangle. The impossible pressure that smothers her.

When it's done, the blinding light dulls, the cold void warms, the gurgling sound ends, Nori finds herself still on her knees, face cast to the ceiling with eyes closed, the points of an unwelcome triangle contained within her. She is an emptied vessel refilled. She no longer cries. She no longer does anything but exist and fights the urge to do so. Fights the urge without knowing why.

It's Kayla's screams that break the silence. Nori snaps her eyes open and stares above her at the light fixture, at the heavy weight hanging there that the triangle had been hiding. There is no kicking, there is no struggle, there is nothing but the gently swinging aftermath. Nori can't stop looking, mesmerized by the simple motion. Even when Kayla runs past, she stares. Even when her father shouts, she stares. Even when she's being dragged from the room while someone uprights the overturned wooden chair, she stares. Nori stares without judgment or question. She stares with all the understanding and acceptance she needs.

Nori's submission to the triangle clarifies what no one understands. That there is nothing for anyone. That there is no escape to later. That this is all there is.

Nori will let it be enough for as long as she can.

Thea Was First

I

Thea was first. We'd found the book in the Tomthål forest only a few weeks earlier, hidden in a split tree trunk painted long ago to look like a tiny house. The bright primary colors were unexpected so deep in the woods, so we put down our packs and took photos. Thea, most of all, couldn't contain herself. *A hjärtahus! A real hjärtahus! The kids at the shelter will love this,* she said, practically dancing in her boots. *I'm going to hang these photos all over the classroom!* But I found the painted house unnerving; we were so far from electric lights or traffic that it felt as though we'd left humanity behind and were walking where no one else had ever been. Yet the painted house proved otherwise, and finding it felt like an invasion. It felt *wrong.* But none of us wanted to admit it. Especially not Yänna, who was barely speaking to me as it was. Instead, everyone smiled and joked to hide their discomfort. And it might have worked had Thea not looked closer at that split and noticed among the ants and fleas the book hidden inside.

But it was her brother, Isak, who removed it. Yänna told him not to in that way she had, but he didn't care. His confidence in his own instincts intrigued me—which was something I couldn't admit in front of Yänna. She'd decided how she felt about him a long time ago, and I couldn't disagree openly, not when she was already mad. So I didn't. But she couldn't stop my quiet fascination. Thea once called him *empathic,* and I wondered what that meant. Did his confidence breed it? Had I been more like him, would things between me and Yänna have been as strained? Were I more like him, would I better understand her persistent anger? Because I didn't understand it; I didn't really understand anything.

At least that made it easier not to care. Isak taking the book from the tree didn't bother me the same way. It *did* make me uncomfortable, but *everything* made me uncomfortable. Pretending to care about it was a waste of effort. I might have tried, though, had I known what we were setting in motion. But none of us did. Not Isak who flipped through the pages and questioned what the diagrams meant, circles inside circles like a spirograph. Not Thea who asked what the book was bound in and if it was some sort of skin or leather. Not Yänna who wondered aloud how anyone could have written so much when their handwriting was so cramped. Not even I who heard a thud echo from somewhere but couldn't pinpoint the spot, then suggested, innocently, that it might have just been a woodpecker driving its head against a tree.

"Woodpeckers don't hit their heads against trees," Yänna informed me. I wasn't so sure she was right.

Thea found the book, Isak removed it, but I'm the one who kept it. I didn't want Yänna to know, so I dummied a step as we left and slipped the book out of the split and into my Norrøna jacket's pocket. Yänna clearly wanted us to leave it where it was, but I had an irresistible hunger to defy her. I didn't know why nor did I care. I took it like anyone would have in my position. I took it for spite if anything.

Like I said: Thea was first. One moment alive, the next not. The time between weeks. None of us heard from her and none of us worried about her. It was just Thea, we thought. Moppy- and platinum-haired Thea. Thea, who didn't have a cell phone and was never home long enough to answer her landline. Thea, who wept over holiday advertisements, who read our palms and told us what great things we had in store. Thea, whose laugh was a high-pitched wheeze and who never stopped grinning. It was Thea who was first, and after her things went bad fast.

Of all people, Isak had to discover her. She was at the bottom of a stairwell outside her place when he stumbled upon her body. He told us afterward he didn't immediately recognize what he saw; it didn't look like a person. He thought it was a large dog who'd been thrown by a speeding car—something that might have been brought to Dr.

Karim to put down while its owner cried and held what remained of its paws. Then Isak saw the mop of white blond hair, so much like his own, clotted and spread across what was left of her lap. It sent him into some kind of fugue state, but he remained aware enough to call the police and sit patiently on a stair until they arrived. I know because he called me, too. We barely spoke, but it was clear he was in trouble, and I ignored Yänna's narrow-eyed judgment and went to find him. I arrived just as he was being placed into the back of a police cruiser and driven away. I asked a gray-pallored officer what happened, but all he could manage was to point a trembling finger toward the stairwell and at the dismembered Thea lying beneath it.

What happened to her? None of us knew, and that ignorance was troubling. For Yänna more than me. At least she became less critical of me for a while. More patient. Asking me to stay over. I sometimes found her crying at odd times, and struggled with how to react. I didn't understand her moods, but I did have other things on my mind. More troubling things. I had to let Yänna's suffocating embrace bury them, though, because she needed me, and I knew that meant I had to be there for her and find some way to make her happy. Or, if not happy, then at least happier. Not that I knew how to do that, either.

"Why do you want me to be happier? Thea's gone," Yänna sobbed. It only confused me more.

Then it was Isak's turn.

The police didn't hold him long. There was no reason to. He didn't remember what they'd said to him, or what he'd said in return, but he knew Dr. Karim had vouched for him, and had driven him home after their questions were answered. Yänna and I didn't find this out for days, not until we received the note about Thea's funeral. It had only been a week since we'd seen Isak—since Thea's death—but he looked as though he hadn't slept in months. Yänna hugged him hard as I watched and tried to make sense of her behavior.

Despite the circumstances Isak seemed in control of himself. I quietly marveled. He was a few years younger than me but was able to navigate the world in a way I never could. I was convinced he could have worked in finance and become wealthy ten times over, but instead he settled for being a veterinary assistant. He said it was a calling, but it seemed like a tragedy to me. But even the control he showed at his sister's funeral had its limits, and the longer I watched him standing in his slim black suit, cemetery dirt ground into his trouser cuffs, the more the cracks began to show. Cracks that couldn't be fixed. Cracks through which something irreplaceable had slipped.

It's why after the funeral I dissuaded Yänna from visiting him, even knowing she was trying to make amends for her past behavior. It was obvious he wanted to be left alone, though I confessed to only understanding his desire, not his reasoning. Yänna said she did and attempted to explain, but eventually she threw up her hands, called me names, and stormed out of the room. Maybe I should have tried harder.

I had no reason at the time to connect any of this with the hjärtahus and the book we found inside its split. Why would I? I'd barely looked at that thin faerie book once we returned home—I hadn't even removed it from my jacket pocket. If I had I might have remembered the discomfort it evoked in me, the nervous sensations, but I felt uncomfortable and nervous all the time so I doubt I would have known the difference.

As the days added up Yänna grew more worried and would no longer listen when I suggested Isak needed more time. I didn't know if it were true or not, but I heard someone suggest it at the funeral and it sounded smart. Yänna reported later trying to visit Isak but not being able to get past his door. Nor would he answer his phone. Maybe Thea's death had broken him open and he didn't know how to close the wound. Doesn't that happen sometimes? Isak's decline worried Yänna in a way I never would have predicted and I wasn't sure what to do. For either of them.

"You're just going to keep going to work like nothing's happened, aren't you?" Yänna decided to ask me, as though there were something else I should be doing and wasn't.

I was in a client's boardroom when Isak's number came up on my phone. I had to excuse myself from discussing their bankruptcy acquisition to take the call. I just ignored their unhappy stares. When I found some privacy I discovered Isak didn't have much to say. All he wanted was for me to come over. He didn't beg, but by the quaver in his voice I knew he hadn't ruled it out. With Thea gone I guessed he had no one else to reach out to. Still, his call was a surprise; I didn't consider myself useful in a crisis, but I knew I couldn't turn him down. It was no casual request. Besides, part of me was flattered to be asked. As much as I envied Isak, I also relished getting the opportunity to have the upper hand. Maybe it was because I so rarely did. So I agreed to go as soon as I could, and he asked only one favor: that I not bring Yänna. He couldn't give me a straight answer as to why, but his indecisiveness told me everything I wanted to know just the same.

I arrived at the scarred wooden door of his downtown apartment and knocked. The peephole's lens rattled, but otherwise I heard no sounds from within. I knocked again, louder, and felt it echo inside me. The hallway smelled strange—tangy, like burnt wood—and I didn't like it. I'd made a mistake going; there was nothing I could do for him and he should have known it. I pivoted away, but before I could leave a loud crash made me leap unexpectedly. My first thought was worry about what Isak had done to himself and if I'd be blamed. I scrambled to my feet and tried twisting the doorknob. It wouldn't turn. So I shouted his name and started kicking the lock until the frame around it cracked.

The door swung open but I didn't rush in. I just stood and stared.

And stared.

It took no more than a second, probably less, but long enough to imprint the horrible image on my eyes. The creature was large, maybe the size of a small car, constricted by the walls of the apartment. Its body was covered in a spatter of malformed cancerous spiracles that drooled a gooey substance and wheezed in a way I first mistook for labored breathing. The thing was curved and thin like a misshapen flea, but where its body tapered sat a head with a face. A human face. *Thea's* face. Smeared with blood, frozen in weepful sorrow, betraying no animation or trace of humanity. The giant creature scurried over Isak, delicately probing his torn chest with its elongated black tibia and sharp tarsi. It was like some grotesque surgeon, spilling his organs and entrails across the braided rug. I inadvertently made a noise on seeing it. That was a mistake. The creature, already startled by my entrance, twitched then scuttled over and across the wall toward me then stopped. Thea's bloodied weeping face hanging from it like an old mask, vacantly surveying me. I squirmed, its unchanging expression evoking an unsettling feeling in me I couldn't describe.

Then, abruptly, the creature fled. Thea's weeping face swung away and its giant body followed, maneuvering inexpertly in the tiny apartment, knocking an armchair aside and a yellowed lamp to the floor. When it reached the broken window it skittered away so quickly I wondered if it had even been there. I suppose I felt berated by the impossibility of what I'd just witnessed. It couldn't be true, I told myself. And yet the mess at my feet that was once Isak told me I was very very wrong.

II

I don't remember leaving Isak's apartment and I don't remember running, but somehow I ended up on the side of the road, hands on my knees, panting so fiercely I thought I might turn inside out. It was all too much, my head was too muddled, so when the black cab pulled up beside me I thought for a second it was that creature and almost screamed. Instead the driver rolled down her window and shouted at me fearfully in a thick Greek accent. I didn't understand it; I just snatched open the door and threw myself onto her back seat. I shouted, ordering her to drive—at least I tried to, but in my panic I wasn't sure the words were in the right order. She just kept saying *"Pou? Pou?"* until I somehow managed to string together Yänna's address. I had to repeat it four times before she hurriedly flipped the meter, and only then did it occur to me that the creature might be watching and might follow us straight to Yänna. I told the driver to wait, but she ignored me and pulled the black cab onto the road too fast. I didn't even know where we were and already we were gone.

I spent the entire ride vigilantly panicked. The driver didn't say anything; she just watched me nervously in her rearview mirror as I darted from window to window for almost an hour, making sure we weren't being chased. When she pulled the cab up to the front of Yänna's building I threw a handful of money at her and tried to leap out. The doors were locked. And she wouldn't unlock them until she counted the bills. *Éna, dýo, tría* . . . Meanwhile, sweat seeped into my collar as I struggled to scan the now-dark streets through the rear window, hyperaware of any unnatural movements. Shadows crept strangely, as though they were circling, and I couldn't help myself. I started wrenching the door handles as hard as I could in an effort to open them. The driver shouted at me, her hands flailing, but I ignored her and kept at it. Then I heard the locks click and by the time she was frenziedly cursing I'd already launched myself out of the door. I stumbled over the sidewalk and dove into the concrete, but she didn't wait to see if I was okay. I was already smelling the cab's exhaust by the time I hit the ground.

But I didn't care. I was already on my feet and hurtling toward Yänna's door.

I'd arrived later than I'd thought. I pounded my fists on the door forever, barely slowing as I checked over my shoulder for whatever was about to ambush me. When Yänna swung the door open, dressed only in an old heather-gray shirt, I pushed past her and charged inside. My limbs were weak, but I managed to stay upright long enough to tell her to close the door. She looked at me as she would at a wailing baby, and no matter how much I pleaded she stayed by the door, spitefully holding it wide open. Beyond her I saw dusk streets and heard the scraping and scratching of things outside. It could have been tree branches, or it could have been something worse. I shouted and she turned, unhurriedly, to look out into the dark. I'd had enough. I sprang to my feet and before she could stop me I yanked the door from her hands and slammed it shut.

I'd never done anything like that before. I looked at Yänna. She didn't speak. She just disappeared into the kitchen. While she was gone

I hurriedly drew the blinds closed and double-checked the door's locks were bolted. Only after I'd rechecked them again did my heart begin to slow. But my legs wouldn't stop jittering. I found it concerning.

Yänna re-emerged from the kitchen and immediately stormed toward me. Her expression was full of both irritation and anger. She wagged her finger in my face as she shouted, "There is something very wrong with you!" and I felt I wanted to wither. But then something in me broke, something hiding in the emptiness but goaded by my fear. I shouted back. Yänna was not prepared for it. She staggered, momentarily wrong-footed and weakened. Without thinking I sprang. I told *exactly* what happened. I told her Isak was dead.

The change was instantaneous. Her face began to tremble, and that tremble moved in waves across her body until every limb shook. I didn't know what to do when she collapsed onto her sectional, her worn and tired face turning red and blubbery. I admit I was thrown; she'd never cared for Isak before, so what had changed?

"God, is there nothing inside that head of yours at all?" she asked between her sobs.

I took the chair across from her and waited for her bout to end. When she'd cried herself out she looked up at me with swollen, bloodshot eyes and I realized I had no idea what she was about to say.

"What happened?" she managed to squeak out.

I hesitated, not knowing how to explain. Not in a way she'd believe. I didn't even believe it. I glanced at the door and the windows to make sure they were in place. I heard a rattle as something scurried past the front door. I didn't like it, and shoved my twitching hands into my Norrøna's pockets to calm them. When I did so I was startled to find something else already there. I pulled it out to see what I'd forgotten.

"What are you hiding?" Yänna asked, her voice rough and suspicious. But she was wrong; I wasn't hiding anything. I told her the truth: it was the book we'd found in Tomthål forest—the one she'd told Isak not to take. I had taken it instead. I opened it randomly to a page full of strange diagrams, held it out so she could see for herself.

Her eyes widened as she stared at my hands. I looked down to find blood had soaked my cuffs black.

Did she think the blood was mine?

"What have you done?" Yänna asked, slowly standing. When I didn't say anything she repeated herself, the quaver becoming something more bitter. More seething. "I asked what you did!"

I stepped back.

Then stepped forward, assuring her it wasn't my blood. It was Isak's. Isak's, not mine. Not anybody else's. Something got him. Something large and strange with a face I still saw whenever I closed my eyes. Thea's face.

That was not something she was ready for. I couldn't describe the look she gave me—wide and piercing, filled with so much anger I didn't think she'd be able to process it. So I held off telling her the worst part: that I believed it was coming for us. I didn't know when or how, but it was.

There was a pause. And then she shouted, and it was so loud I thought for sure we'd been found. I spun toward the window in terror.

But no. It wasn't that.

She demanded to know what really happened to Isak, what I'd done, as though there were some answer that would make sense. Maybe make her feel better and more in control of her world. But there was nothing I could tell her. All that I knew was it had something to do with the hjärtahus.

Surprisingly, that quieted her. She looked confused.

The hjärtahus, I said. In Tomthål forest. The painted tree with the split. The one where we found the book.

She shook her head.

"What book?"

Before I could make sense of what she'd said there was a crash outside. Something big and destructive. I rushed to the window, pushing past Yänna and ignoring her protests. I saw shadows moving everywhere, but I couldn't see what caused it. And Yänna didn't care. She asked me again what I'd done and what happened to Isak and Thea. The same unreasonable questions, as though our lives weren't in immediate danger. I thought maybe she was panicking, so I did what I guessed was right: I stepped closer and tried to hug her.

She shoved me away, then glared at me coldly and with vicious incredulity.

I didn't understand what I'd done. And she wouldn't tell me.

She just demanded I disappear.

My mistake was grabbing her shoulders. I just wanted her to calm down and realize the danger we were both in, but she started screaming and clawing at my face. I let her go, my hands flying up to protect myself, and when I drew them away I saw they were streaked with blood. That's when my wounds began to sting.

I don't know what I said to her then. The memory is lost in the heat of my rage.

What I do remember is that Yänna remained suddenly cool throughout my outburst, waiting. When I returned to my senses she told me simply to leave. By then I was too exhausted to fight it.

Only when I was outside, in the night, the door slamming behind me, did my rational fear return. I swung around and pounded my fists as hard as I could on the door. I had to get back inside.

I tried everything I could think of to make her listen. I told her the creature was coming for us and we needed to escape. I told her splitting up was a bad idea and would get us killed. I told her without me she'd never make it. All of that failed to act as a key. I looked up at her neighbors' windows, surprised they hadn't told me to leave.

The final kick was when Yänna turned out the porch light, smothering me in darkness. That's when I screamed my final curse, not caring who might hear. I told her she'd come running to me eventually. She'd come running and crying when it came for her. And when she did, I promised on Thea's and Isak's graves I wouldn't open the door.

To my surprise, that failed to move her, so I kicked the door as hard as I could. It accomplished nothing but made the street erupt with the terrifying chirping of millions of legs drawing like bows against one another.

A shadow across the street caught my eye. It moved across the side of a neighboring building. Something big and darker than the night around it. I heard crackling, clicking.

I didn't wait to see what it was; I just ran.

I made it maybe to the end of the block. I definitely made it around the corner. Just far enough to find my escape suddenly blocked by a slippery black shape filling the sidewalk. I pivoted, trying to avoid it, and to avoid driving my face into rows of leaking cancerous spiracles. But my balance was thrown and I tumbled onto the concrete, rolling and skinning my hands. The impact shook me, and I was too dazed to make sense of what was seeing. I thought it was Isak rushing in, extending a long arm to help me up. But that arm was thin, dark, and vibrating, and when the spinning world slowed I realized it wasn't Isak at all. It just had his face.

There was a scream. It could have been mine. I lashed out and the creature reeled back, Isak's lifeless face shuddering. For a moment it staggered, unsure, and I used its hesitation to get on my feet and bolt.

It was quickly on my heels and stayed there. I don't know how I managed to keep ahead of it, but I knew my adrenaline was going to wear out quickly and I had to find some sort of escape. It was pure luck that I spotted the chain-link fence at the back of a small house's lot. I made that my focus.

But the lead I had was narrowing—I could practically hear its skittering inside my head—and when I reached the fence and vaulted it I felt something tug at the leg of my trousers. It pulled me short, but not enough to prevent me from rolling across the top of the fence—the metal jabbing into my back—and onto the other side where I landed in a crumpled heap.

I didn't feel the pain, though. I was too full of fear. I shot up to see the corrupt flattened creature pacing back and forth, pushing itself against the chain-link. It creaked so loudly under the weight I raised my hands in hopes they might protect me. I didn't lower them until I saw the fence was clearly going to hold.

Isak's dead white eyes were rolled up in its head but nevertheless they were fixed on me, the creature's pacing growing more frantic. I stared back unblinkingly as I backed away, terrified it might figure out how to get to me. It pushed its face against the fence again and one of us started to scream. I turned and bolted away, refusing to look back with the childish hope that what I couldn't see couldn't hurt me.

III

I quickly realized I had nowhere to go but home. There was no one left to help me who wasn't dead. I checked over my shoulder the entire journey, making sure the shadows following me weren't anything more than shadows. The barren streets didn't ease my mind—and neither did the sound of dry leaves rattling on the asphalt, pushed by the frigid autumn wind. When I reached my house I dashed in and slammed the door behind me, then immediately threw the bolts and shut off the lights. Even then, I didn't feel safe, so I retreated into the house as far as I could without losing sight of the door. There, in that corner, I let my body crumple to the ground. I was exhausted. Yet I couldn't keep the images of Isak's torn-up body and Thea's dead unnatural face from my thoughts. I didn't think I'd ever understand what happened; it was so large and impossible an idea I could barely comprehend it. What I saw was ghastly, and I couldn't describe its effect on me. Because, maybe, it was a *lack* of effect . . . if that even made any sense.

The longer the front door remained intact, the more the balance between by terror and my exhaustion shifted. My eyes refused to blink at first, but after an hour of staring at an unchanging door I couldn't keep them open any longer. I fought it, but somehow, at some time, in some way, without my fully realizing it, they closed and I slipped into a kind of sleep.

When I woke the darkness of the house was so absolute I didn't know for sure I'd opened my eyes. The curtains were drawn, the lights were off, and maybe every light in the world had gone out, every star in the sky collapsed. I felt worse than alone. I felt trapped.

I reached into my Norrøna's pocket for my phone and instead found the small book I'd taken from the hjärtahus. It flew from my hand as I fished it out, tumbling across the floor into the nothing around me. I heard pages tear free and spill out, and I blindly swept the floor with my hands to find them.

But I couldn't. I couldn't feel them at all.

So I sat back in my cramped corner and tried to pick out the door's outline in the dark. Almost immediately that dark started to churn. To change. The shadows twisted and assembled themselves into shapes, and those shapes into an image. A tree. It was a tree.

That tree.

The one from Tomthål forest. Split right down the middle.

Before I could stop myself I reached out my hand and placed it in that phantom cleft where we'd once found the book, but now I couldn't feel anything at all. Just an emptiness I knew shouldn't be there yet had always been.

Then a noise shook me awake from my half-dream. It was so loud I thought the world was ending. I leapt to my feet, startled and confused. The door. It was the door. There was something *pounding* on it.

Yänna. It had to be. She must have escaped and was injured. Injured but alive. Lying on my stoop, bleeding, desperate for my attention just as I'd promised she would be. But what if that creature with Isak's face was nearby? I inched forward as though I were nothing; empty, light as air. As though there were nothing to me at all. And when I reached the door I carefully put my mouth against that small crack between the door and its frame. And I whispered out to her. I whispered to Yänna.

There was no response. So I tried again. Louder.

That's when I began to doubt.

Because how did I know? That it was her? Out there, pawing at the door? Shouldn't I have felt it?

Shouldn't I have felt anything at all?

Isak would have. Thea, too. Even Yänna. Their faces hovered before me. Judging me.

Outside there were gasps. Dying gasps. Or maybe it was the wheeze of oozing spiracles pushing air like bellows.

No. I couldn't doubt myself. I knew. I was sure I knew. It was

Yänna. No matter how we left things she had come running to me. Just like I told her she would. I had to open the door.

But maybe I'd open it just a crack. Just to be sure. I knew I didn't need to, but what could it hurt?

Carefully I slid back the locks. I put my hand on the knob and cautiously started to turn.

Slowly, slowly, the latch retracted into the frame, the strike plate came loose. The hinges were barely audible when they unstuck. I pressed my face against the frame until the crack of the door opened wide enough. Until I could see through it.

The process seemed to take forever.

But maybe it's because afterward everything moved so damn fast.

IV

The first thing I saw was Yänna's face. Just for an instant. Just long enough to be confused. Then the door was shoved open, knocking me off-balance. The frame filled with something so black it eclipsed the night.

I didn't wait to hear those long ebony legs scrambling to get inside. I ran. Behind me, brick and plaster cracked with the sounds of destruction. The horrible chirping was so loud my ears screamed at me.

I stumbled over my furniture as I fled, trying to get to the staircase, hoping it wouldn't be able to follow me to the second floor. Against the dark of the house I saw Yänna's face projected. But it was as I'd just seen her—devoid of any life, an immovable expression of sorrow; eyes misaligned and staring somewhere past me. I tried to push the memory down, but it wouldn't go.

I don't know how close that creature was. But I thought every step I took would be my last. Each followed by the echoes of crashing as that thing climbed across the walls and the ceiling, spiralling through the rooms, funneling toward me. I managed to slide myself through the half-closed kitchen door before it caught me. The opening, too small for it to fit through. I had a straight line to the staircase.

But I didn't make it. I managed to leap up no more than four stairs before there was an excruciating pain in my calf. My leg wouldn't move. Confused, I tried to wrench free it, but instead I was yanked backwards, thrown. My hands clawed uselessly at the walls as I twisted through the air. I hit the floor so hard I felt my nose pop, my cheekbone fracture.

Above me bobbed Yänna's dead vacant face. Haloing it were a dozen long black tarsi, frantically stabbing into me, pinning me down. I knew it was the end, but I desperately didn't want to die. I didn't. Anyone else, please, but not me. But there was no one else left. I feebly swatted the creature's legs, somehow hoping to discourage it. I refused to give up. Then those bladed interlocking tibia pressed into my ribs and, like dozens of knives, flayed my flesh.

From Yänna's frozen wailing mouth dropped a rough bifurcated tongue that curled sideways in opposite directions. It pressed against my sternum and I yelped with pain—the burn was like nothing I'd ever experienced. Excruciating flashes of Tomthål forest, of the hjärtahus, of the book, seared my brain. As much as I'd fought it before, at that moment I gave up. I begged for death.

Yänna's re-embodied face leaned closer; sharp tibia sliced red lines in my chest. I closed my eyes and awaited what was next.

But there was nothing.

I opened my eyes.

The creature rose up. Yänna's head cocked. Her blank face confused.

I didn't understand, either.

Giant black legs plucked themselves free from me one at a time, lodging themselves instead into the walls for purchase. And when the last was removed the giant creature lifted its body and scrambled sideways across the wall. I heard it crash its way through the house, back the way it came, leaving me prone and bleeding on the floor.

Bleeding but alive.

I don't know how long I lay still, my body on fire as pools of blood clotted around me. Everything hurt, but as deep as that pain went it didn't go everywhere. There was one place inside me that remained numb. It was from that place I gathered enough strength to roll over, then a moment later to pull myself to my knees. Using the broken furniture around me, I climbed to my feet and staggered to the open door.

I thought I wanted to lock it before that creature came back to do to me what it had done to Thea, Isak, and Yänna, but when I reached the empty doorway I stood there, agog and confused.

The other houses of my street. Their lights were burned out, and on their stoops, or their roofs, or their lawns was a creature that mirrored my own tormentor. Large and flat, a human face so slack you'd think it was dead yet still on the verge of tears. But I didn't recognize any of them. All their faces were mysteries to me. And there were so many.

But at least I wasn't among them.

In the red glow of the dawning sun, my body weeping blood as theirs wept something worse, I put my hands in my empty pockets and watched, waiting for the inevitable mayhem and screams.

A moment later I pulled my hands out. Looked at them.

They were dirty and they were bloody and they were empty.

Completely empty.

And I couldn't tell you why.

Black Bequeathments

My father and I didn't have the kind of relationship you see in the movies. We didn't play catch, he didn't help me with my homework, and we never went to ballgames. We were two different people living, for a time, in the same house. Some of this was likely due to my late mother, who seemed to regret marrying him almost as much as he did her, and her way of getting revenge for ruining her life was to attempt to turn their only child against him. But most of the reason my father and I didn't connect was because he didn't belong. He was a foreigner, a tobacco farmer from a small village in Portugal, who found himself living across the ocean in a family that held none of his values, and though he quietly railed against it as best he could, he was never able to overcome the pressure I was under to be the most westernized version of myself, watching *Dukes of Hazzard* cartoons while eating Frosted Flakes or grilled cheese sandwiches.

Since my father didn't know how to relate to me or my mother, he became a ghost. He still lived in our house, ate our food, contributed to household expenses, but did most of these things during those hours I was at school or asleep. The rest of the time, he clung close to his old-country friends in those small bare-walled cafés that litter rundown subdivision strip malls, the sort that somehow make enough to remain open, all the while hosting illegal low-stakes card games in the back all day. At these places, my father was warm and gregarious and well-loved by everyone. I know this, because those friends told me so at his funeral, while I silently wondered what the man they described had to do with my father, lying in his casket only a few feet away.

My father was a cipher to me, despite how many awkward years I'd spent sitting with him, trying to come up with something to talk about, wondering if he was doing the same or if the idea of connecting to his son never occurred to him. Sometimes I'd ask him questions about how he'd met my mother and what life was like before coming to America, but most of the time I'd give up with a shrug and find something else to do, never understanding that just because he'd always been there didn't mean he always would be. Even after my mother died, five years before him, it still didn't sink in. But why would it? How often does one contemplate the death of an acquaintance? Of a relative rarely spoken to or seen? In many ways, that's all he was, and the failure for that lies as much with me as it does with him. Perhaps more with me because I should have known better.

Maybe if we'd been as close as a father and son ought to be, I would have understood what I found in his house after he'd gone. I spent every weekend and most weeknights trying to make a dent in the clutter that had taken over my father's life since my mother's passing. I thought I knew about hoarding and what it looked like—a world of stacked newspapers and saved trash settled in layers of sediment, just waiting for some future archeologist or bereaved child to sift through—but all I knew were its extremes. There was true hoarding, and there was my father's hoarding, where small items were stuffed into drawers to get them out of the way, and the effort to throw them out was always more than the effort just to start another drawer. With much of my late mother's belongings gone or donated, there were a lot of those drawers to use, so when I arrived to the house after his death, the house that had been my childhood home, I found it as much a burden as it would have been had both my parents gone at the same time. Of course, that would have been impossible; they were never together in the same room long enough to suffer that sort of tragedy.

But it wasn't the hoarding that was the biggest surprise; it was what I found in those drawers and closets of hidden things. I'd spent the first few weeks gamely sorting the clothes from the garbage so I could donate anything of use, but the task was too overwhelming and slow. Eventually I had to give up and started bagging everything by indiscriminate handfuls to take to the dump. This was how I almost missed the box. Made of dark blue cardboard and measuring a foot and a half long and almost as deep, it was sandwiched between a bundle of folded, smoke-stained blazers and a stack of white tablecloths that had that sour mothball smell that old cotton seems to get. It was only by luck I unearthed it, and only because of a momentary curiosity amid my depression that I paused long enough to open it.

I expected one of my mother's old ceramic vases, part of a collection that I'd learned held no value after she'd gone; or perhaps another box of photographs, black and white memories of distant relatives from the old country, dressed in black dresses and matching scarves. Instead, what I found was the strangest thing I'd even seen—a cheap-looking statue of some impossible animal, with arms that ran around its body like rays of a sun, and an elephantine trunk that was curled like the letter R to form a handle, although there was no reason to carry the statue anywhere. Its surface was rough and pocked, highlighting the visible signs of human hands that shaped the clay as it hardened, and the entire piece was spraypainted the sort of dull crass gold you get from a clogged can that has been kept too long. Rivulets of paint dried in solid lines over its bulbous body. I took the statue out and thumbed its crumbling edges, confirming what I suspected: it wasn't even fired clay.

I saw my father do a lot of things over my life. I saw him paint our house, I saw him fix our plumbing. I saw him landscape our tiny yard, and saw him install us a new linoleum floor. I saw him watch television into the night and saw him sleep into the day. I saw my father doing nearly everything a man might do to idle his days away, one after the other, as though death were never coming. But the one thing I never saw my father do was look at a piece of art, let alone craft one. Despite its homemade appearance, I knew that whatever that statue was, it didn't come from him. But if not, then where? And why was it in his house?

I couldn't allow myself the luxury of sorrow and regret over how much I didn't know my father; I had a house to clean and prepare for sale. So I put the lid back on the box as I did on my own guilt and despair—haphazardly—and pushed them temporarily aside. Sometimes I think back to that moment and wonder why I didn't just drop it in a black garbage bag along with everything else. Would it have spared me from what was coming or only end up making it worse?

It was a week before I noticed the box again, stacked on a small table alongside an ancient clock radio and bundles of still-wrapped socks. I only dimly remembered finding it, and I had to lift the lid again to recall what it contained. The statue's gold coating looked even duller and cheaper than I remembered, and I could see small fractures along its appendages as though the paint had shrunk as it dried. There were no markings or labels anywhere inside the box or on the statue that told me anything about where it came from or what it was.

To say I was puzzled would have been an understatement. It was as though I were on the cusp of multiple worlds: one where my father was gone, the last remaining connection I had to my youth; one where I held in my hands a nightmarishly bizarre statue, bordering on the grotesque; and one where I was dressed in old and torn clothes, surrounded by the stale odor of cigarettes and cleaning supplies. These three worlds were incongruous, and yet they congregated anyway.

I felt the eyeless statue staring at me, judging my ignorance. I racked my brain trying to remember if I'd seen anything like it before, but drew a blank. It all meant nothing. Yet its presence filled me with something like nausea, as though I'd been spun around in circles and released back into the world, unable to find my footing. Still dizzy, I placed the lid back on the box and considered what to do.

There was no denying part of me was curious. Why my father would keep something so unlike him? There was more to that oddity. There had to be. But what that more was had me baffled.

I was still baffled by the time I returned to my empty home. The emotional turmoil of the day, of sorting through my father's things, of slowly dismantling my childhood, wore on me worse than had my father's actual death. I was more depressed than ever, wanting only a long drink before settling into a numb stupor. But I also knew from time-worn experience that my stupor would not be peaceful, and I'd be haunted by half-imagined demons until the worst of my drunkenness passed. If I truly wanted to forget the world for a few hours, I had to do it sober.

But the alcohol could promise me one thing sobriety couldn't: freedom from thought. And as I lay in the dark I couldn't keep my mind from racing. The lingering effect the clay statue's misshapen face had on me pressed into my thoughts and obscured everything else. Even when I tried to focus on other things, on other people or events, it was always there, waiting in the periphery for my concentration to waver. My sleep was as fitful as if I'd been drunk, and in those brief periods where I did manage, through sheer exhaustion, to slip away, I always awoke suddenly, the image of that statue dissolving from my thoughts. Soon, the only thing I could do to tame it was to dwell on how adrift I felt without my parents, as though the stars around which I'd always orbited had vanished, and without that gravity I felt myself spiraling outward and away. And, worse, one day I too would be gone, probably in a similar hospital gown in a similar overcrowded room, only unlike my father and mother, there would be no child attending to me in my final days, no one who would lovingly and callously sift through all my treasures and decide which were merely sentimental trash. It was these thoughts that put an end to my sleep, at least until the darkness began to break. Once the light started its creep over the horizon, my eyes finally closed long enough for me to rest.

I returned to my father's house after work midweek to cart the garbage cans to the end of the driveway. Inside, the house was finally starting to look cleaner, as though I'd finally made a dent in the piles of detritus that had been building over the years my father had been living alone. I'd managed to clear and bag enough so that I could shift items around—one bedroom was designated for garbage, another for donatable furniture, and so on. It made it easier to clean when there was a fixed destination for everything. I also created a pile for the items I intended to sell if possible—some small kitchen appliances, my father's power tools. And that statue, of course. I didn't know who would want it, or even why, but there had to be something appealing about it. Why else would my father have saved it?

You never know who's going to want the things you think are junk, no more than you can predict how few people will want the things you think have value. There's just no way to know. I put those small appliances and tools into various online auctions, and never found a single buyer. The whole lot of them ended up at the Salvation Army, and who knows if they were ever able to move them. That statue, though . . . That surprised me. I put it up for auction and within a few days I had a bid. It wasn't a lot of money, but it was something, far more than I expected, and immediately I suffered remorse. That statue was a symbol of the gulf between me and my father that I never tried to bridge. I cried when the bid came through, then laughed at myself for crying. It was just a clay thing I hadn't even known existed a few weeks before, so why suddenly could I not be without it? Things were just things, intrinsically devoid of worth except what we assign to them. I'd made it this long without the statue and I would continue to make do without it. These are the things I reminded myself of over and over, but not once did I feel as though it weren't a lie.

The buyer was the only person to bid on the statue if you discount the request I received once the auction had closed, asking if I'd make an exception and sell to them instead. I didn't bother replying. Instead, I swallowed my sadness and emailed the buyer with my congratulations and arranged how she or he wanted to pay. I waited a half hour without a response, then turned in for the night, amazed at the things people wanted, while part of me wondered what it was about the statue that I'd missed. It bothered me, this oversight, enough that each time I broached the edge of sleep, my curiosity woke me again. This went on for at least an hour, at the end of which I was more awake than when I'd turned in. The only thing I could do to dispel my curiosity was to sate it, so I threw aside the covers and shuffled in my slippers to the shelf where the statue sat waiting. I carried it to the kitchen and turned on the blinding light. When my eyeful of stars faded, I inspected the statue top to bottom, front and back. I even shook the thing, but no sound penetrated the clay. If there was something more to the weird figure, I wasn't able to see it. All the same, I carried the statue into the bedroom with me, telling myself I wanted it close in case I was struck by a midnight revelation, but understanding it was because I needed to feel connected to what I'd lost.

I was back at my father's house early after having taken a few days off to rebuild some of my defenses. Visiting my childhood home and watching it disappear, actively taking part in said disappearance, all while struggling to accept the loss of the last vestige of family I had, quickly wore me down, and the bouts of depression were growing more and more exhausting and debilitating. I needed time to readjust and recalibrate before subjecting myself to it again. When I entered his house, though, it immediately crashed back into me, and that sense of loss was again all I felt. All I really wanted to do was leave, but the longer it took me to clean, the longer I'd have to suffer.

I didn't realize there was a knock at the door at first. All I heard was a tapping, and houses make all sorts of noises all the time, enough that you stop paying attention. Pipes heat up or cool down, refrigerator compressors switch on or off. The pilot light of a furnace. But when I paused from my cleaning to catch my breath, the repeated sound tripped my attention, and I turned to see the shadow of someone with their hands up to the sidelight of the door, peering in at me through the frosted glass.

I assumed it was someone my father knew—maybe a neighbor wanting to express condolences while also sniffing around as to when the house might go up for sale. But when I opened the door I knew immediately it was neither of those things, which is why I didn't open the door wider than what the width of my body could block.

I didn't speak. I waited for the small brown gentleman in the mauve suit to do so first. I didn't have to wait long.

"Please excuse my interruption. I wasn't sure if I'd find you at home."

His voice was light and breathy, and his eyes protruded like a pair of glass marbles as they studied me. I didn't like it.

"Do I know you?"

"Oh, please forgive my manners. My name is Clifton Bees. I'm here in search of an item I've been led to believe you recently acquired, an item I'm hoping you might be willing to part with. For the right price, of course."

I was genuinely confused. And irritated to no small degree.

"This really isn't a good time," I started as I began to close the door. Before it traveled very far Bees's foot was in its way. I looked down at his highly polished shoe, then back up to his smooth baby-skinned face.

"The statue, my friend. I've come about the statue you have for sale."

"What? How did— Never mind, I've already sold it," I said. "Now please remove your foot."

I stared until he hesitantly pulled it away, then closed and locked the door, leaving him standing on my father's stoop. I kept my body pressed against the frame until his shadow in the sidelight wavered, then disappeared, the clacking of his shoes following shortly after.

It was a bizarre encounter, and I had so many questions. How had he known about the statue? He must have seen the online auction, but how would he have tracked me down to my father's house? And if he'd known my father, why wouldn't he have said so? I didn't like it, not at all. The entire encounter left me baffled and compounded my irritation and malaise. It also reminded me that I had yet to hear back from the buyer of the statue. I checked my phone for any messages and still there were none. I wondered how long I should reasonably wait. It occurred to me that Clifton Bees and the buyer might be the same person, but that seemed unlikely.

But they might know each other. Then the coincidence of the buyer's disappearance shortly before Bees's arrival seemed something less than coincidental. I turned and looked out the window at the door's stoop, but it was thankfully empty. Nevertheless, I checked the deadbolt was drawn one more time.

*

My precautions seem foolish in retrospect. Bees was hardly an intimidating person. I was fairly certain I could have pushed him over with hardly any effort. I still didn't like him, but I didn't have to: I doubted I'd ever see him again. And once that statue was sold it would be one less thing to worry about.

I'd always wondered, while my father was alive, how he would die. It didn't matter that we'd spent so little time together and even less talking; he was still a part of my life and I worried about the day he would leave it. Every time I visited the house I ran through scenarios of how I might find his prone dead body, each worse than the last. Maybe he'd be in bed, passing in the night while he slept. Maybe he'd be at the bottom of the stairs after having tripped, or face down on the floor after accidentally cutting himself too deeply. So many ways, so many things I couldn't control even if I'd devoted my life to it. His inevitable demise hung over me every time I saw him, tainting our every interaction, so when the doctors discovered his cancer and its severity, I felt a strange peace set in. I finally knew how he was going to go. There was no chance ever again of a surprise waiting for me as I walked through his front door.

If only I'd known the surprises the house had in store for me would mount after his death.

One of the biggest, or perhaps least expected, was when I returned to the house one last time to prepare it for my real estate agent's inspection. As I pulled into the driveway, I saw the front door standing open, and I asked myself if I'd forgotten to close it when I last left, knowing full well I hadn't. I could taste the dread gnawing at my stomach.

That dread intensified when I saw the state of things. The house had been turned upside-down, my careful organization ruined, and someone had rummaged through it all, tearing open garbage bags and overturning boxes and pails. Everything was a mess, nearly as bad as when my father had left it, not knowing it was for the last time. Exhaustion suddenly overwhelmed me, and I sat down on the floor, no longer able to trust my legs to keep me upright.

I didn't make the connection to Bees, not at first. At first, all I wanted to do was tidy up the house as much as possible before Tricia, my agent, arrived. I didn't know if I should tell her there was a break-in; I didn't know if that was something that needed to be disclosed. I doubted it, but I wanted to be careful and keep her in the dark as best I could. She was due soon, so I rushed through the rooms, collecting and rebagging as much as possible. I couldn't wrap my head around what happened. Nothing appeared to be missing, and I'd already moved or given away anything of value, so it all seemed so pointless. Just another undoing of my life. There were so many pains now stored in that house that I was going to be relieved when it finally sold. It was only when I came across the tinted business card I'd left on the mantel previously that the various loose threads connected and I realized who must have broken in and what he'd wanted. I was sickened, violated, and confused. I should have called the police, but what would I have told them? My dead father's house was broken into and I suspected the culprit was a small Asian man with a weird name who wanted to steal a cheap clay statue I found hidden under some clothes, but don't worry because he also left me his business card? It was ludicrous. And I had no proof; after all, nothing was actually stolen. The only tangible evidence I had was the card, but it didn't even have an address on it. All it had was a phone number, but I knew the chances were high the line would be disconnected. I didn't know what to make of any of it. There was definitely something strange going on I didn't like. I peeked out the window at the street and saw nothing unusual or out of place, which only made things worse. Somewhere, eyes were watching me.

Tricia's arrival a few minutes later made me feel better, or at least less alone and spied on. After a tour of the house, she gave me an idea of what it might sell for based on its state, and a few small things I could do to increase its value. It was probably only politeness that kept her from asking about the pronounced mess she had to navigate, but had she done so I was so rattled I probably would have admitted there was a break-in and laid out my suspicions as to who committed it. I would have come across as an unstable paranoiac, despite how confident I was that I was right. When Tricia finally left, the sudden silence caught me off-guard, and I suffered an immediate and utter deflation of all happiness and joy. While it wasn't true that everything in my life was vanishing over the course of a few weeks, it certainly felt that way. At that moment I understood the reason Bees failed to find anything. I'd already lost it all.

I drove home with my eyes on the rearview mirrors, alert for cars that might be following me. I was convinced I was leading Bees right to my house, but if he was behind me, I couldn't see him. No one was there long enough to be suspicious. Still, to be sure, I drove past my house and circled back using the quietest side streets I knew. If he was there, he wouldn't be able to hide.

Satisfied, I returned home, but instead of going in right away I sat in the driveway, just in case. In my solitude I looked at my front door and had the cold fear that Bees wasn't following me because he had already found my house. I wondered if I'd left the blinds open or closed, if I'd left the front room lights on or off. I couldn't see movement inside, but was it possible someone was there, quietly waiting? Or maybe they'd come and gone with it in hand. I didn't know any of it for certain, but after a while I realized I couldn't remain in that parked car forever; I'd have to face my fear and go inside. I steeled myself for any outcome. Any outcome, except everything being as I left it, undisturbed. That called for a celebratory drink. And then another.

I was on my third when I decided to look again at the statue to see what all the fuss was about. I removed the box's lid with my drink-free hand and picked up the statue by its golden trunk. I set the thing down on the table across from me. It was even uglier than I remembered. The gold spraypaint was supposed to make the statue look luxurious, but instead the clay absorbed the paint, giving it a rough satin texture that was distinctly unappealing. I tried to remember why I hadn't thrown it out at first sight, but there was no good answer. It looked like trash. And yet I kept it. And my father kept it. And some stranger had broken in to get it. And for the life of me I couldn't understand why.

Three drinks was a lot more than I'd usually allow myself, but this situation warranted it. It helped me feel better, if more muddled, and in my increasing dullness I decided it would be wisest to put the statue away before something happened to it. I took hold of it by its curled trunk, and when I lifted it didn't travel more than a few inches before the appendage cracked right at its base, and the whole thing broke off in my hand. The statue was suddenly in two pieces and I wasn't sure what to do. It was a serious issue I was in no state of mind to solve. So I dropped both fragments in the box and carried the whole thing with me to the bedroom. I hid it in the cubby above my closet, deciding I'd deal with it in the morning when I wouldn't be quite so exhausted or drunk.

I woke in the morning in a fit when I realized I hadn't locked the front door. I got to my feet faster than did my head, and my legs almost spun out from under me as I dashed to the door to throw the deadbolt. Relieved, I turned around to find the statue was no longer on the table, and for a few addled moments I was convinced that Bees had found me and taken the statue. Mild panic attacked my limbs; combined with the hangover, I felt nauseously enervated. It was only once I started piecing together the night that I hazily remembered storing the statue in the cubby to keep it safe. I sat on the edge of the bed relieved nothing had happened, but it didn't help me feel confident that nothing would. There was a sense of foreboding growing inside me I couldn't shake.

I tried to remain vigilant, but the thing about vigilance is it's taxing and requires a level of concentration that's difficult to maintain. It's why car accidents happen, and why after weeks of dealing with my father's sudden death and the dismantling of my life, when strangers were appearing at his door and ransacking his house, I found myself walking along the street after work autonomously while my mind was somewhere else entirely. I was so in that place that I didn't immediately notice the young man who was following me. He was dressed in a slim tan overcoat and wore thick-rimmed glasses beneath his large, blond eyebrows, and he hovered about thirty paces away, hands in his pockets. I probably wouldn't have noticed him if I hadn't suddenly chosen to jog across the street on an amber light, which caused a litany of horns to sound when he did the same on the red. But once I noticed him, I continued to do so out of the corner of my eye—enough to become concerned. At the next opportunity, I turned down a side street, then ducked into a grocery storefront before he could see where I'd gone. I waited by the window for him to pass, but he never did—not after two minutes, nor after six. After fifteen, I felt confident I'd misread the situation, and noticed the queer look the cashier was giving me, and the way she cleared her throat disapprovingly. I offered her an apologetic smile and nod, then slipped back out the door and straight into the young man who had been waiting for me just out of sight. He locked onto my arm.

"Mr. Slant wants to see you."

"Who's Mr. Slant?"

"He's Mr. Slant. Let's go."

There were many reasons why I went with him. None of them had to do with being physically intimidated, because this kid—and the more I looked at him the more I realized he really was a kid; maybe twenty, I suspected—was no more than half my size. I'd never punched another person before, but I was fairly certain I could overpower this one relatively easily. But I didn't want to try because I didn't know. I didn't know if he was carrying a gun, or if he was a boxer, or if there was something dangerous about him. So I went where he told me, even though I had no idea who Mr. Slant was. But I did have an idea about what he wanted with me.

"I already met Clifton Bees. Does Mr. Slant work for him?"

The kid laughed. It wasn't with the sort of guffaw other people laughed with. His laugh was mirthless. Not really much like a laugh to anyone except maybe his mother.

"Good joke, buddy. I like it," he said, no longer even smiling, then nudged my back to make me move faster.

He marched me two blocks to a small hotel nestled between a boarded-over convenience store and a barber shop complete with rusted striped pole in front and sun-faded posters of out-of-date models hanging in its dirty windows. There was no elevator in the hotel, so the kid nudged me first up the stairs, tempting me to turn and push him down a flight or two, but I kept it together and did what I was told. When we reached the fourth floor, the top floor, he took me down the hall to an undefined door and rapped on it twice. There was a jovial voice from within, urging us to enter. I suddenly had no interest in doing that, but the kid insisted without making a sound.

"Hello, my friend!" said the tall man in the middle of the room. He was pale, with a long, pronounced nose and an unruly head of white hair. He looked as if he might be an albino, but I immediately dismissed the thought. The smile he had on seeing me was so wide and warm that it made me uncomfortable. It was too familiar to be genuine.

"Please," he said, "come in! I trust you didn't find the climb up the stairs too taxing?"

"No, Mr. Slant," I said. "It was fine. I had no problems. And if I did your man was right there to make sure I didn't lag."

He chuckled. "Oh, dear. You may call me Fitzroy, or Fitz, if you prefer. I'm sorry if Edna frightened you. He can be too taciturn and too eager to please me at times. I've asked him to be more polite, but what can you do?" He shrugged innocently, then shot a glance over at the kid, Edna, with his lip slightly curled.

"What am I doing here, Fitz? What's going on?"

"What's going on? Well, only the most important thing there is, my friend. What's going on is no less than an opportunity for you to make a healthsome amount of money by doing hardly a thing."

I knew what he wanted, and I suspected he knew I knew as well, but I wanted to hear him say it because of how ridiculous it was. Somehow I'd become trapped in an absurd nightmare and felt that the only way to accept it was to hear the words spoken—out loud and unvarnished. Maybe if he said it, it would begin to make sense.

"I don't know what you're talking about. Your assistant, Clifton—"

"'Assistant'? That's hardly the word I'd use to describe that sniveling miscreant. What he is is a junk dealer, pure and simple. He wouldn't know the value of a dollar bill if he were holding it in his hands. I'd caution you to stay away from him."

"So you *do* know Clifton Bees."

"Alas. Intimately and unfortunately."

"But you want the statue, same as he does."

"I've been looking for this statue for a long time. I traced it half-way around the globe to your father, but I was not able to secure the funds to travel here before his untimely death. Believe me, I was heartbroken when I heard and wish to extend my deepest regrets for your loss."

Nothing could have confused me more than the idea that this tall pale man operated in circles that may have overlapped with my father's. To call the two incongruous would have been an understatement. He was the opposite of swarthy, the antithesis of the small-time crooks with whom my father often did business. And yet Fitzroy's comments on his death seemed genuine. There was too much about my father I didn't understand. But I wanted to.

"I don't know what you need from me, Fitz. By my math, you're the third person to try and get that statue over the last few days, and I hate to tell you but the statue has already been bought and paid for by someone else. It's no longer mine to sell, even if I wanted to."

This is where Fitzroy Slant's lips curled again into a smile, and I could see through their parting a thin window of coffee- and nicotine-stained teeth. The way he looked at me—with serious amusement—made my skin crawl.

"You can't hope to sell something like the statue online, my friend. Objects like that, they don't travel through normal means between owners. It's much too pedestrian."

"How—?" I was confused, retracing our conversation, and the one I had with Bees. I was certain I'd never mentioned selling the statue before, let alone to whom.

"My friend, as I told you, I've been chasing this statue a long time. There is not much about it I don't know. You needn't worry about that other buyer. He won't be asking for his money back. I, however, am prepared to make you a quite handsome offer on the same prize. Think of it: you'll keep that money, plus my payment. You'll make out like a bandit, if I do say. So what do you think? Do we have a deal?"

"Why is this statue so important to you?"

"My friend, I might ask you the same. You're going through a lot of trouble to forestall a simple transaction."

"It's not, but it was my father's and I want to understand where he got it from; why he had it. It must have meant something to him."

Fitzroy chuckled again, glancing at Edna.

"Children can be too nosy for their own good. Believe me, I know. Your father had the statue, but it was never his. He only thought so, and only for the most mundane reason: he won it in a poker game. The man from whom he'd won it didn't know what it was and neither did your father, otherwise he wouldn't have kept it. Had I known where it ended up, I would not have let him take such a risk, but the fool who lost it went and died shortly after playing that game, and before revealing what he'd done with the statue. It was quite unfortunate, wasn't it, Edna?"

Edna's head slowly nodded. The rest of his body didn't.

Fitzroy never let his display of joviality drop, nor did it ever seem sincere. I glanced over at Edna and wondered what might happen if I refused to turn over the statue. I suspected Fitzroy wouldn't attempt to reason with me. He'd let Edna do it, and Edna looked as if he was just waiting to be taken off his leash. I swallowed, wondering if I could overpower the kid after all.

The knock on the door startled me. Edna was laconically unfazed, and Fitzroy's pale forehead wrinkled as he appeared cross for the first time. Fitz nodded to Edna, and Edna took his cue to check the door through the peephole, then open it slowly. He stepped out then stopped, and we watched him slowly back into the room again, Bees following. In Bees's hand was a small single-shot derringer, and as he advanced his eyes moved rapidly from Edna to Fitzroy. He never once looked at me, which told me all I needed to know about the level of threat I engendered.

"I'd hoped I'd have longer before you appeared," Bees said.

"There's nowhere the statue goes that I won't follow, old friend."

Bees nodded facetiously as he patted down Edna and checked his pockets. I wondered if there was going to be a scuffle, but Edna knew the drill and just waited it out, the whole time watching Bees with dead eyes. Bees's search turned up nothing; information I filed away for later. He motioned with the pistol for Edna to join us on the other side of the room. Edna moved fluidly, his mouth half-cocked with a smile as his stare bore into Bees.

"I must admit," Fitzroy said, "I'm surprised you've made such a threatening entrance, considering there are three of us here, and that pistol holds only one bullet. One would think you'd be more discreet, being so outnumbered."

"That may be true," Bees said. "But I only need the one bullet to make my point. Should anyone make a sudden movement, it's you, Fitz, who will be on the receiving end."

At this, there was a pause, then an enormous laugh erupted from Fitzroy. Neither Edna nor I joined in. I found the entire situation terrifying. I'm certain Edna felt a different emotion.

When Fitzroy was done, he wiped away the tears from his eyes. "Dear me, I've missed you, my old friend. I've missed you and your wit terribly. I don't know why you ever left us."

"I didn't leave, if you recall. It was you who left, and right when the gendarmes were closing in. I escaped only by a stroke of luck. But enough of this. Hand over your father."

Fitzroy laughed again. Shook his head. "My dear friend. Always one step too early or too late. We don't *have* him. No one but this gentleman has Father right now."

I muttered something as confused as I was.

"I already searched his house. He doesn't have it."

The sigh from Fitzroy was enough to waver Bees's confidence.

"You do understand that house belonged to his father, don't you? The man who's been hiding the statue all this time? Don't look at me like that; it's not terribly complicated. The statue was not there because our new friend had already moved it. And now he's going to sell it to us for a tidy sum that will cause him to forget it and all our faces. Isn't that right, new friend?"

I nodded, and he nodded, and Bees looked as us both. Edna looked only at Bees, stared at him like a dog awaiting the kill command. It all sounded easy when Fitzroy said it, but I wasn't stupid enough to think there was much chance of me walking away with their best wishes and a suitcase full of money. The only suitcase I'd be seeing would be the inside of one as Edna was carting my body parts down to the river.

"I don't know where Fitz's father is—" The words stuck in my throat as Bees's pistol slow moved from pointing at Fitzroy to pointing at me. "—but I do have the statue, and I'm happy to give it either of you. *Both* of you. It's just a cheap clay statue painted gold."

"My dear friend," Fitzroy said, chuckling as though Bees didn't have a pistol aimed straight at me. "Don't you understand? The statue *is* my father." He paused. "I can see this confuses you; it's written in bloodless lines across your face. Of course, I don't mean the statue itself is my father. Rather, it holds the remains of my father. My dear, cremated father, Hieronymus Slant."

"I—"

"It's a shock, I'll concede. Especially if one has seen the statue. It hasn't always looked that way—so monstrous. It's taken on that shape after years of being transported from owner to owner, city to city, country to country, all in an effort to disguise it from me, its rightful owner. It was in Budapest I learned that the trunk had been affixed, somewhere in China the small arms. Rome had the urn covered in a clay veil and nowhere else but in America where it took on that spray-painted shine like some dime-store bust. It was all a trick—a ruse. A case of hand-waving misdirection to keep me off its trail. And, for a time, it worked. It gathered so much bulk, so much weight, as might a snowball rolling down a mountain side, that eventually the whole thing grew overwhelmed and sank out of sight. It was only by luck that it surfaced now, in the hands of you, a gentleman—and forgive me for saying so—too ignorant to see its worth. Placing the item for auction online was comically suicidal. Had I not seen the listing myself, we might be attending your funeral right now."

"How—?" I wondered. "How did my father get mixed up in this?"

"I told you before, my friend. He gambled his way in. He wasn't the man to steal my father's remains, and he certainly hasn't been hiding them for the last forty-nine years, at least not knowingly, but he's been holding them all the same. And now that he's gone, I'm sure you can understand why I'd want them back. Of course, there are always obstacles to overcome . . ." He looked over at Bees and his pistol. The small man did not see the same humor in the situation that Fitzroy did. If anything, the story had only made him angrier.

"Keep pushing me, Fitz, and see what becomes of you and your treasured Edna."

I didn't bother looking at Edna; I already knew the expression on his face. I could hear the kid growling underbreath.

"So, my old friend, here we all are. What do you propose happens next? Have you given that any thought?"

"I've given this all tremendous thought, you can be sure," Bees said. "Finding this statue and keeping it from you might be more important to me than the statue itself."

"Ah, but how are you going to exploit your find without me? You need me, Bees, as much as Edna and I, regrettably, need you. Put that pistol away and let's talk sensibly, all four of us. Who would like some tea? Edna, why don't you boil us some water?"

"Don't anybody move," Bees said, not that there was any threat of that. "We *will* be having that sitdown, but not until I have the statue in my hands. You say you have it at your house?"

Bees looked at me and I nodded.

"Then it looks as if we'll be taking a trip. But first, there seems to be a surplus of bodies here. Perhaps one of you would like to tie this youngster to a chair? He may get the wrong idea about what we're doing and try something that none of us would like."

"Don't be silly, my friend. Edna is of no threat to anybody. I don't think we need to resort to anything quite as drastic as tying him up. I have no doubt he'll sit here like a good boy until we return."

Bees shook his head. "The only way we leave this room is with your Edna secured to a chair, or with one of you needing an emergency trip to the hospital. Perhaps I should just take this one with me and leave you and Enda to decide if it's more important to follow us or visit the hospital to treat the hole in your neck."

The smile on Fitzroy's face dropped suddenly, an actor discarding his mask once it was clear the show was over. As false as I'd found him until then, the undisguised Fitzroy was not someone I wanted to be near.

"We both know that would be a grave mistake, my old friend. Perhaps your gravest."

To this Bees shrugged, then looked at Edna. I could see Edna's confident glare twist to disbelief, then to hurt, before settling on acceptance, all in fractions of a second. The betrayal was all that remained there as Fitzroy, too, shrugged.

"My friend," he said, nodding at me, "would you do us the honors? Enda, we'll be back soonest. Once we have the statue, all this will be a fading memory."

I'm not sure if anyone actually believed that.

Edna did not struggle as I looped a length of rope through the arms and back of a hotel room chair, nor when I pulled it as tight as I could on Bees's insistence, so tight that Edna's hands turned nearly white. The sum emotion Edna conveyed was a sharp wince as I yanked, and the icy stare he gave both Bees and Fitzroy.

"I'll be back soon to free you," the latter said, with dubious sincerity. It made me nervous, if only because Edna struck me as the oily type, and I felt confident he was going to slip out of the ropes I inexpertly tied at some point and hunt us down. I just didn't know when it would be, or how much blame he attributed to me. I tried to read his face, but it was pouting when I first saw it and continued to pout until the last. If there were any emotions rolling around inside his head he wasn't letting anybody see them.

Bees led us to his car, a small white sedan with out-of-state plates, and motioned for me to get behind the wheel. He sat in the front passenger seat, his derringer continuously pointed at me, while Fitzroy slid into the back, his neck kinked to avoid the low ceiling. No one spoke to me—there was just the wave of the pistol, indicating I should drive forward and head toward my home or wherever the statue might be hiding. I did it because I didn't know what else to do, because I didn't have many options open to me. I considered what might happen if I drove too fast, then hit the brakes suddenly. Would the pistol fall from Bees's hand? If I purposely drove into a tree, or the median on the highway, might the ensuing accident give me the chance to escape? Or would the most likely outcome of any scenario be me bleeding out in a ditch along the way while the two men found and raided my home? Part of the idea appealed to me—there was a circular beauty in joining my parents again—but I bristled past it. Despite the issues they had between them, I knew they'd agree that I should do my best to live as long as possible. I found myself agreeing with them, too.

When my chest began to vibrate, I first worried death was coming for me in a different way. I was startled, which sharpened Bees's attention as he watched me, and it was only when the vibrations stopped, then started a moment later that I realized what was happening. I pointed at my breast pocket.

"Should I answer my phone? Someone is calling me."

Bees looked to Fitzroy. I couldn't see the back seat, or the pale tall man in my mirror, but whatever silent communication they had was enough for Bees to nod his head.

"Don't say anything that would get you in trouble," he warned. "Nobody wants to see things go poorly."

I swallowed, then pulled out the phone. I kept my eyes on the road as much as possible and hoped nothing unexpected happened.

"Yes, who is this?" I asked.

"It's Tricia," she said. "We got an offer on the house!"

"You what? How? The house hasn't even been shown yet."

"Sure it has. Remember? Today was the first day I was showing it."

I glanced at Bees, who was watching me closely. Tricia was too quiet for anyone else to hear, something for which I was thankful.

"Ah, I see," I said, trying remain as vague as possible. "And what did they say?"

"They offered twenty over asking, no conditions, no inspection. And they want it in six weeks. You'll have your money next month!"

Tricia was happy with the speed and success of the transaction, but my emotions were mixed. Leaving aside the two men actively plotting to kill me and despite my haste to get the house ready, I found myself unprepared to give it up. I knew, rationally, it was just a house, but it was *my* house. My parents' house. The place I grew up in. It had been the central point around which my life had always and forever rotated. And suddenly it was being taken away, and I'd have to find a way to deal with such an integral piece of my life vanishing. I didn't want to lose anything at that moment, and when I thanked Tricia and thought about it I realized that statue was no different to me than anything else in my father's life. They were all things I didn't want to get rid of, didn't want to lose. Instead, I wanted to hold them as tightly as possible so I wouldn't forget anything, forget anyone. I wanted to cling to my past like a child to its mother—terrified of ever letting go. Because if I let go I'd surely become lost.

"So will you be at home?"

"Pardon me?" Tricia had been talking but I hadn't been listening.

"I need to get the paperwork signed. Can I swing by your house?"

I glanced over at Bees. Then at his gun. I heard Fitzroy's impatience in the back seat.

"Right now is not good," I said. "I'll call you later tonight."

"But—" was all she got out before I disconnected. I needed to keep her as far away from what was going on as I could.

"Should we be worried?" Bees asked.

"Was that someone else looking for the statue?" Fitzroy asked.

"No," I said. And then, "Why are your father's ashes in the statue? I mean, why in a cheap clay statue painted in gold, as if a child made it? A broken statue, too."

Bees turned pale. Looked at Fitzroy. "You never told me it was broken," he said, his voice trembling. "It can't be broken."

"Don't worry, my friend. Your imagination is getting the better of you. Our new friend only means one of the extremities has been—how can I put this—*liberated* from the body of the statue. There's been no real damage done."

Relief engulfed my captor. Even his pistol arm momentarily relaxed.

"But why are they there?" I said. "In the statue. And why do so many people want them?"

"I take it you've never heard of my father, the great Hieronymus Slant? It's not surprising, but it is unfortunate. The greatest men are often unheralded in their time. And my father was certainly unheralded by many. Considered strange by even more. You see, my father was what one might crassly call a 'wizard,' were the term not already thoroughly corrupted. He was the Grand Magus of the Order of Valzerial, follower of Monteligro, and spent all the life that I knew him immersed in various forms of alchemy, faith healing, and investigations into the supernatural. In short, my father was very much respected and revered by those in his circles, and he repaid that adoration by explaining to us the unlocked secrets of the universe."

I saw him looking at me in the rearview mirror. He couldn't see more than my eyes, but he seemed to see them wholly and completely.

"I can tell you are having trouble accepting the magnitude of what I'm saying. It's to be expected, of course. The world is so much wider and larger than we give it credit for being, and yet it's also so small a chance encounter can have reverberating consequences throughout one's life. My father was, arguably, the most powerful man alive for a time, and he revealed miracles—true, undeniable miracles—to the Order that proved there was more to the world than what lay within the ken of men. Sadly, though my father's vision was transdimensional, his physical form was all too bound by this world and its rules, and his body could not take the punishment he inflicted upon it in his advanced years. When I found him, his essence had already nearly drained, leaving him close to an empty shell.

"We, the Order and I, cremated my father by the practices he instilled into the organization, wrapping him first in treated papyrus gauze and stuffing him with natron powders, incense, and spices. He was then burned in a kiln built strictly to act as his pyre, and the ashes collected into a Vessel—a sacred urn made of Tinaldam clay mixed with his blood. That part was important, you see, because it was the only material that could contain his remains afterward. Those ashes, over the following forty days, were transformed into something more. The Order prepared for the Vessel's arrival.

"But that day never came. We had spent so much time protecting the Order of Valzerial from external threats that we failed to ensure there were no rogue agents in our midst. On hearing about the power developing within the Vessel, this splinter plotted its theft. They were eventually caught and punished, but not before smuggling the Vessel away from us, disguising it more the further it traveled around the world.

"What none of them knew at the time was that just as only blood could contain the power in his remains, it was only blood that could subsequently free it. What they got had value, but without a living relative of my father they had nothing.

"That statue has been outside my grasp for nearly sixty years, but that time is nearing its end. Can you feel it, Bees, my old friend? Can you feel the end of the road we've been traveling on for so long? I must say, it feels right to be traveling it together, just as we did in old times."

He put his hand on Bees's shoulder, and the small man smiled, glanced back at his tall partner, then looked back at me with a face that no longer betrayed any of that warmth.

"How much farther do we have to go?" Bees asked.

"Not much farther," I said.

Bees raised the gun and pushed it into my face. I shrank away, nearly twisting the wheel into oncoming traffic in the process.

"Bees," Fitzroy said, "what are you doing? Stop this at once!"

"Do you think we're fools?" Bees said to me. "I recognize that corner. How long have you been driving in circles?"

"I'm not—" I started as he tapped the pistol against my skull. My hands shook uncontrollably. My foot left the gas as I lost control of it and the car began to slow. The drivers behind us leaned on their horns.

"Think very carefully about what you do next," he said.

"Okay, okay," I said, raising one hand from the wheel in defeat. "We'll be there in ten minutes."

"Good," he said, removing the pistol from my face and leaning back into his seat beside me. I glanced again in the rearview mirror and saw Fitzroy's bloodshot eyes there, watching me mirthfully.

My house came into view fewer than nine minutes later. It looked so normal and routine that I found the sight jarring. So much had happened, so much continued to happen, that transformed my life into a chaotic mess. And yet the house was still the house. It had not changed at all, and I realized that no matter how different everything felt, my real life, my day-to-day existence outside my father's sudden illness and death, outside the mysteries he stored between the blankets in his home, was just as it had always been. The tragedy I was suffering through had done nothing more than pause my daily life, and it now waited in patient status for me to return. It was reassuring—or at least would have been were Bees and Fitzroy not behind me, waiting for their spraypainted treasure, holding my life in their hands.

"Let's go inside, my friend, and see what you've been holding onto for us."

It was too much to hope that a neighbor might happen to notice I was being marched by gunpoint into my home and call the police for assistance. And I knew without that intervention I didn't have much hope for rescue, so I did as I was told and marched like a death-row inmate toward my inevitable end. Fitzroy was speaking, but I didn't listen. I couldn't stomach the explanations or platitudes. If anything, what I needed was for all this to be over once and for all regardless of consequences.

Fitzroy took a seat on my oversized green armchair while Bees remained standing, his nose upturned at the squalor in which I'd been living since my father's death. I wanted to explain myself, but I doubted either would listen. Fitzroy rubbed his dry hands together, the sound like starched sheets.

"It's been quite an exciting day. An exciting day. And now here we all are at the end of it. Friends, the lot of us, all in business together. I must say, when I woke this morning I never expected it to wind up like this."

I stood silently, waiting for instruction. Bees was still holding his pistol, but it was no longer pointed at me.

"I think you can put that away now, my old friend. I don't think our new friend is going to try anything foolish. Are you, son?"

I shook my head.

"Besides," Fitzroy continued, slapping his knees with his hands, "we have *business* to attend to. And whoever heard of conducting business at gunpoint? It's not done. No, sir. It's not. I won't stand for it. Utter rubbish."

"Fine," Bees said, narrowing his eyes and looking into mine as he pocketed the weapon. "But I'll have it right here in easy reach."

That still made me nervous, but without it in the open significantly less so.

"Now," said Fitzroy, "why don't you bring us what we came here for."

"And don't try anything funny," Bees added. "In fact, why don't you give me your phone before you go. Just in case."

I took my phone from my pocket and handed to Bees. He glanced at it, then put it down on the end table.

"The Vessel?" he said.

It took all my willpower to avoid sprinting from the room.

With the way my luck was going, I fully expected to open the closet doors and find the box missing, but it was there, right where I'd left it, the broken statue still inside. I exhaled the breath I'd been unknowingly holding. I'd once had so much curiosity about the thing, but that had gone a long time ago. All I wanted now was to be rid of it, be rid of Bees and Fitzroy and the whole lot of them. I wanted everything to go back to the way it was. Go back to normal, because everything had been not normal for so long that I honestly didn't know how much longer I could handle it. I stopped worrying, though, when I heard the deafening clap. It startled me so much I nearly fumbled the box holding the statue. By the time I wrestled it back under control, the air stank with a metallic and sulphurous tang. Like an idiot, I dashed back to the living room to see what happened. Bees stood there, trying to stop his hands from shaking long enough to wipe the derringer with a handkerchief. On my couch sat a slumped Fitzroy Slant with a spreading hole in his chest, gurgling words that the blood and coughing made impossible to understand. Not there was much time, as he was dead only a moment or two later.

"What did you do?" I asked.

"Get me a towel," he said, and I went, not thinking, not sure what else to do. I was trembling as much as he was, and probably in no small amount of shock. I took a small hand towel from the closet and brought it over to him. Bees snatched it from me, then gingerly laid it down of Fitzroy's cooling body. A dark stain appeared instantly, then Bees stood up and walked into the kitchen. I dumbly followed, statue in hand.

He rifled through my drawers until he found what he was looking for: a box of plastic zip-top freezer bags. He took one out and walked back to the living room with me in silent tow. By this time, the towel had transformed completely from white to dark red, as though it were some sort of magic trick. He lifted it by a corner and dropped the sopping wad into the zip-top bag, then sealed it.

"If you knew what I've been through with him, you'd understand." This he started telling me without prompting and without looking at me. I half imagined he'd be saying it even if no one were in the room to hear. "You'd probably have done the same. Fitzroy Slant wanted to be his father, but he wasn't and could never have been. His father understood how important everyone in the Order was. Not just because they were necessary for his plans to reach fruition, but because without them there was no power. Fitz, if he'd abandon me, the one person willing to help him find the Vessel and his father's remains, he'd abandon anyone and everyone. That's not what the Grand Magus is, power or not. That's nothing anyone wants. He could have learned so much from his father, but he chose not to. Did you hear that, you ignorant old man? You wasted your chance and you'll never get another."

He continued to berate Fitzroy's cooling body. I kept quiet and backed slowly toward the doorway, hoping to get out of his sight, until I realized he'd fired the only bullet the derringer had. The gun was empty. As though a blind had been lifted, I was suddenly reminded of how small Bees was. Or, rather, how much bigger than him I was. I stopped backing away and looked for anything I could use as a weapon. Something blunt and heavy and to the point. I couldn't see anything. Not until I looked down into my hands and noticed I was still tightly clutching the broken statue.

I didn't even realize I was creeping up on Bees until I was doing so, statue held above my head. I could sense more than see the cheap gold shimmering above me, absent from the rough white spot where the trunk had been broken. I didn't know exactly what I was going to do, or even if I was capable of doing it, but something motivated me on, pushed me forward to where the small man was going through the larger man's pockets, looking for something. When I was within striking distance I hesitated, the statue growing too heavy. All the grisly outcomes flashed through my mind, and when I accidentally glanced at the face of Fitzroy on my couch, the muscles slowly relaxing and becoming plasticized, I was struck again with the recollection of my father's face, moments after he'd gone, while I ran my fingers through his graying hair. I lowered the statue and stepped back. Bees turned then, holding something in his hand he'd taken from the dead man's coat.

"Here," he said, tossing a wad of folded bills on the floor in front of me. I could see it was soaked with Fitzroy's blood. "I'm not sure how much is there, but it's more than Fitz promised you. Hand over the statue, please, and let's put an end to all this."

Bees stepped toward me, his brown hands grabbing for the statue, but I jerked it away. Strangely, it was only when his pistol could no longer cloud my judgment that I began to worry what was going to happen next.

"If I give you this statue, how do I know you'll leave? How do I know I'll never see you again?"

"You have my word, of course."

"Your word? You've killed a man in front of me. In my house. What am I going to tell the police?"

It was here he shrugged, as if to suggest he didn't see a problem. Or, if he did, it was my problem, not his. His reaction angered me and I raised the statue above my head again.

"What if I were to smash this stupid statue on the ground? What would you do then?"

I thought I'd see terror in his eyes. Instead Bees glared at me, and I could almost hear the gears in his brain grinding, his mind weighing various scales, and I could see in his eyes when he came to a conclusion. He sighed, then sat down on the armchair across from what was left of Fitzroy Slant.

"Go on," he said. "Throw it down. Destroy it."

I was confused. Bees waited until I faltered before continuing.

"You think it makes a difference? Any of it? Do you think destroying the statue will bring Fitz back? Do you think it will bring Hieronymus Slant back? Even this"—he held the bag of blood up for me to see, waved it so I couldn't miss it—"it doesn't mean anything. I'll take it back to the Order, we'll concoct some other vessel for the old man's ashes, put it up on a shelf where no one will touch it, and they'll go on doing what they do, asking it questions, sacrificing to it, wishing they could commune with Hieronymus even though he's long dead, and even if the spells are right and they somehow bridge that gap to the otherworld, so what? What does it mean? So many questions, but there aren't answers. There are never answers. It's just another load of questions."

We both heard a clatter coming from the hallway behind me. We turned and saw Edna there, an automatic pistol in his hand. He had sneaked into the house, intending to rescue Fitzroy or maybe kill Bees or me, but he clearly saw Fitzroy dead on my couch and it threw his plans out the window. That stoic face I'd seen earlier was now crumpled and wrought.

"Edna—" Bees said, and Enda shot him through the eye.

I remember a scream, and I'm pretty sure it was mine. Everything I'd lost, and now to be staring at Edna and his gun—it all became too overwhelming. I'd reached my breaking point, and beyond it was an unknowable void. I don't remember much of what I did or said. I might have just kept screaming. Whatever it was, I didn't stop until Edna slapped me hard across my face.

"Stop. I won't kill you. It's a waste of time. Give it over."

He reached for the statue. I didn't protest. He lifted it up to inspect it, turning it over in his one hand while the other held the still smoking gun. I was vaguely aware of the crumpled body of Clifton Bees on my floor, and the spread of gore that covered everything behind him. I didn't know if I'd ever be able to turn around again, so I kept facing Enda. I knew, deep inside my head, that I should be terrified, but I couldn't be. I didn't have any more terror left. I didn't have anything left at all.

Edna stooped down and picked up the zip-top bag of blood that Bees had dropped and put it in the box along with the statue. Then he looked at Fitzroy's body and paused for a moment in reverence before walking to it and putting his hand on the dead man's cheek, and then, hesitantly, ran his fingers through Fitzroy's hair. I recognized the gesture, and recognized what it meant.

"I'm taking these now," he said without looking at me, without motioning to the box.

"I have no intention of stopping you," I said. "I'm sorry I had to tie you up."

He shrugged as though he had already forgotten what I was talking about. He had the look that I knew too well—the look of someone suddenly cut adrift, unmoored and unsure of what he was doing or what he should do. He just stood, not making any motion to leave, while he looked at Fitzroy's body. I needed to do something, to say something, but I didn't know what. All I could think of was how the room smelled of rust and seared flesh.

"You know, my father wasn't around much when I was growing up," I said. The words were just spilling out on their own in a babble. "My mom would make him take me places sometimes—I remember having steak fries in a basement strip-mall restaurant where no one spoke English and everything smelled like old cigarettes. She made him take me, I think, so he'd form some sort of bond with me, a connection that fathers are supposed to have with their children, a connection she'd had with her own father before they moved here. But it didn't work; my father was always this unknowable being in my life, like a living, breathing secret with which I interacted only superficially and sporadically. An unknowable life in the periphery of my own. And when he was gone I found myself wishing I'd taken time to understand those mysteries, because maybe they would have told me something I didn't know about him. But I wouldn't have. Even if I had him back, even if there was some magic way of resurrecting him and talking to him again, it wouldn't be anything different. There wouldn't be anything new to say, anything to learn I didn't already know. It would just be one last grasp at disappointment. Maybe it's better to let the past go. Let it turn to dust and fly away."

"Maybe," Edna said, then wiped something off his cheek. It was probably blood.

So Much Potential

Hilda did not like the look of Blake. He was tall and broad, with brutish features clumped around a crooked nose. Underneath his heavy lids sat a pair of flat black marbles that fixed on her and didn't move. None of him did. From the moment she saw his giant square hands laid flat on the table between them he didn't move an inch. It was as though he were a statue. Or, more worryingly, as if he knew he couldn't trust himself not to lose control of those hands and strangle her.

And the worst part was, he had nothing to say. Hilda should not have come. She could have stayed home, worked on another proposal, or studied another marketing book. She couldn't afford to waste time. So why had she allowed herself to be convinced to go on a fix-up in a sketchy restaurant across from a man like Blake? He just wasn't right. She'd been on plenty of bad dates, but even the worst of her ill-suitors had at least tried to start a conversation, even if that conversation was about how hard it was to be a man nowadays. Too many complaints and too much overreaction about a bit of friendly and misunderstood flirting. These men were monsters, but at least they were the sort Hilda had encountered before. This one was different. He didn't have to say a word to scare her, because all of him scared her. From his dirty fingernails to his scuffed shoes. Where did he get that suit, she wondered. A yellowish gray, he must have rolled in dirt to get it so filthy. Or crawled out of a dumpster.

"Roxanne tells me you're from out west. Did you grow up there? Just outside of Evenston, is that right?"

Nothing.

"I used to know a pair of girls from Evenston. We'd go round the pubs in college, but eventually they failed out and had to go home. I managed to get myself back on track, thankfully. How about you? Did you go to school nearby?"

Nothing still. Just dead black eyes; his giant hands, bigger than her face, flat on the table.

Was it too soon to leave? That was the question swirling through her head since she'd arrived and found him waiting there. How long was the right amount to ensure she didn't upset him? Ten minutes? An hour? His existence terrified her. Just sitting near him was enough to make her feel ill; he seemed perpetually on the edge of utter and unbelievable violence. But would it be safe to leave? She didn't want that violence turned against her. Please, let it be directed at anyone else, anyone but her. She didn't care how horrible it was to wish it.

"I should freshen up," she said, pushing her chair away from the table. "I'll only be a minute. Don't get up," she quickly added, not that she'd needed to bother. Her emerald dress with its white floral pattern draped over her knees as she stood. If he saw through her ruse her escape would be thwarted, so she tucked her small purse under her opposite arm as quickly and discreetly as she could and headed straight to the restrooms where she hoped there might be a back door waiting. It was cowardly, but that's what she was. Ahead she saw a steel emergency exit door propped open by a sweating cook in a greasy white apron. She knew if she looked back, even for an instant, Blake would be standing there, watching, so she didn't. She pushed forward toward the cook and squeezed past him before he could say a word.

The alley behind the restaurant stank of garbage and freedom. Wonderful freedom.

*

Never had being at home behind her locked door felt so good. She'd looked over her shoulder the entire commute—from subway to bus, from bus to second bus, then on foot ten minutes more—ensuring no hulking shadows followed. Even in the elevator of her building, she feared he'd be waiting when the doors opened. But all that waited was the mirror on the opposite wall, reflecting her sad struggling face. She pushed it out of her mind until she was inside and throwing the locks into place. Only then, once secure in her armchair, glass of wine in hand and an eye on the door, did she take a moment to reflect on her aborted evening.

Why had Roxanne done this to her? It was true they weren't more than office acquaintances, but Hilda hadn't asked her for a fix-up or even hinted at it. It was Roxanne who came running in saying she had found her the perfect man, and it would be a crime for the two not to meet. Hilda should have been warier, but things had been going better lately for her—at work she was complimented twice by a client and once by Brion—and she thought, perhaps naïvely, that it might be okay to try meeting someone. Or, if not okay, then at least tolerable. She expected an accountant, or an insurance salesman, or something equally boring and benign. That was how the women at work saw her—unchallenging, unexciting, a bit of a bore—and maybe they were right. They were probably right, which is what made Roxanne's fix-up so odd. Blake Massas was anything but those things. He reeked of cheap cigarettes and cheaper booze, of old leather and oil. He smelled of danger, of risk, and those were the last things Hilda needed.

*

The morning arrived with an unseasonable chill against which even two coats weren't enough. Nor was her cream knitted hat. She hadn't slept all that well. After another glass or two of wine before bed, she found herself waking periodically to the sound of thumping from somewhere nearby. It wasn't loud enough to warrant getting up, and sometimes she wasn't sure if she was still hearing it or it was just the echo in her somnambulating mind, but in the end it didn't matter because it was there, waiting for her when she faded back in. As a result, the night dragged on for an eternity and ended far too soon. Even after showering under water as cold as she could stand, she found herself in battle with her eyelids to stay awake.

Her cellular phone had been blinking all commute with a message she dreaded playing. She didn't recognize the number, but felt she knew who it would be and had no interest in hearing apologies or justifications. All she wanted was for it to be over. Hilda stared at the blinking light for a moment, wishing she could go back in time ninety minutes, back before she saw the light. But what difference would it make? She'd still be sitting there, holding the phone, ninety minutes later.

Better to get it over with than let it hang over her, she thought, and pressed play. There was the sound of shuffling, muffled speaking, and far off shouting. The rumble of a motor, louder than that of the bus she was on. Maybe a wrong number? A clicking sound over the line, like static. Then a voice.

"Hilda, it's Brion. Great work on the Bressack proposal. It really knocked the partners' socks off. Can you drop by my office for a chat this morning? I'd like to talk to you about your future. I'll send over a calendar invite. Again, great job!"

Hilda stared at her phone, wondering what she'd heard. What did he say? She must have misunderstood it. Because what it sounded like was . . .

Hilda replayed the message to be sure she had heard it correctly. Then once more to grasp all the words, but they were too many. It was too big to fit in her head. The idea pushed everything else out, leaving her brimming with terrifying hope. She wanted desperately to change her lot—had been working so hard to be in a position to do so—but suddenly it seemed real, and she wasn't sure. Not at all. Should she dance or flee? Either way, she wanted to scream. But there wasn't time. She needed to prepare for the most important morning of her life. At least it would give her a distraction from thinking about Blake Massas.

But he was not so easily forgotten. As the crowd standing shoulder-to-shoulder around her swayed with the motion of the train car, it parted for a moment to reveal brutish features staring angrily at her. Before she could utter a scream, the gap closed and Massas was gone. Hilda trembled, raised her arms to adjust her glasses, and stared into the crowd, but found it too thick to reveal anyone more than a few feet away. Nevertheless, she searched each face, intent on proving she'd been mistaken. How could he have found her? Was it possible he followed her from the restaurant? She didn't see how. He knew Roxanne, but she only knew her as a co-worker—they'd never exchanged addresses or even phone numbers. As far as Hilda could tell, there was no way to find her unless she wanted to be found, and she most definitely didn't. So Blake's appearance had to be Hilda's sleep-starved mind playing tricks. It had to be. And yet she couldn't stop staring into the crowd, waiting and worrying it would part again and give her a less-welcomed answer.

But it never did. The crowd continued to slide back and forth with the train car's motion, but it never broke the same way, never revealed Blake Massas or someone who might be mistaken for him if glimpsed for a brief instant. There was no one at all, which Hilda found both reassuring and distressing.

*

At work she turned off the ringer on her phone and put on her headphones. She needed to concentrate on preparing for her meeting, and that meant forgetting her terrifying aborted date with Blake Massas. Brion and the partners had been impressed, which intimidated her endlessly. Her instincts screamed at her to run and hide, as they had the night before, but this time she wouldn't let them win. This time she was going to face the threat, because if she didn't she would remain at her desk for the rest of her life. It might be her only chance for something more; she refused to believe this was all there was.

And yet she couldn't banish the phantom of Blake Massas from her head. If anything, it grew stronger; even when she blinked, she saw that crumpled face pressing toward her.

When Roxanne appeared in Hilda's cubicle, it was in a sudden and startling cloud of fluttering sheaves. She wore a pale green frock and an inscrutable look of contrition. Hilda knew why she'd come, and there was no time for it. Hilda was not ready to discuss what happened with Blake. But Roxanne's stare demanded attention, and she would not leave until she received it.

Hilda peeled the headphone from her ear.

"I'm just in the middle—"

"I want to apologize."

"You don't need to," Hilda said, though it wasn't true. She *did* want an apology. And even more, she wanted an explanation. But she didn't have time. Brion was expecting her in minutes.

"But I do. I'm really sorry. Blake is really sorry, too. He wanted me to ask you for a second chance."

A second chance? "No, I don't think that would be a good idea." She remembered how his dull eyes still looked angry. How his thick fingers looked as though they should be covered in blood. "I don't think that would be a good idea at all."

Roxanne looked crushed. "But he's so sorry! And you two would make such a great match. I know it. You'd be perfect for each other."

"I really need to get back to work, Roxanne."

"Please tell me you'll give him another chance? Please? It's not his fault. He's not like this normally."

Hilda did not like the pressure. She was already on the precipice of falling apart, and the more Roxanne pushed, the more it felt as though Hilda were teetering.

"He doesn't seem my type, Roxanne."

"Why? Because he was late?"

Was he? He'd been there when she arrived. Had she been late?

"Roxanne—"

"Give him one more chance. Please? He's a very sweet man, and says he'll make sure he doesn't stand you up again. He promises. See? He's as excited for you two to meet as I am. That's a good sign!"

"Thanks, but I think I met him enough last night."

Roxanne gave Hilda a queer look.

"What do you mean?"

There was no way out of this. Roxanne was not going to leave Hilda alone. The only way to get free was to be rude. The question was how to do that inoffensively.

"To be honest, Roxanne, I'm surprised you two are friends. He seemed different from how you described."

"That's really strange. Blake says he never saw you. He says when he reached the restaurant you weren't there."

"But that's not true. We talked."

But had they? Hilda remembered talking to him, yet couldn't recall him answering any of her questions. In fact, he hadn't spoken a single word. No, he must have. He must have said something.

"And you're sure it was him?" Roxanne was still confused.

"Yes, it was. Why would I lie about that?"

But Hilda's vehemence felt phony and full of doubt. She didn't know at all what to believe.

"Hang on," Roxanne said, and went to her desk. Hilda remained standing, wondering what she was waiting for. But after a few moments Roxanne returned, her wallet in hand.

She opened it and flipped through, then pulled out a photograph from a small stack.

"Here," she said. "Is this him? The man you met?"

Hilda squinted. It was a photo taken around a campfire, a small vignette illuminated by an orange flicker surrounded by night. In the corona of firelight sat six people, all dressed in summer clothes that hadn't been fashionable in about a decade. Even Roxanne looked different, with longer hair cut in an unflattering bob. Behind her, half-lit by flames, was a wide dark face. He was staring at the camera, his teeth barely discernable in the grain of the film.

"I don't know," Hilda said. "I guess it is if you say it is. But—"

"But what?"

That was the question, wasn't it? Hilda squinted hard at the picture. She wasn't sure. It could be him, but it could just as easily not be. The person in the photo was younger, but so were they all, and the difference in complexion could just be the reflections of firelight. But there was something different about the face, something that Hilda couldn't immediately discern but felt in the pit of her stomach. Or, rather, didn't feel. The person in the photograph didn't fill her with utter and consuming terror. It couldn't be the man she'd met, because the man she'd met was something less than a man. He was only shaped like a man.

"If you have to look that long, then it wasn't him. Blake's pretty memorable. I don't know who you were talking to, but next time you should be more careful. Besmirching my friend's name isn't right."

"I'm sorry, Roxanne," she said. The photograph still haunted her, as did her lack of confidence in who its subjects were. But worse was the mystery of who she'd met the night before, and what he'd wanted. And still might want.

Hilda's computer chimed. On the screen, a small dialog box appeared. A reminder for her meeting with Brion.

The panic returned.

"Oh, no! I'm sorry. I have to go. I have—I have a meeting with Brion right now."

"Brion, huh? Look who's suddenly important."

Hilda ignored Roxanne's turn. She had to. If she didn't she'd only grow angry that the woman had stolen her preparation time with her stories about Blake. Who else could it have been, though? Who else would have met Hilda at that exact time, at that exact place? And why he had lied to Roxanne afterward was a mystery. Maybe it was to cover his tracks? Hilda couldn't worry about it at the moment. She had to focus on her meeting with Brion. Focus on the future hurtling toward her.

*

She was at the elevator when she realized she'd forgotten her folder of notes and had to go back. Precious time was ticking past. Being late, even by a few minutes, would not look good, not look professional. By the time she reached the fourteenth floor, she felt the beginnings of sweat creeping along her hairline, but she managed to keep it together long enough to let Brion's assistant know she was there. She took a seat and wondered if it were possible for her heart to beat any faster. After a few moments, it did just that.

Brion didn't keep her waiting long.

"Come in, Hilda. Let's chat."

She followed Brion into his office. She had never been inside it before. It was probably larger than her entire apartment, filled with dark oak furniture and a bookcase spanning the wall behind his desk. Along the length were a series of giant windows that would have overlooked the city if there weren't a sister building across the street with matching floors. Each of its windows reflected enough daylight in to brighten the room. Was this what her future was going to look like?

He led her to a pair of leather couches, then motioned for her to sit. The reflected light shone in from behind, silhouetting him and making it hard for Hilda to see without squinting.

"You may be surprised to hear we've been watching you for some time, Hilda. You've consistently proven yourself a valuable asset to the company. Your work on the Bressack proposal showed a thorough understanding of the client's needs, and more importantly you took the time and the hours necessary to understand why those needs were important, and how we could best address them. I've looked at the numbers, and your projections for their costs savings are significant, but more importantly you outlined and implemented a methodology that allowed us to deliver those savings in a smaller budgeting envelope. You showed not only ingenuity, but also thoroughness and accountability. You saw the entire project through while not allowing that oversight to affect your day-to-day. You assembled and deployed teams strategically and coordinated their efforts effectively. Your project not only came in on time, but under budget. Frankly, the partners agreed it would be foolish for us to overlook what you've put into the company. As a result I've called you in here for this meeting."

Hilda smiled, she hoped convincingly as Brion droned. It was all too much, too fast, as her stomach confirmed with its churning and twisting. She didn't know how she felt about what was happening—a sickening combination of excitement and dread that made her want to scream. Even the clouds seemed wary, shifting in the sky to block the sun and deaden the glare off the building opposite. The reflection from each of its windows blinked out a row at a time, allowing Hilda to finally see, not only Brion clearly, but through the large windows behind him.

"Now, I'm not sure how much you've been paying attention to the goings-on of management, but we've been through restructuring that's moved Karris to a different division and created a new opening for an Intradivisional Operations Manager. I've reviewed your current compensation, and this position would come with a significant pay raise. Of course, since it's a newly created seat, there will be some tinkering involved, and will probably require an investment in your time to plan the restructuring of the various departments and how they interrelate, but based on what you've shown us so far we're confident you're ready to meet the challenge. The question is whether you feel the same way."

Hilda nodded without thought, her eyes transfixed on the building out the window. Across from Brion's office she saw a figure standing there, unmoving. She squinted even though she didn't want to, even though she knew what she was going to see. Brion's voice drained away as she witnessed those crumpled features glaring at her across the divide. They bore into her.

Blake was coming. Blake was coming straight for her. And she worried he might jump across space to get her.

"Are you all right?" Brion asked, concerned. But Hilda didn't respond. Her heart beat so fast it thundered in her head. The sickness was unbearable, ratcheting up her body in convulsive waves. She trembled, tried to force her eyes shut to keep from screaming. She had to escape Brion's office. She had to get out before Blake found her. She had to go any way she could.

"I'm—I'm sorry, Brion. I'm not feeling well. Do you . . . do you mind if we cut the meeting short?"

"I—" he started, unsure what to say. Hilda knew it was a mistake, but she couldn't stay there another moment under Blake's stare. If she didn't leave immediately she wouldn't be able to contain her terror any longer. She stood without waiting for his reply. Brion stood, too.

"Thank you for this opportunity," she rushed out. "I need—I just need . . ."

She just needed time. And there wasn't any. She did her best to offer the sort of smile a normal human might offer, and didn't dwell on how she'd failed as she fought the urge to sprint from the room. Brion said something she didn't hear. His assistant, too. But it was just noise drowned out by her thudding terror. It didn't stop as she jabbed at the elevator's buttons, and continued when it let her off at her own floor. A steady thunder following her into the washroom, staying with her as she locked herself in a stall and covered her ears with her hands. With eyes squeezed closed she counted down and prayed her heart wouldn't seize from terror.

When she was calm enough to emerge, twenty minutes had passed. She was drained. She slunk back to her desk, the dissipating adrenaline making each step harder than the last, and tried to ignore her overwhelming sense of shame. She had hallucinated Blake Massas, she had fled from Brion and her future. Was it her fear that cast the illusion in the other office? How could she both want and be afraid of something so desperately? Her head wasn't working, and she didn't know what to do.

It felt as though the entire office knew about her panic. Every set of eyes on her belonged to someone snickering. Even her cubicle, the one refuge in the building that was hers alone, had been staked out by a hovering Roxanne who whispered with others at surrounding desks. Roxanne glanced up as Hilda approached, half a smile still clinging to her face, and waited until she was sitting before she spoke.

"How did your meeting go?"

"Fine, fine." All Hilda wanted was to be alone.

Roxanne's eyes narrowed.

"You don't look fine. Are you sure you're okay?"

Hilda looked at Roxanne's inscrutable face and decided she'd been tortured enough.

"You know what? No, I don't think I am. I think I need to call it a day."

She stood and began to pack her things. Roxanne stepped back, but continued to hover.

"Go home. Rest. Maybe take a bath. We'll be okay here without you." Her words seemed supportive, but the tone betrayed them. "I'll tell Blake you'll have to postpone things. He'll be very disappointed."

Hilda smiled weakly, then put her phone in her pocket and picked up her bag.

*

Once on the street, she inspected every face for Blake Massas. Or rather the man she'd thought was him. There were times, on her travels home, she imagined she saw him: a lurking figure in the corner of her eye, an errant shadow across a distant wall, the sensation of being stared at when no eyes were cast her way. Each instance was easily dismissed, yet compounded kept her on edge, expecting violence at every turn, down every block. By the time she reached home she was a jittering mess, barely able to hold her key still enough to unlock the door, and even as she did so she kept peering back to be sure the shadows gathered around her were just shadows. It was only when she was inside, the locks drawn, that she could relax. Her home had become her only haven from that thunderous man and whatever vile harm he intended to inflict on her.

Hilda pulled shut her curtains and drew a bath. She lit scented candles, too, with the hope that they might help soothe her, but the smell was overpowering, and she blew them out before they could make her head hurt worse than it already did. Turning down the lights helped, but the bathroom had no windows, and without candles it was too dark, so she left the door ajar to light her way.

Hilda slid into the hot water, the heat wicking away her anxieties. The preceding days had been confusing and torturous, and as much as she wanted to sort through everything that had happened, what she needed now was to put it out of her head. To let her eyes close and allow her mind wander to anywhere but where she was. Any place that disconnected her from her travails.

She did her best to ignore the thudding. It was just a noise, something outside the cocoon of wet warmth she'd made for herself. She refused to let it in. But it persisted, a discordant sound that drilled into her thoughts, pulling her back from whatever mild tranquility she'd been able to secure. Eyes open, she looked through the narrow of the door into the rest of her apartment, as though the source of the noise was within its walls.

It certainly sounded as though it were. The pounding grew so loud it shook the organs in her chest. Everything seemed to vibrate with each strike. But no; it wasn't everything. It was only one thing: the door. The sunlit door shook as though being struck by a powerful force, over and over again. Hilda caught her breath, pushed her body against the far side of tub. Someone was trying to get into her apartment. She was too terrified to speak, too terrified to move. All she saw was that door, vibrating over and over, giving way a little bit each time. Her body prickled with all-consuming fear. She knew who it was. She knew who was coming.

The telephone rang. The sound was a needle puncturing the tenuous membrane that held back her terror. She screamed, blinded by white as fear spewed out of her. It went on and on, a steady stream that would have continued forever if her lungs could have sustained it. Instead, her body shut down and she slid deeper into the cooling water. Her head remained buoyant, though, long enough for her to realize the pounding had stopped, that the locks and knob were no longer shaking. All that was left was the shrill of the ringing phone.

She felt with her jittering hand for the bathrobe hanging beside her. Wet footprints followed her as she made her way to the telephone, answering it midway through its ring.

"Hello?" Her voice quavered.

"Hilda? This is Brion. I wanted to check on you. Is everything okay?"

Her heart sank. Brion. The partners. The meeting. She'd been trying so hard to avoid thinking about it that she hadn't had time to process it.

"I'm—yes, I'm okay. Thanks. I . . . um . . . what I mean is I don't feel great, but I don't think it's anything serious. I'm really sorry about running out of the meeting."

"Not just the meeting. Apparently the office, too."

"Yes," she said. She wished she were dead.

"I want to reassure you it's okay. Don't worry about it. Also, to be clear, it *was* a meeting, not an interview; I was offering you the promotion. That's on the table, regardless of what happened today. I know it's not indicative of your work ethic. And, as I mentioned, the partners and I think you'd be a great fit."

"You do?"

"Of course we do. The only reason I'm calling—other than to make sure you weren't too overwhelmed—was to find out when you'd be ready to start. We'd like to get moving on this soon, you understand."

When would she be ready?

When?

She heard a footstep in the kitchen.

"I—I don't know, Brion."

"What do you mean? Isn't this what you wanted?"

"I thought I did. I mean, I do. It's just . . . it's just that there's a lot going on right now."

"Hilda, I have to say I'm surprised." His voice took on a different tone; a faint thread woven through. "We need someone to step into this role as soon as possible. I'm frankly surprised it's not an easy decision."

"It's just—"

"Just that things are going on right now?" he parroted. Hilda cringed. Her life was unravelling before her and she had no idea how to stop the tumult. How could she concentrate on anything Brion had to say when she was certain she heard heavy breathing behind every wall in her apartment?

"Maybe if I had some more time . . ."

The sound over the phone grew muffled. She could hear Brion's voice, faintly. Who was he speaking with? She held her breath.

"How much time?"

There was no way of knowing. How long did it take to get over the perpetual feeling of imminent death? How long until the sounds from the other side of her apartment stopped sounding like someone large shifting their weight? She glanced around, saw nothing amiss. But nevertheless it felt different. Wrong. She had a sense the space where no one stood was the opposite of empty. It was like a shadow, occupied by the echo of something that had just left or was about to arrive.

"Brion, hang on a moment. I'll be right back."

There was a pause on the phone. A pause not unlike the space on the other side of the room. Full of more than the nothing on its surface. And when she heard the definitive sound of scraping, she didn't know from which world it came: the one on the other end of the phone or the one in front of her. She dropped the receiver to her side so she could listen more closely to the apartment around her.

Brion replied, but Hilda didn't hear him.

Still dripping, one hand clasping her bathrobe closed, she placed the receiver on the table and crept forward. The wall seemed to expand and contract in slow rhythmic waves as though breathing. Hilda's skin was cold and numb, and tightened the closer to the kitchen she stepped. She noted a peculiar scent in the air that left a bitterness on her tongue. Going forward was a mistake, but something waited for her ahead that had been waiting for a long, long time, and it wasn't going to wait any longer.

She turned the corner of the kitchen. The room was empty, the dim yellow bulb leaving pale shadows on the island between her and the sink. She could see out the window into the oncoming dusk filling the sky, veins of color running through it like cracks in stone. Nevertheless, they tinted the color of light seeping through, turning the cupboards and table top a pale shade of dusk.

There was no movement, and yet the room was full of potential. It was building, whatever it was, like a low thrum increasing in volume and intensity until it overtook all her senses. Hilda raised her hands against her temples to soothe the pressure but it didn't help. The sound was coming from within her. There was nothing to do but turn away and wait, but that became very quickly impossible when the man pretending to be Blake Massas slowly rose up from behind the island, lifting his enormous hands one at a time, followed closely by his long scowling face.

Hilda didn't speak. Didn't move. Didn't breathe. The world had been violently torn away, leaving the two staring at each other in the void. The hulking man didn't utter a sound; he only stared with his flat black eyes. So many thoughts collided in Hilda's head that she could utter none of them. Her panic transfixed and immobilized her just outside the penumbra of light from the kitchen. His long shadow reached out and blanketed her.

"What are you doing here?" she asked, her throat fighting each sound.

But he had no reply.

"What do you want?" she begged him.

But he had no reply.

"Why are you doing this to me?"

But still he had no reply.

There was no humanity there. The sum of him was a monolithic concentration of potential violence. It vibrated on an obscure frequency that irradiated and liquefied what was inside her. Hilda looked at what passed for his face, doughy and crudely molded, and realized what she hadn't earlier.

He hadn't come for her; rather she had summoned him.

The imitation of a person she'd called Blake Massas came because of her. Because she had not fought hard enough to stop him when it was still possible, when he hadn't grown so large, so intimidating, so inevitable.

"What are you?" she whispered, but she knew.

The thing that wasn't a man, that wasn't Blake Massas, wasn't looking at her. He couldn't. He could neither see nor hear her. And yet there was no escaping him. Not anymore.

Hilda watched his poorly constructed face ripple, his features swell improbably. The crack where his mouth should have been grew larger, splitting his molten face. At the sides of his head his eyes protruded oddly, what might have been the bones in his jaw jutted outward. From beneath his nose another crack formed, climbing from mouth to his brow, and at once the various points of his face unhinged, peeling back to reveal a throat deeper than anything she'd ever seen or imagined. And still his face peeled further, the opening widening until it consumed the entire kitchen, floor to ceiling. It grew so large, so deep, she couldn't see anything else. And when the thing that was not Blake Massas moved to envelop her, Hilda found herself stepping forward autonomously into the deep nothing that awaited.

Circle of Blood

I'd been staying at the Y for a few weeks, trying to keep a low profile. I signed in under the name "Robin Littlejohn" not only because the name made me laugh, and sometimes laughing was all I had left, but also because Detective McCray was on the warpath and the name *Owen Rake* on the register would have stuck out. McCray was built like a solid wall, and wanted me like I was the one who put that scar on his face. Sometimes I think he and Mrs. Mulroney had something going on and that was why he was so mad at me. Other times I think it's just because my screw-up got her killed, but either way the cop was gunning for me. For some reason it seemed like the best way to avoid the law was by turning tricks in the dark of the YMCA.

Jake Rasceta was the kind of suited douchebag you see on the street all the time—a Bluetooth earpiece in wherever he went, speaking at a volume one decibel higher than everyone else. He was about a foot taller than me and a foot wider. When he approached me as I smoked by the emergency exit I'd propped open, I thought he was there to kick my ass. Instead, already sweating, he looked me dead in the face and said, "I'm looking for a blowjob." I told him I knew where he could find one.

Afterward, things were awkward. He wanted to leave but had to get dressed. I wanted him gone so I could gargle for a million years but I couldn't leave him alone in my eight-by-eight. The last thing I wanted was anyone going through my stuff and finding something they shouldn't. So I waited while he put his suit back on, noticing how much more he was sweating than before. He was silent, especially compared to the shit he'd been saying to me only ten minutes earlier, and in that silence I heard the traffic outside my closed widow and the coughs and gags of my neighbors. It was a peaceful Sunday morning, I thought. Not at all when I expected to see something bizarre. It caught my eye as he opened his thick wallet to pay me for services rendered. There, tucked within a clear plastic envelope, I saw his gigantic face mugging for the camera, behind him some cheap department-store backdrop. He stood with his wife and what I assumed was his kid, but the photo didn't show all that; at least, not clearly. It showed him and his wife, and something else I wasn't seeing right.

Most people don't notice these sorts of things—Rasceta hadn't—but I've been around too much crazy shit in my years to let it go. Rasceta was fixing his tie around his throbbing throat when I got out of my chair and went to investigate what I saw. Rasceta immediately hid his wallet from me, glaring, and shoved me away, hard. His skin was red from overheating, but he continued to add more layers of clothes. I wondered if my ass-kicking hadn't been so much canceled as delayed, and started babbling small talk in hopes of avoiding a confrontation. If I got thrown out of the Y, I had no idea where I'd end up.

"Hey, take it easy. I just wanted to see that picture. Was that your family?"

He seemed startled by the question. He wasn't really paying attention. I saw it in his glassy bloodshot eyes.

"In your wallet. The photo?" I said again, louder in case he hadn't heard me the first time. "Do you mind if I take a glance at it?"

He looked at his pocket, then at me strangely. "Why, uh, why would . . . No, I don't—"

He was trying to protect them; I respected that. But it was clear something was seriously wrong with Rasceta, and I suspected that photo would give me an idea of what.

"Seriously, let me see it. I'm trying to help."

For a second he hesitated as though he was going to do it. Maybe he knew, subconsciously, he needed help, and wanted to reach out, but I guess his programming kicked back in because his face scrunched in anger and he increased a foot in size. At least, that's how I remember it.

"Fuck off. You have your money."

Which I did, but that wasn't the point. I would have explained if he hadn't stormed out of my room without even a thank-you, slamming the door hard enough his cash lifted up and floated around the room. It was probably a good thing I'd closed the window.

Here's the thing: people don't always know what's best for them. They know what they want, but there's a difference between *want* and *need.* I saw what Jake Rasceta needed, and all he could see was what he wanted. There was little I could do to stop him.

I should have let things go and forgotten about the guy. He'd almost taken my head off when I tried to help him, but that photograph in his wallet wouldn't stop haunting me. Whenever I closed my eyes, I saw his child squirming like some deformed reptile breathing slowly while mucousy black eyeballs rolled in its head. I knew if someone didn't do something about it there would be dire consequences. And I was the only one remotely qualified for the job.

Nowadays it's amazing how much information you can find about people using the Internet. But what's equally amazing is how much is available off the Internet, and always has been. My life would be a hell of a lot harder if it weren't. It's there for anyone to dig up if they know where to look and aren't afraid of getting their fingers dirty. Or taking their time, too. A whole lot of time. Luckily, I met all the qualifications. Jake Rasceta didn't try too hard to hide who he was, but guys like him, guys who help me pay my rent when I have rent to pay, they don't usually plan their actions too carefully. I make my money in more of a spur-of-the-moment fashion. Kind of like that chocolate bar at the cash register you don't know you want it until it's in your face, and less than an hour after you've swallowed the thing you start to regret it. But, oh, during that time nothing tastes better. At least, that's what I imagine. For me, it was just a means to an end. And I knew Jake was going to come close to his if I didn't get to him soon.

Finding where Rasceta lived and getting there were two different stories. At the time I was traveling lighter than usual, and the price of two buses—one out of the city, the other through suburbia—ate up more of Rasceta's money than I wanted. I would have hitched it if I could, but few drivers are interested in picking people up anymore. Still, I made it to Collingwood in only a few hours. Everything was so quiet and still, and the trees on the streets weren't in tiny concrete planters but in a long string along the side of the road. I felt horribly out of place, as though I was wearing a neon overcoat and marching to the beat of a bass drum. Those few couples I passed on the street stared at me like I was from Mars, and they were right; we were from different planets.

Rasceta's house was one of those split-level ranch houses you see being built along the highway north of the city. It looked like every other house on the block, its bricks painted a godawful fake terracotta. It was still early in the day, so I figured I'd catch him before he left for his sales job. I knocked on the door and waited. It was a nice morning out, which made it strange that I couldn't hear any birds. Maybe they were avoiding the place? I rang again, then knocked.

When Rasceta answered the door he only had enough time to say, "What the fu—?" before the door slammed in my face. That half-second was enough to see the guy already looked worse. His face was sallow and sweaty and his shirt was plastered to his chest. I hoped he wasn't dumb enough to call the cops; the last thing I needed was any cockeyed company. I rapped on the window when he didn't come out and then looked inside. There was a dark-eyed woman there, terrified, hair plastered to her sweating face, holding tight to a familiar little boy. I was terrorizing them, which wasn't something I normally liked to do. I would have felt worse about it if I hadn't realized too late they were trying to distract me long enough for Rasceta to slip out the back door and sneak up on me. It was a stupid mistake, and I paid for it when his sweating hands reached around my neck and choked me. Everything went light and wobbly and in my oncoming daze I saw the face of that little boy in the window starting out at me. It seemed impossibly big, flickering as it filled the pane edge to edge, and it slowly turned. Then I realized it wasn't the face that was turning but the world. In the distance I heard a voice cursing me, calling me names, telling me to stay the fuck away from his family. It was a normal reaction, considering. Weird how you can have a guy's cock in your mouth but never really know him. I'd had enough of what he was dishing out, mainly because I knew that if I lost consciousness I'd probably never wake up again, so I did the only thing I could think to do. I grabbed hold of his balls and squeezed as hard as I could. He let go instantly, and as the blood pumped back into my head my skull felt as though it was on fire. I coughed, my eyes a river of tears, and I knew better than to stick around long enough for him to recuperate. Instead, I stumbled down the driveway and out into the street. I half expected him to follow me, and if he had there wouldn't have been much I could have done, but he stayed away and I was able to find a backyard overgrown enough to hide in. Needless to say, the whole intervention could have gone better.

I licked my wounds and wondered what I was going to do. I would have liked to hop on the next bus out of there but that thing was stalking Rasceta, and I wanted a better look at it. Besides, the way that kid had looked at me—maybe it was a choked-out hallucination, but it didn't seem right. The kid was *flickering* when I looked at him, for fuck's sake. That sort of thing wasn't normal, and it was worth investigating. I stayed in those overgrown bushes for a few hours, though, just to make sure neither Rasceta nor his wife called in any sirens. I didn't hear any, but I haven't survived this long without being careful. Once I was sure no one was looking for me I straightened myself out as best I could and started walking back to the Rasceta house. The road was quiet in the middle of the morning, and when I got closer to their place I saw there was still a car in the driveway. If he was smart, Rasceta would have taken his wife and split, but something told me the guy was too big to think straight. He probably felt invincible, probably told his wife I'd never come around again. Probably told her lots except about how he met me. I bet the last thing he wanted was for her and me to talk. As for me, I wanted nothing more. At the very least, I wanted a piece of their kid. But when I got back to the house, it looked empty. I peeked in as many windows as I dared, but Rasceta and his wife had gone. What passed for their kid nowhere to be seen.

Normally, in the city, I pretty much disappear on the street, which makes life a lot easier for me. And the city is like an open book to me—its secrets are my secrets. The suburbs, though, are like another galaxy, one where I'd stand out less if I wore an actual astronaut suit and scowled at the primitive Earthlings as I strutted around. I felt people peeking out their windows at me from behind their silk curtains. All curious who I was and what I was doing there. I didn't think I could stand the scrutiny for very long, so I did the thing I do best: I gave up and went to find somewhere to sit and ponder.

There was a park not too far from the Rasceta house, one big enough that I wouldn't be too conspicuous. Suburban parks are little oases, filled with green grass and flowers. Just the sort of thing to make you forget about cockeyed cops and weird things that look like children but definitely aren't. I almost felt normal sitting there, listening to the kids on the playground close by, ignoring the mothers henning it up on the benches around me. Had I found a bed there, I might have lain down and taken a nap. As it was, the day was getting to me and my eyes were already feeling heavy. I wanted to close them but was afraid of what might happen if I slept. I shook myself to keep aware, and once I did I realized something was wrong. There was a lot of noise, as though the volume on the world had been turned up two notches. I heard the kids louder, and the birds were kicking up a storm. I half thought I heard ants crawling across pavement because there was the sound of footsteps moving quickly but I couldn't see anyone around who might be walking. I might not have noticed it if I hadn't run into crazy shit like that before, but I *did* notice it, and whatever it meant I knew wasn't good. As though on cue, as soon as that thought had formed, the sound dropped out. And this time it was noticeable, and not just to me. Even the hens stopped henning and looked around.

The birds were dead silent again. Have you ever seen a bird when a snake shows up? It was like that. Eerily silent, waiting for the predator to move on. Then I saw the Rasceta kid standing in the middle of the playground, staring right at me, his worn-down mother and sweating father not around. That did not inspire hope in me for their safety. Why else hadn't they called the police after I showed up at their door?

Why else had the house looked so empty when I went back later? The kid didn't say anything or react at all to me. He simply stood there watching, and damn if I didn't see something other than a boy in his place. He looked at me with a sort of soulless gaze, an empty vessel steered by something malignant, and part of me wanted to go over and take the bait he was trolling, but before I moved I heard voices clucking behind me. The hen party had made me their concern.

"Excuse me, but is one of these your child?"

I only barely paid attention to her. I wanted to keep my eye on the Rasceta kid.

"I said, do you have a child here? Sir?"

When I looked at her, at her fat rubbery face, I almost said something vile but noticed the lineup standing at her back, all in pecking order. Suddenly I didn't feel as inconspicuous as I'd hoped. Even the kids had slowed their games to watch me . . . except for that Rasceta kid. He didn't do anything at all but stare. Things were suddenly worse.

"Why are you looking at our children? Who are you?"

"I'm just relaxing in the park, lady." I hoped my indignation allayed their suspicions. The Rasceta kid went back to playing, but it was calculated. He wasn't watching me directly but he knew exactly what was going on.

"I'm not relaxing until you tell me your name and why you're watching these children."

"Goddamn it, will you back off? I didn't—"

"I will *not* back off," she said, and I knew I'd slipped, that I'd made too much of a spectacle of myself. It was time to get gone.

"Fine, fine. I'm leaving, see?" I held my hands up and turned to walk away. She clamped down on my arm to stop me while her hens advanced.

"Oh no, you don't. Not until the police get here."

This wasn't going to end well for anyone. Especially anyone around that Rasceta kid when he started feeling murderous again. I had to make a choice: fight now or fight another day. As usual, it wasn't much of a choice at all.

I have many faults, but not being aware of all the tools at my disposal isn't one of them. I know what I can do and I have a good sense of how far I can push things. This woman who was grabbing my arm, for instance: I knew how far I could push her. I could push her right the hell over. She was a sight, falling backward after I shoved her, throwing her into the grass and dirt, stunned like I'd just slapped her across the face. It shut her up, and her hens too. Long enough for me to hightail it out of there, but not before I gave them all the stink-eye. I hoped it would be enough to buy me some time. I didn't know for certain if they'd called the police when they said they had, but if they hadn't they sure were going to once I was out of sight, so I had to make myself scarce until things blew over. It was back to the bushes for some cover. My home away from home.

Things were a mess, and I wasn't sure why I was bothering. No one had asked for my help; even if Rasceta had, it wouldn't exactly have done much for him or his wife. I wasn't completely sure what their kid was, but I suspected it was what I like to call a cuckoo situation: something had managed to finagle a flesh-and-blood suit and use it to infiltrate this world. It was probably just biding its time, and my unfortunate appearance caused it to escalate its plans. That, or once again I was in the wrong place at the right time. If I were smart, I'd have left Collingwood right then and there. I was already a suspected thief. Last thing I needed was to be accused of being a child molester, too. I needed to get back home. I even missed Detective McCray, that righteous bastard. But I couldn't do it; I had to stay. If not to keep that thing from destroying Collingwood, and afterward probably the world, then at least to satisfy my curiosity.

Two things happen when you hide out in bushes for a long period of time, listening to sirens and chatter from somewhere outside your vision. First, you get bored. I used to carry a paperback in my pocket to read when I was just sitting around doing nothing, but I'd read everything I really want to read and couldn't find anything new. It was all just trash, really. Instead I ended up drawing over the tattoos on my arm with the stem of a leaf. For some reason, tracing those wards relaxed me. That led to the second thing: you fall asleep. I'm not quite sure when I slipped out, but I know when I woke up. It was when I was being dragged into the open by the scruff of my coat.

It took me a few seconds to figure out what was going on wasn't good; by then I'd received a few kicks to the ribs to clue me in. Around me stood a circle of men, screaming at me to stay out of their neighborhood. For a brief moment I wondered if I could suck my way out of the situation, but I didn't think they would go for it in front of each other. So instead I curled up and tried to cover my face and my balls. I didn't get kicked more than a few more times, though, and when it stopped everything went quiet. So quiet that I didn't really want to uncover my eyes and see why. But I did, because I realized that was *exactly* what I wanted. One of my eyes was already swelling shut, so it wasn't as easy as I'd hoped, and I hurt like a son of a bitch, but I managed to stand up and look at what awaited me on the lawn: about a dozen men, all lying in pieces on their backs, dead eyes wide, staring at the empty sky.

Across the lawn I saw the Rasceta kid. He was crouched down over one of the bodies, doing something to it I had no desire to see up close. His tiny arms were covered in gore, but not nearly as much as his face. For a second I forgot that beneath that little-boy suit was something old and soulless, until he looked at me with a gaze that made my nuts crawl up into my chest. He ran right at me, those smiling teeth getting sharper with every step.

Imagine being charged at by a vicious dog. Then imagine something worse, all long teeth and crazy eyes. The kid was practically on four legs and moving quicker than he had any right to. He leapt at me—and my brain finally kicked in and my closed fist connected with the side of the kid's face. He fell, but it only knocked him off balance temporarily; I'd done no real damage. So I dropped down and wrapped my hands around his blood-caked throat. His jaws opened and closed, revealing at least three rows of the craziest teeth I'd ever seen; his tongue darted out, short but seriously forked. His eyes were cloudy to the point of white, but they focused on me while I struggled to stay on him, although not at the same time. Like a lizard's, those eyes moved independently of one another, while the kid hissed and spat and tried to push me over. I felt the muscles in his neck as I squeezed—they were like rock. I couldn't even dig my thumbs into them, which did not bode well. There was nothing I could do to contain the kid and yet I was stuck on top of him. If I let go and ran, how far would I get? No more than a few feet before he tore me open. If I stayed, could I really outlast him? Already my strength was leaving me, but his bucking and thrashing did not seem to be slowing down. I'd put myself in bad trouble and I had to figure out a plan quickly to get out of it. Otherwise, I was going to end up on the menu. But I didn't need to bother worrying; the kid's bucking made the decision for me. With a final jump he threw me into the air and I careened forward over the dead men on the ground. The kid watched me like a hunting dog watching a wounded duck.

I was better prepared when he charged at me again. I'd already removed my coat and when he got close I tangled him in it, then dropped him to the ground. He was strong, but I didn't need to hold him forever. Just long enough to cinch the belt tight and form a makeshift straitjacket. He still bucked with unheard-of strength, so I put my knees right into his ribs, where I knew they'd be weakest, and put all my weight down on them. I heard the thing's muffled screams as it died in agony, shattered bone cutting though flesh like a thousand razor blades. Beneath me my coat turned the darkest shade of red, and though the bucking stopped the gurgling didn't. It took the kid a lot longer to die than I expected, even after I jumped on his chest to make sure, digging my knees in deeper each time. Eventually I had to stand to prevent a cramp, so I stomped on his head a bit to change it up. That ended things a lot quicker.

I wiped my forehead. There was no way I was getting my coat back. I reached in the pockets and took out whatever I could. The rest couldn't identify me anyway. Still, to be safe, I lit the kid on fire. Then, for kicks, I took off the pants of some of the dead guys lying there. I figured it was better for all involved if it looked like some crazy circle jerk that had gone horribly wrong. At least people would understand that. I felt bad for them, but I felt worse for Rasceta. He hadn't wanted my help, and in the end it probably got him killed sooner. At least I did a favor for the rest of the people in Collingwood. They'd never know it, but I saved their lives. More or less. Still, I wasn't going to wait around for a tickertape parade. Instead, I got myself to the station as quickly as I could and then caught the first bus out of there. It wasn't until I saw the Welcome to Collingwood sign fading in the rear window that I began to calm down. To be on the safe side I needed to lie low for a while. I checked my pocket for the rest of my money before realizing I'd left whatever I had in my coat pocket, the same coat I'd burned along with the kid.

I knew a way I could make some more cash, at least enough for a room at the YMCA. This time I vowed: *no more small talk*. It wouldn't be the last time I had to remind myself of that. I ought to get it tattooed across my fucking chest.

Doused by Night

I'm late for dinner, so I hurry home. Rain is falling like an avalanche of cold stones on asphalt, and the droplets kicked up beneath my fogged glasses make it hard to see. It's all a kaleidoscope of amber light. Lorianne is going to be angry and won't understand, even after I explain that the useless car won't start.

"Couldn't you change the tire or something?"

"Don't you get it? The car doesn't go vroom vroom!"

I keep imagining things like this—things I'll never have the nerve to say—to distract me. I don't want to deal with her tonight. I don't have the energy to face the whirlwind of abuse and its destruction of my soul. I walk past bar after bar in the downpour, each promising liquid warmth and neon fun, but I can't afford it. Even a moment would mean days of Lorianne's accusations and threats, of her throwing my past weaknesses in my face. She demands so much of me that I barely have anything left for myself.

I arrive to find a dark house with locked doors. I can't work my fingers, so I press my cramped cold hands against my pockets, feeling for my keys. I know I had them when I left. I think about Lorianne lying in bed, the stub of a cigarette burning out beside her, and weigh my options: knock or find somewhere else to spend the night. Rain pummels me as I debate which would be the greater mistake. But there's no way to know. So I turn my soaked loafers until they're pointed in the direction I came from. The bars are still open, which means there will be flickering blues and reds I can sit under and dry out. Somewhere the drink and the rain will help me forget until one of them stops flowing. I don't know what I'll do at that point, and I don't care. I don't care about anything the future has in store. For once in my life I'm not going to worry about goddamn tomorrow.

*

I wake up and don't know where I am. I've blacked out before, but not like this. Everything is bright and the quiet rings my ears like alarms. I try to sit up and my stomach rolls over, pokes itself up my throat gingerly as a warning. I drop back into the thin foam pillow and moisten my dry lips. Everything sounds distant. I only have the strength to close my eyes.

When I open them Lorianne's face eclipses the world. She's mouthing words that I can't make out. Annie Oakley? I repeat it back to her. She turns red as she boils.

"Are you okay?" she shouts, enunciating each syllable into my face with sour breath. I don't know what she means, but she's angry.

"You promised me you were done."

"I didn't do anything," I say, but I don't remember and the fuzz on my tongue says I'm lying.

She looks up, then looks at me and shakes her head. Mercifully stands back.

An Asian woman steps into my tunneled vision. She has the thickest eyebrows I have ever seen and there's a stethoscope tucked in her white coat pocket. Her ID says "Dr. S. Maharaj." Suddenly it all makes sense.

"Am I in the hospital?"

"Yes, Mr. Edmund. You were admitted late last night."

"What?"

"You've been here since last night, Miles," Lorianne repeats at an unhelpful volume. I cringe, head throbbing. Dr. Maharaj says something and Lorianne shakes her head angrily. The doctor does not flinch. She hasn't dealt with Lorianne as long as I have. Give Lorianne enough time and she'll wear down Mt. Everest. But Dr. Maharaj is insistent, and Lorianne eventually storms out the door crushing a pack of cigarettes in her hand.

"Mr. Edmund, do you know how you got here?"

Is it hard to hear her because of the drumming of the rain on the window, or because everything feels so far away?

"Mr. Edmund?"

"No," I muster. She nods her head; writes something in her book.

"You were found slumped in our Emergency Wing. We admitted you with what appeared to be severe alcohol poisoning. You may have noticed the charcoal on your bib?" She points to my chest with her pencil. I don't follow it.

Her story sounds impossible. I ask if maybe she's mixed her charts up, but she's adamant. When I think back I realize I can't remember anything from the night before. The footage in my head has been erased. My worry almost distracts me from what Dr. Maharaj said.

"Wait. What do you mean it *appeared* to be severe alcohol poisoning?"

This is where Dr. Maharaj pauses, catches her breath. I try to study her upside-down face hovering above.

"We're still waiting for more tests to come back. We'll know more this afternoon."

*

Later, the light in the room is gray down to the fixtures, and my skin ripples with a thousand insects that radiate from the base of my skull. There's something wrong with me. The cardiac monitor panics as my chest heaves in and out. I scramble for the remote beside me and jab at its button. No nurse comes.

Lorianne does, though. She arrives in a dervish, smelling of damp smoke, and after one look at me she's ready to lose her goddamn mind.

"What's wrong? Are you in pain?" I nod and reach for my chest, but my hand is jerked back by my tangled intravenous tube. Lorianne steps forward and does what I couldn't: she puts her cool hand on my chest. My heart slows, the dizziness in my head ebbs. She only removes her hand to run her fingers through my hair. It's comforting, but not enough. I'm terrified, and I want a drink.

Dr. Maharaj arrives. She's shorter than I remember. Her eyebrows thicker.

"Mr. Edmund, we've reviewed the test results. There's no trace of anything wrong with you." The news should be reassuring. Lorianne exhales and responds with her fastest voice. I don't listen, because Dr. Maharaj isn't finished.

"If the tests are clean," I say, "then what's wrong?"

She glances at the window of my room. All that's out there are wet bricks. The hospital's other wing.

"We found something when we examined you," she says. "A mark behind your right ear."

I look into Lorianne's wide terrified eyes. That can't be good. I reach up and feel behind my ear. The skin is sore, and touching it pricks deep into my tender flesh. Lorianne no longer looks at me.

"What kind of mark?"

"It's some kind of symbol. No one here can identify it. But the mark isn't what's important. There's something else."

She clears her throat, looks down at my chart, adjusts her glasses. Her fidgeting makes me nervous. I usually feel this way when Lorianne is in one of her moods. It's the inevitability of an oncoming storm. The cardiac machine's beeping jumps in tempo.

"You said he was okay."

Dr. Maharaj doesn't acknowledge her.

"We've seen the mark at least a dozen times before. Each time, the patient appears healthy with no visible signs of trauma. Within twenty-four hours— There's no easy way to say this, but the patient has died."

I wait for the punchline. Then ask her to say it again to make sure I'm not hallucinating. She does, but I've already stopped listening. All I'm thinking about is another drink.

"We've called the police, Mr. Edmund, and they're on their way. This mark has been on every patient so far, and the homicide detectives need to question you before it's—what I mean is, before we discharge you so you can get your affairs in order. I'm sorry to be delivering this news, but anything you tell the police may help them find who's done this to you and put a stop to it."

Things suddenly click into place. "Wait. Homicide detectives? Someone's done this to me?"

"That's right, Mr. Edmund. This isn't something that's just happened. This was deliberate. In effect, you've been murdered."

Lorianne sits down. I'm lucky I'm already lying in bed.

But I don't feel lucky.

*

Dr. Maharaj leaves and we wait for the homicide detectives. Lorianne shakes. I shake, too. And can't stop probing behind my ear.

"What happened to you last night? Why didn't you come home?"

I hesitate, not sure how I should answer.

"It was raining and I didn't want to wake you. I went for a drink. I'm not even sure where."

I can't describe her expression. She's simultaneously mad, confused, and terrified. Each emotion strikes her face in time with the storm. I shrink, worrying what she's about to say. Instead, the storm abates and exhaustion seeps in. I've never seen this before. I don't know what it means.

"You must remember something."

"I don't," I say. I don't remember anything at all. I return to the spot behind my ear. The tingle makes my head swim and insects crawl down my back. But I'm numb otherwise. Is it normal to feel numb when you've been marked for death? There's no time to wonder. Before I notice, Lorianne is on me, removing my oxygen hose and disconnecting my electrodes. The beeping gives way to an alarm—the sound of my stopped heart.

"We're so out of here," she says, abruptly yanking the intravenous needle from my arm. I flinch.

"But the police—"

"To hell with the police. We aren't staying."

Lorianne fetches my clothes from the locker and throws them at me. No one has come by to check on the alarm. I think about how lucky I am that I wasn't actually dying, considering the lack of response. Then an idea occurs to me that makes me sit back down on the bed. Maybe they didn't come on purpose.

"Let's go!" Lorianne is impatient, already at the door. I nod and slip into my trousers.

*

We're running through the halls. Lorianne wheezes, and my feet are too numb to keep me balanced, but if we don't get out we never will. My skin ripples and crawls with each footfall. My teeth chatter. No one bars us from leaving. No one prevents us from getting into Lorianne's tiny Ford Fiesta, or slams the parking lot gate closed before we reach it. No one does anything. I wonder if it's because they know I'll be back.

The adrenaline of our escape ebbs quickly behind the wheel. I know, because we haven't gone more than a couple of blocks and I'm rifling through the glove box for a half-bottle of anything. Anything would go down good right now. I hear Lorianne's breath hitch over the torrential rain. She's watching me instead of watching the road. I glance at the side mirror and am startled by my pallor. I'm a ghost.

"Miles, I'm worried."

"Don't be. It's going to be all right." I say it with conviction, though she won't believe me. She rarely does when I contradict her. Part of me doesn't believe it either.

"Of course it's going to be all right," she scoffs. "That doctor was an idiot. And she was talking out her ass. But I'm worried about how you're taking it."

I shrug my shoulders and pretend she's right. But she's not. I can feel it. I don't know how to make her listen, so I keep quiet. I don't say all the things I need to say to her; those things that need saying while I still can. But maybe if I don't say them I'll have more time. Maybe speaking the words, closing the loops, is what brings on my end. What if I don't say goodbye and instead postpone it indefinitely? Maybe then I won't ever have to leave. I touch Lorianne's leg and notice my hand is shaking. It's probably from the vibration of the road.

"Christ!" Lorianne shouts. I snatch my hand away as she stomps on the brake. The car skids on the wet asphalt, the tail swinging out into the middle of the street. My heart doesn't stop rattling even as she straightens the Fiesta and pulls over to the curb. I'm relieved no one else was on the road, otherwise we may not have survived. The irony isn't lost on me. Every inch of my skin vibrates at a different wavelength; I'm out of step with everything. The sensation takes time to subside.

"What did—?"

"There," she points.

I'm not sure what she's pointing at. There's a series of boarded-over storefronts cloaked by curtains of rain. The only visible lights are the red and blue neon of the neighborhood watering-holes.

"Look," she says, stabbing the air with her finger.

"Lorianne, what is it?"

She looks at me, angry and excited and frightened. And smiling? The raindrops leave shadowy pools on her face, making it hard to tell.

"Over there," she says. "It's the same mark."

I look through the sheet of rain at the twisted neon tubes and see what she's talking about. Crudely painted on the brick behind the glowing tubes, the graffiti is hidden in plain sight. It looks like an interrobang with six lines radiating from its curved crest. I have never seen it before.

Though I wonder if that's true.

Lorianne dashes from the car and my stomach sinks. The street is empty and the neon lights it like a Christmas decoration.

"What are you doing?" I shout into the storm. She doesn't look back.

"I told you this is bullshit. What was that doctor talking about? You're one hundred percent healthy, and you're going to die by tomorrow? No, I don't accept that. That's idiotic. But somebody put that mark on you, and we're going to find out who and why."

"Leave it alone. Let the police handle it. I just want to go home." The rain pummels my skin, but beneath the sensation everything buzzes faster with each step I take.

"I'm tired of this bullshit. And who does that Dr. Maharaj think she is? She doesn't know everything. Screw her. Screw all doctors. It's just another example of the way people are classed by society. Like, I'm supposed to listen to her because she has a stethoscope. Why? Is she more valuable to society than me? I guarantee you I do as much in my job as she does in hers, but I don't have a Ph.D. after my name so I get ignored or harassed. And I have to watch this so-called expert tell you that there's something wrong with you when there clearly isn't. And you believe her because she has a fancy piece of paper and makes lots of money. It's one of the oldest fallacies in the book: the appeal to authority."

The storm intensifies alongside her rant, the heavens drowning me in it. She continues until we reach the bar, at which point her face twists into a grimace, and her shoulders lift as though she's taking a breath. It lasts less then a second before she reverts to herself.

"Bringing you in here is a bad idea for so many reasons."

"We don't have to go in," I say, but all I want is a drink. A drink will make all of this go away.

"We do," she says.

We enter the bar drenched. Lorianne pushes her soaked hair back and looks at me, but my memories don't return. I don't know what happened last night or how I got this bizarre mark. Nothing is familiar: not the crooked knick-knacks pinned to the walls, not the line of curled football pennants around the mirrored wall, not the row of old men draped like lost coats over their chairs, eyes blankly fixed on the stuttering television. No one glances at us. Lorianne snatches my wrist and drags me to a booth along the outer perimeter.

We sit and Lorianne lights a cigarette. She leans back and blows thick smoke into the air separating us. She squints through the cloud at everyone in the bar. Then asks me to do the same.

"Is there anything that you recognize? Anything that rings a bell?"

The drinks are all I see, but I don't admit it. I pretend to stare, since it's too hard to concentrate. I'm sopping wet and I don't want to be in this place. I want to be at home, dry and alone and apart from the world. Lorianne has no confidence in Dr. Maharaj, but I can't shake the feeling there's something else going on. Something inevitable. I have less than a day left in this world, fewer than twenty-four hours above ground. I can't process how frightened I am—it's so overwhelming my mind keeps sealing it off. But like a cracked dam, I can't hold the growing pressure forever. Every inch of my flesh writhes and struggles to escape my body. Scratching brings no relief.

"Well?" she asks.

"Nothing looks familiar. I don't think I've ever been here before."

She purses her lips. I don't want to hear whatever she has to say next.

"You have been here before."

There's no question in her mind.

"Lorianne, maybe we should just go home. I don't want it to end like this."

"We need to get to the bottom of what happened to you, Miles."

"But why? Why can't you just leave it alone?"

She looks at me through a cloud. I can't tell if her eyes are wet or angry.

"Anyway, you need to stop worrying. If you were sick, you'd be getting worse, and you're fine."

Except for the ants crawling over me.

The bartender notices us and throws a white rag over his shoulder. I turn away, pretending I'm not desperate for a drink, but Lorianne doesn't bother. She crosses her arms at the elbow and rests them on our table while her cigarette dangles between two of her fingers. I can't tell if she's too distracted to notice the bartender or doesn't care. Neither would surprise me.

He arrives at our table with eyes swollen and red like two fresh wounds. I wonder how long he's been awake.

"What can I get you?" he says. His attention is focused on Lorianne.

"Nothing for me. Miles, what do you want?"

Before I can tell her, there's commotion behind me. I turn around, but no one in the bar has moved. I glance back at Lorianne, whose face is inscrutable. What does she want? Does she want me to keep playing the game or be who I am?

If ever there was a time to splurge, this would be it. On the eve of my death.

"What's the best Scotch you have?"

She looks at me. The bartender doesn't. I don't care: my mouth is watering.

He rattles off some choices, but I'm not paying attention. I'm busy imagining the taste of it, smoky and peaty. I run my tongue over my eager lips.

"Give me the Lagavulin."

He nods. As soon as his back is turned, Lorianne's face is a mask of unbridled excitement. She stubs out her cigarette, and I worry she's about to lay into me. She has other things on her mind. She waits until he's far enough away before she says anything.

"He wouldn't look at you."

"What do you mean?"

"The bartender wouldn't look at you. I was watching him the whole time he was here."

"Are you sure?"

I turn and watch him going about tending bar. He never looks our way.

"He knows something," Lorianne says. "I don't know what, but he knows something. He probably recognizes you from last night. He has to. He recognizes you and he's worried you recognize him. He's trying to figure out what to do about it."

"He doesn't look worried. He looks bored."

"Maybe, but he isn't. He's panicking and trying really hard to hide it. Now shut it, he's coming." She leans back into her torn leather seat with feigned indifference. My hands are sweating.

The bartender arrives and drops the tumbler before me with a muted thud. I stare at it greedily, not certain it's not a mirage. But it feels real enough. I take a sip and it burns in my nose the way the good stuff should. For a moment I forget all about Lorianne and everything else. There is only this. This beautiful instant.

Lorianne's voice nudges me out of my reverie.

"So," she says, "do you get a lot of business here?"

The bartender hovers above us. Shrugs. Lorianne keeps going.

"I assume it gets busier than this, usually. I mean it must, since you're still in business. Like, it was probably really busy last night, right?"

I study his weathered face, and there's only the smallest hint of impatience. He nods at the *Employees Only* door behind him, then looks at Lorianne. Then at me.

My head swims.

"You can go try again if you want."

That's it. That's all. He says it, then walks away.

I don't speak as he goes. I can't. My skin is skittering over my body, my heart racing. Everything spins as though I'm in a dream and have been since I woke in the hospital. Nothing makes sense. I push the tender spot behind my ear and the world flips sideways.

*

It rights and once again I'm lost. The stairs at my feet are lit by a dim bulb, but it can't disguise how much paint has flaked off every surface. Lorianne is ahead of me, descending into the dark. She never looks back at the coils of smoke that follow her. I piece together that we're still in the bar and we've traveled beyond the locked door. The problem is I have no memory of how it happened. I don't know where my Scotch went, either.

"Where are we?" I whisper.

Lorianne shushes me, then points into the darkness ahead with a cigarette pinched between her fingers. I hear something. A voice quietly murmuring.

Maybe it's hesitation or dread or fear, but I wonder what we're doing. Why is Lorianne working so hard to find out where the mark came from if she thinks I'll live? And if I think I'll die, why am I wasting these moments in a grungy stairwell? It's not who we are, but it's who we used to be, who we both think we should be. We're stuck, our reflections failing to match how we are seen. I desperately want to pull Lorianne back and tell her we need to go, but it's too late.

She pivots the corner at the bottom of the stairs, the lit tip of her cigarette an ember doused by night. When I reach the foot of the staircase I look down that long hallway, but she's no longer there. There is only a single shoe a few feet away, chewed and worn through.

Thin light falls down the stairwell behind me and highlights the edges of stored cardboard boxes. I open one and find it full of musty clothes, folded neatly. In another, jewelry and accessories in unsorted tangles. I've packed my own life so often into similar boxes, compressed it and expected a future new life to spring forth. But wherever I ended up, when I opened those boxes nothing was different. Everything I hoped to escape was right where I left it.

"Lorianne," I whisper with as much volume as I can muster. The sound reverberates off the peeling walls and damp floor. "Lorianne, where are you?"

There is more murmuring. A tiny square of light penetrates the dark at end of the hallway.

All I want is to be anywhere else, but my flesh won't let me leave. It pulls me by my bones, drags me forward. I don't want to hear the voice. I don't want to know about the mark behind my ear or if I'm about to die or when. I don't want to be confused or disoriented. But most of all, I don't want to die in the dank and the mildew, surrounded by puddles and concrete. I don't want the last thing I see to be sodden cardboard boxes of clothes stored for so long they can't hold themselves together. Like pupae splitting open.

A pale specter moves in blackness. I detect familiar smoke.

"There you are," Lorianne says, emerging from the dark. I can barely see her face. "Only you could get lost in a hallway. Come on." She grabs my wrist. The skin beneath her touch buzzes and radiates in waves.

"We should go home, Lorianne. I think—" I check my forehead to convince myself I'm not lying. "I think I'm actually sick."

"Don't be an idiot," she says. But what she means is, don't be a sucker. Don't believe Dr. Maharaj just because she's a doctor. Doctors are only people and people are no smarter than me.

But Lorianne doesn't know about my blackouts. She doesn't know how fast my heart races. She doesn't know my skin won't stop moving or my head thumping, especially now that she's leading me toward that square of light. She doesn't know anything and I don't want to tell her because everything since I woke in the hospital has been leading me deeper and deeper into a nightmare, and if I say something—if I admit the truth—then I'll have accepted it's all real and I'll never wake up. So, instead, I bargain.

"Let's turn around, Lorianne. Let's go home and hide in bed and forget everything that's happened. Let's for once pretend that we aren't angry or scared or worried or unhappy. Let's let all this go and be something we're not. Just this once. Just for tonight. Let's forget everything else. Please, Lorianne. Please, let's just leave."

My voice warbles once, and it stops her. She turns, her face lit by a long drag of her cigarette. She's practically a shadow now, framed by the solitary light at the hall's end.

"We have to keep going, Miles. Otherwise, how are you going to know this was all bullshit? Or do you want to worry for the rest of your life? Because I don't. I don't want to worry about it, and I don't want to watch you worry about it. We might as well never get out of this basement, if that's the case. We'll be stuck down here forever."

I don't know what else to say. I don't know how else to move her or change our direction. I don't know what else to do but continue toward the square of light.

At the end of the hall there's a room. It's not a large room—it's no more than twenty feet in any direction, and the floor is made of uneven concrete; the walls, pale scratched brick. There are piles of clothes everywhere tucked in shadow. On the far wall is the square of light, and only when I'm close do I realize it's a mirror. No bigger than two feet square, it's the only furniture in the room and is reflecting light from somewhere.

The floor in front of the mirror is slick, and my shoes make tearing sounds as I lift them. I barely recognize my reflection; I've aged since I woke in the hospital. My skin pulls, sallow and loose, an outfit that no longer fits. Lorianne's voice is behind me, but she's not in the mirror. There is only me.

"Look at this," her disembodied voice says. I don't turn. "Are these your keys?"

Metal clinks and jangles, but I'm distracted by my reflection. It's untethered and glitching, and I wonder if it's caused by the throbbing behind my ear.

Fingers find the tender flesh where the mark should be and I push, unleashing waves of scurrying insects under my skin. They ripple across my body with the turn of my head and the bending of my ear. I need to see the mark. I need to see my oncoming death. I pull back the skin and the cartilage and finally look in the mirror.

"There's nothing there," I say.

"What are you talking about?"

"There's no mark. The spot behind my ear isn't even red."

Lorianne whispers her protest, but the truth is obvious. It's reflected right back at me.

There is no mark, but there is a spot in the mirror. Some smudge on the glass that reshapes as I waver on my unsteady legs; a spot that grows the longer I stare. I reach out and put my finger on it. The glass is warm and soft and my finger feels as though it's sinking in, as though nothing in the world is solid. Lorianne's voice is behind me, emanating from a deep hole, uttering shrill words I can't make out before they slip away.

I push harder against the spot on the mirror and my finger suddenly punctures the membrane. Electric shocks travel the length of my arm. I vibrate, lose control. My body activates and pulls toward the surface. I frantically struggle but only sink deeper as staggering pain burns through me. My hand is already two knuckles deep, but the flesh has not followed. Instead, the skin has split, then buckled, muscles and thick-walled veins collecting against the smooth mirror as I'm yanked inch by inch farther in. Lorianne is screaming somewhere as I reach out with my other hand to stop my descent. But the mirror is now too wide, and I can't reach the wall in time; I plunge my other hand into the plastic surface. Both hands are electrified and angry, and the remainder of my burning flesh shrinks from my bones, further stripped by each jerk deeper into the glass. I'm soon at my wrists. Then I'm at my elbows. If the pressure I feel on my shoulders is Lorianne, struggling to pull me free, it's too late. Each successive tug leaves more flesh gathered against the glass, the evacuated sleeves of my Miles-suit hanging lifelessly. I don't know anymore if the screaming I hear is mine.

There's a momentary chill when my elbows are taken, right before I cry out in torment. The mirror is inches from my face, and through my tears I see light refracted there. Another world, faintly superimposed on this one, a new image on old film. My face is wrenched closer still and I see another face staring out from behind the glass, looking into mine. His mouth is open and stretched wide, his eyes burning with tears. I look deeper and see all the grooves carved around his features. That man is so close I can almost touch him, our faces an intimate inch apart.

Then I am yanked again. I open my mouth and can't breathe. Everything burns as the surface breaks and I am submerged.

*

Everything is blank. Empty. Nothing. A yawning void forever of blinding white. I stare and stare and stare and stare and the white goes on forever. There is nothing. I am nothing. There is only nothing.

Then suddenly there is something. Into the white creeps a shadow. I stare into the void until the shadow thickens and congeals. It takes millennia to form. It takes aeons. But the shadow becomes a shade, the shade a blur, the blur a body. And other shadows emerge, colors touch and paint the blank canvas. A gradual painting is created, words becoming thoughts becoming images. The endless nothing ends as the vast white contracts until it is no larger than a light bulb hanging above my head in a stark white room. I blink and sit up.

The world wavers then settles. At the foot of the bed, flipping through my chart, stands Dr. Maharaj. Her brow turned up at the ends in a hirsute smile.

"Welcome," she says without glancing. I scratch my head. There's the distant echo of a cry. "How are you feeling?"

"Fine," I say, though I don't remember what fine feels like. My voice sounds strange. Dr. Maharaj nods and scribbles.

"Well, you're awake. That's a good sign." She reaches over, checks my pulse; takes the stethoscope from her pocket and pushes the cold disk into my chest. Satisfied, she scribbles again in her book, then points at the open locker by the door. "Your clothes are in there."

"How long have I been here?" I wonder. Time is moving slow.

She waves away my question.

"You're perfectly fine. You can leave as soon as you're ready. There's already a backlog waiting for the bed."

The room's brightness fades gradually. Beyond the window the sun bakes the side of the other wing.

"What happens now?"

She looks up from her clipboard at me. Her skin is a deep brown. Mine is as red as a newborn's.

"Now? Whatever you want to happen, I suppose. It's up to you."

I open my mouth, but her pager beeps before I speak. With a finger posed to quiet me, she bends the pager upward and glances, then the ends of that brow draw together as if someone pulled a loose thread. I ask her what's wrong and she doesn't answer. She wordlessly storms from the room.

I sit in silence and wait. I can see my clothes folded on the open locker shelf, but they don't look familiar. I doubt they're mine, but I'm not sure what they're supposed to look like. All I know is I should get dressed and leave.

Sunlight beams in through the room's window, drawing a bright square on the tile. I carefully stand and pace to where I can see clearly outside.

From the bed, I can only see the brick wall of the other wing, but as I step closer to the window that wall moves, and an overlooking view of cityscape and its waterfront is revealed.

"Whatever I want," I repeat aloud as I survey what's below me.

Before I leave the hospital, my eye is drawn once more to the crystal clear sky. It's breathtakingly cerulean and nearly perfect as it hangs over the world. It harbors but one single flaw: the solitary dark cloud moving just above where the great lake meets the infinite curved horizon.

Antripuu

There are four of us left huddled in the cabin: me, Jerry, Carina, and Kyle. And we're terrified the door won't hold. Carina shivers so uncontrollably, her teeth sound like stones rattling down a metal chute. Kyle begs her to quiet down.

But her teeth aren't making enough noise to matter. Not compared to the howling storm. It comes in gusts that build in slow waves, rhythmically increasing in both volume and strength until a gale overtakes the cabin, pelting the windows with hard rain. A cold draft pushes past us while we tremble on the floor, wishing we were any place else.

Still, the draft's not the issue. It sneaks beneath doors and crawls down the chimney, and these are things we may not like, but we expect. It isn't the storm that bothers us, despite its deep-throated howls and the way it screeches around the corners. The problem, instead, is what's beneath the storm, mimicking the howls of the storm, trying to coax us into opening the door and letting it in.

The others are quickly losing hope we're going to survive this.

Not me. I lost hope a long time ago.

*

Kyle, Jerry, and I have traveled up north together, three former workmates who still get along. Kyle, tall and lean, with a confidence born from getting everything he wants without much difficulty; Jerry, his opposite in a way, maybe trying too hard to remain detached from life's upsets. But both are good people, and I need to surround myself with good people. I meet so few of them.

It was Kyle who suggested we hike through Iceteau Forest for a week. Collectively we've spent too many nights in downtown bars and pubs, and he thought time outdoors would do us good. I suspect, though, it was his and Jerry's plan to get me outside my head for a while. Give me something distracting to do, some good stories to focus on for a change. Since all three of us left the socket company, I haven't landed on my feet the way the two of them have, and I know they're worried.

The trip to Iceteau was long, mostly sunny and pleasant. The forecast promised long warm days and short cool nights in that brief window between the rise of the mosquitoes and the fall of the black flies. The perfect time to hike into the woods, Kyle said, and when we left our car at the side of the road I felt buoyed enough to wonder if I'd ever want to return to it. Maybe we'd leave that life behind and start anew, become one with the grass and bushes and trees. But it was clearly a dream; my desire to give up and do nothing resurfaced quickly once we started walking.

The good weather didn't last long. No more than a day; long enough for us to hike too far to make turning back reasonable. As the storm commenced, we rooted through our backpacks for our waterproof shells and trudged through the deepening mud and the increasingly heavy downpour. After a while, the white noise multiplied on itself, becoming as deafening as it was maddening, as though it were trying to prove something to me: that no matter where or how far I went, my misery would always follow.

Maybe that misery was why I didn't notice it. Maybe being unhappy makes it harder to speak. I know the longer we walked through the mud, the less we wanted to talk to one another. Misery loves company, but the miserable just want to be left alone. The wind was hot and drove the rain against the sides of our drawn hoods, creating an impenetrable racket, loud enough to cause hallucinations. Kyle did his best to convince us the storm was abnormal and temporary; that it would be sunny again soon. It sounded like just another story to me.

We hiked single file, picking our way between tall old trees. Kyle led the way, Jerry close behind, but I couldn't keep up with their strides. The mud was too thick and sucked my boots down no matter how many stones I stepped on. Wet leaves clung to me, their weight slowly building. I heard only my panting breath over the rain, interrupted by the scratching of low-hanging branches against my hood, and I saw only the gray of heavy sheets of rain. With each deaf and blind stumble forward I sensed something was wrong, and that sense quickly turned to fear; cold, irrational, debilitating fear.

I kept quiet, told myself the story that everything was fine; that it was only my depression rearing up. But when I peered ahead I saw the shimmer of movement, like some giant thing unfurling. I screamed and Jerry spun, but I knew he saw nothing. Even Kyle asked what was wrong. I was dumb, unable to do anything more than point. The two followed my hand, saw what had until then been camouflaged by old trees.

The thing had to be twenty feet tall, yet couldn't have been more than a hand's-breadth wide. Its limbs were thin and elongated as a stick insect, except an insect that towered over us on two narrow legs, and instead of a head there was nothing.

There was nothing.

Just a mouth, too wide, lined with a dozen rows of tiny sharp teeth embedded in undulating flesh. It reached toward us with one of those long creaking arms, and only Kyle had the wherewithal to move. He yanked me and Jerry back, breaking the spell of disbelief and terror that had enthralled us.

I chased after Kyle, Jerry behind me where I couldn't see him, but I could hear his boots throwing themselves frantically into the mud. The howling wind grew louder around us, as though the storm were strengthening, yet the rain didn't fall heavier, the sky didn't grow darker. Whatever caused that noise was not the wind; it was merely pretending to be the wind.

We scrambled through the downpour, chased by the sound of trees being uprooted and tossed aside. Jerry shouted hysterical gibberish, but I heard nothing from Kyle. Both their reactions were frightening, but I couldn't allow myself to succumb to the fear. I had to concentrate on escape.

Sighting the cabin was more blind luck than anything else. Kyle saw it first, pivoting mid-stride toward the ramshackle structure. I followed without thought, Jerry close behind. I prayed the door would be unlocked.

Kyle stumbled ahead of me, just avoiding the black iron rod driven into the ground. He reached the cabin a few steps before me and wrenched open the door. I dived in, followed close by Jerry and Kyle. They tripped over themselves, tumbling into a heap on the floor, and I scrambled to slam the door shut against that twig creature and its horrifying, undulating teeth. The three of us then froze in place—I curled against the door, Jerry and Kyle tangled in each other's arms—and we stared at the cabin's buckling walls, its trembling windows, waiting for the defenses to inevitably fail. But they didn't. Not when the storm howled louder, not when the cabin rattled with anger. I didn't understand why, but I also didn't understand any of what was happening. The swelling of wind and rain against the cabin eventually subsided, and we three instinctively knew that whatever that half-seen thing between the trees was, it had retreated back into the woods to wait for us. Kyle and Jerry hoped, for the moment, we might be out of danger. I didn't share their hope.

The two disentangled themselves from each other and stood. I thought Jerry might be crying but didn't want to ask. I was worried the truth might cause me to do the same. But the whimpering wasn't coming from any of us. It came from behind the closed door of a rear bedroom. It was Kyle who decided to open it despite my protests, and Jerry who stood close with a wooden chair held over his shoulder as a makeshift weapon. I stayed back and waited for whatever they were letting free to kill us.

And Carina and Weston behind the door waited for the same. We found them kneeling on the floor, clutching each other in fear. Carina's eyes were pressed closed as she repeated *"Antripuu"* below her breath. Tears streamed over her quivering lips. She screamed when Kyle touched her shoulder, awakening her from whatever refuge she'd retreated into during the storm's onslaught.

Carina was petite with dark hair that matched her dark, harried eyes, while Weston was tall, blond, with a football player's shoulders. We found out they'd been hiking in the woods as well, and like us they'd become lost in the unexpected storm when their compass failed to steer them out of it. They were in the midst of staking their small tent when the wind took it and lodged it in the trees. Then one of those trees proceeded to eat that tent.

Carina knew what she'd seen even if Weston didn't. And what she was still seeing whenever she closed her eyes. *Antripuu.*

It was the name she'd said earlier, though she denied it. None of us knew what it was, and Carina didn't want to talk about it. She would only say the sight of it sent her and Weston running, their gear left behind in the forest to rust and rot.

The five of us sat in a circle, Carina and Weston on the couch, Jerry on a small stool he dragged over, and Kyle and I on the floor. I had tried to light a fire earlier, but the stove wouldn't open and even if it had, seeping water had already made the pit an ashy swamp. No one said anything for a long time. We just listened to the howling and the rain as it ebbed and flowed. Every so often one of us would startle, certain we saw something at the window, but it turned out to be nothing.

When all that was left was darkness, I thought we should sleep in that rear room, hidden and protected, but Kyle wouldn't entertain it. He did not want us to give in to the fear. I didn't know how to tell him I already had, a long time ago. Nevertheless, I sat in the front with the rest, sharing my sleeping bag with Jerry so Carina and Weston could use his. I was so exhausted from the hike and the subsequent terror that even my anxiety couldn't keep me from sleeping until morning.

When I woke, there was still no sun, but the black had given way to dark, drab gray. I felt the opposite of rested as I struggled out of my shared sleeping bag. Carina was already up, looking out the window at the half-dozen black metal rods planted in the ground and encircling the cabin. Each had a chain leading from the top into the mud. I asked if they were what was left of a fence, to which she shrugged. Then I asked her if they had something to do with *Antripuu*. She shuddered.

An *Antripuu* was a spirit, she whispered. A forest elemental her grandmother had told her about. But it wasn't real, she said. It was just a story from the old country. What did the *Antripuu* want, I asked, but Carina wouldn't answer.

Kyle woke then, but I suspect he'd been pretending to sleep while listening to us, because he rose unmoored. We didn't repeat anything and he didn't ask. All he did was sit quietly with his face in his hands. When Jerry woke, he looked at the three of us and moaned.

Only Weston appeared inured to the storm, emerging from the room chipper and relaxed. He decreed the night before an aberration, a shared delusion that leapt from him and Carina to the rest of us, or vice versa. Despite our arguments he assured us that we hadn't seen anything but the storm playing tricks on us, but now the storm had weakened. It was already getting brighter, he claimed, though it seemed no different to me. He laughed then, maniacally, as though in the grip of depression or delusion. I was understandably concerned.

He suddenly announced he was leaving. We urged him to reconsider, but he was decided, and even Carina's pleas would not deter him. Weston assured us that once he reached a park ranger or some authority in Iceteau Forest, he'd report what happened and insist on our rescue. We told him again it was too dangerous, but he asked about our alternate plan. Was it to stay hidden until we starved to death? None of us knew how to respond. We looked to Kyle and, after a moment, he acquiesced. Weston was right: someone had to go.

With great trepidation we unlocked the door and he stepped out, invigorated by his imminent escape from captivity. Clouds hung overhead, heavy and potent, while mist had risen from the ground to mirror them. Weston kissed Carina and shook hands with me, Kyle, and Jerry, and again told us not to worry, and that he would see us soon. We stood in the doorway and watched him walk off with the pack we'd assembled for him, following the makeshift path toward the trees. He whistled something jaunty as he passed the black iron rods, the sort of tune one might whistle on an invigorating summer's walk. When he was almost at the trees he stopped and turned to wave at us, and from the mist behind him rose the *Antripuu.*

We screamed, but I don't know if there was time to hear us. A roar like howling wind, and Weston was up in the air and gone. Swallowed whole in a single motion.

I came to my senses inside the locked cabin while around me Carina was trembling and Jerry sobbing. That was when I understood how bad things had become. Once the *Antripuu* appeared, Kyle had dragged us inside before we were noticed, but now he stood at the window stone-faced, watching the day increasingly darken. It was too early for night's approach, so it had to be clouds gathering, blocking the remaining day while lightning flashed and thunder jolted the ground. We looked at one another, then crawled and shuffled toward the middle of the floor and huddled together as a deluge of rain hammered the cabin. When the wind returned, in volume and in force, howling as it had the day and night prior, I was tempted to surrender and follow Weston out the door.

I couldn't take it anymore. I couldn't do it.

That was when Carina slapped me across my face so hard I tasted blood for the next hour. But at least my head was screwed back on right.

*

We won't escape the forest. That was clear the moment Weston was devoured. Our car is days away, and Carina doesn't know where she and Weston left theirs. Even if she did, he carried the keys. We will not be rescued, we will not get away. Which means there is no consequence to anything we do. Nothing could be worse that what already awaits us.

So we spend the night arguing what we should try and when. Jerry wants to wait the storm out, but I don't think that will stop the *Antripuu.* Carina called it a storm-bringer, and as long as it stays, so will the rain and wind. As Weston said, there isn't enough food to hold us long. We pile it in the middle of the floor and there's no more than a day's worth. We could ration, but the more we stretch it out the hungrier and weaker we'll be, and we need our strength. It seems so impossibly insurmountable, but Kyle forces us to press on. It takes him until dawn, but he rallies us. Even with the sound of the storm outside, even with the flashes of lightning, and the *Antripuu* circling, he tells us we can make it, that we can survive. We just need to stick together and stick to the plan.

Once we lose hope, he says, we're dead.

It's a good story. I'm not sure I believe him, but I want to.

We distract ourselves from the howling by sharing bits of ourselves. I learn things about Jerry and Kyle I never knew, such as how when Jerry was eight he lost his father in a bar fight, and how Kyle never graduated high school and got his GED much later. And I learn things about Carina. I learn that she and Weston met at a peace rally only a few months ago. I learn that she's struggled with anxiety for most of her life, and her medication was a godsend. I learn she'd wanted to be a poet, but ended up selling pharmaceuticals because of how much more money she makes. And I learn that she is terrified of the *Antripuu* and desperately wants everything to be over. That revelation, if it can be called one, brings a somber air to our night, and we get down to business planning what we'll do once the day returns.

If it returns.

*

Our plan is not complicated. It can't be, because we have nothing. There is no fighting back. There is running, and there is dying. The only hope we have is seeing the *Antripuu* before it sees us. We will walk in a cluster, a set of eyes in each direction, and head for our car. Kyle will be our point person, the leader, the one we follow if we have to run. We dress him in all the red clothing we collectively have so he will stand out. Be unmissable in the rain, between the trees. If the *Antripuu* appears, Kyle will run, and we will follow him like a beacon. It's a terrible plan, but it's all we have.

We leave as soon as the sky has turned from black to gray. It's the hardest moment of our escape, when we most question our judgment. For me the second-guessing is nothing new, but for Kyle it must be strange not to be sure of something. It takes our cluster some time to find our rhythm, and we worry with each stumble or falter that the *Antripuu* is readying to strike. But it doesn't, and we are in step by the time we reach the black iron rods.

We don't stop long enough to inspect them, but in the morning light I see they are not the remnants of a fallen fence. The chains are not linked together, but instead to metal collars partially sunk into the ground. Poking through the waterlogged mud are yellowed bones, and I shift my eyes away, not wanting to think about why the animals were chained. Or if they were animals at all.

I hear only rain pelting my shell and the howling wind. I concentrate on the trees, scanning for the *Antripuu.* There isn't energy left to speak, and if the others do, the din is too great to hear. It doesn't take me long to conclude we're fools, and that we should turn back. Out in the storm, with that thing stalking us from behind the branches, my anxiety coils tight and threatens to explode. I can't imagine how Carina is faring. I feel her trembling beside me. I want to tell her the only way through is to ignore the fear, push it down and forgets it exists, but I can't help her. I can't help anyone. I'm on the cusp of losing everything, and I don't know how to stop it.

The four of us move as a unit through the pouring rain. Jerry is surprised the tree canopy doesn't better protect us, but it's clear the trees have given up. Alone in the middle of Iceteau Forest, insignificant and alone, I wonder if they're any different from me.

It's as though my every suspicion about the world has been proven true. There is something out there that wants to destroy me. I haven't been imagining it. No job, no partner, no prospects for either; watching my friends excel while I fail repeatedly. Until now I assured myself I was wrong and things would get better, but now that I'm trapped in this downpour, surrounded by deafening winds and stalked by a creature who craves my destruction, it's become clear I'm right where I belong.

The screaming is sudden, but I don't know from whom or

where—the sound is sliced by the savage winds and rain. Kyle is already a red blur bounding ahead through the storm, and I am running before I'm aware I'm doing so. I don't turn to look for the *Antripuu*. I don't turn to look for Jerry or Carina, either. I just pray I'm running fast enough. The mud tries to slow me but I defy it, hurtling over logs and debris. Kyle's red clothing slips in and out of sight as he moves between the trees, looking for the swiftest path to safety. The forest spins, my vision confused and disrupted in a perpetual state of vertiginous mayhem. Then, at some point, I realize I am still running but the red blur ahead of me is gone.

I cannot panic. I will not panic. I keep running straight, hoping to catch another glimpse of Kyle and his red clothing, or of anybody at all. At least anybody real, anybody who is not a mirage of streaming water and shadowy branches, a ghost from my past skittering in the spaces between the trees. Repeatedly, I see an illusion of the *Antripuu* hovering overhead, but I don't stop running as hard as I can. I run until I can't do it anymore, until the adrenaline boost wears off and I find myself staggering through the woods, nearly falling over every root or upturned stone. When I can't go on, I throw myself into the mud behind a tree and wait for whatever is coming.

It's only when I've stopped that my body demands more breath. My limbs rattle and my digits spark as I try to get myself under control. I will not think about the others. I won't. I close my eyes and listen for the howl of the *Antripuu*, but if it's there it's hidden behind the static of rain on the leaves.

I hold no hope I'll see anyone again. Not Jerry, not Carina, not Kyle. I could call out their names, but I don't have enough breath to pretend. The *Antripuu* has found them. I am utterly alone.

We did not plan for this. I have only the vaguest notion of where the car might be, but I start moving nonetheless. Without hope, there is nothing left but the illusion of hope. The treetops above creak and bend, but I do not see the *Antripuu* looming amongst them. I take a hesitant step into the open, then another, and still there is nothing.

As I move through Iceteau Forest, my equipment, food, and friends gone, I question why this happening, what I've done to cause it. The thought consumes me as I watch the trees, hoping I'm still moving toward the road. Toward the car. Toward escape and salvation.

I catch sight of red again between the trunks ahead, the briefest glimpse of Kyle. I yell, even though it is impossible for him to hear me through the rain, and he stops. I stop as well. I can make out a red blur through the haze, waiting for me to catch up, and for the first time I feel hope. Kyle has survived. And if he's survived, the others have survived as well.

They have to have. They have to.

I squint, hand on my brow to keep the streaming rivulets out of my eyes, but I can't see any sign of them. They're not behind me, either. But maybe, I hope, they found their way past me when I became lost. Maybe they're up ahead. I turn back, calling out to Kyle to tell him I'm coming, but he's gone; the red blur is gone.

I run forwards, screaming his name despite my breathlessness, each footfall a jarring thud in my ears. The trees ahead cluster tighter, their branches springing lower to the ground, and the mesh of twigs and leaves scrape my skin. I raise my hands to protect my face, sacrificing them to the long scratches and tears. Everything in Iceteau Forest is hungry for my blood.

When the lattice of branches suddenly opens, I'm spit out over an unexpected ravine, and I spin and flail over the edge. I don't remember the fall, only coming to my muddled senses sitting waist-deep in rushing water, staring up at the narrow opening too far above my head to reach. Dazed and bruised, my head buzzing, I raise my aching hand and it's clear my arm is broken. It's much too thin, and flexing it feels like someone slowly pushing a dull knife into my flesh. I cough and everything hurts.

In the gap above there is a glimpse of movement, a momentary red blur. It's Kyle. He's found me. I see his arm stretch over the side for me and I'm elated. I call up through the rain as I reach to take his hand. My ringing head, though, keeps insisting something is wrong, something I'm not seeing, but I can't focus on what, not until my fingers graze Kyle's overlong arm and I jerk my hand away.

The *Antripuu*'s body resolves between the drops of rain, standing astride the chasm's opening, its unhinged mouth grinding against the crevasse's opening—too wide to fit through, but wide enough to show me the row after row of undulating flesh and teeth within. I smell its fetid breath, the odor compounded and worsened by the rain, and I slide my broken body down farther out of reach until all but my head is submerged in the water.

The *Antripuu,* frustrated, struggles against the solid rock, stretching its long spindle arms to snatch at me. I can see the tattered remains of the clothing we'd given poor Kyle tangled around its knotted limbs, and the sight unleashes the anger and frustration I've been carrying much longer than I've been in Iceteau Forest.

I scream at the *Antripuu* to leave me alone, to ask it what I've done that's so horrible, so absolutely vile as to deserve this, any of this. What have I done to deserve having my only friends taken from me? To deserve losing everything I've ever loved? My home? My career? My sense of self? What have I done that's so awful that my dreams should fail, that any promise I ever had should wither away? What have I done to deserve sitting here, alone, deep in water and muck, pounded by rain so heavy it's like rocks, chased by a spirit or a god or figment of my imagination until my body is destroyed and I have no choice left but to curl up and die? What have I done that is so bad that I deserve this life?

The *Antripuu* doesn't have the answer. All it has is a howl like a thunderstorm, and a hunger to consume me.

Hopeless, broken, and alone, I wonder why I even bother to fight.

The voice beneath the howls is a mirage. It must be. Small and pitched barely above the *Antripuu*'s roar and the ringing echoing in my head, it can't be ignored, even as I focus my attention on the creature pacing above and wonder how much longer I can hold on. The voice sharpens, grows insistent, and needles into my thoughts, forcing me to turn my head, to take my eyes off the *Antripuu.* On the edge of the ravine's crevasse a short distance away, disheveled and panicked and skittish, is someone it takes a moment to realize is Carina.

Through the heavy storm and my concussion I see her eyes are wide and fearful as she watches the *Antripuu*. If it sees her, it's too busy grappling with how best to reach me to care. She creeps near enough to ask if I'm able to move. I tell her I'm not sure. She tells me I must.

I wait until the *Antripuu* steps away from the crevasse in search of a solution. First I try to straighten my bent knee stuck in the ravine's muddy bottom. It's painful and exhausting, but I manage to free it, and immediately the rushing water carries me forward. I use my one good arm and the drag of my legs to slow myself before submerged debris tears me open. Carina races along the bank to keep me in sight while I try to remain as silent and as invisible as possible.

The *Antripuu* returns to the place I was shortly after I've gone. I can see it through the widening opening of the crevasse—circling the spot it last saw me, frustrated and confused, and I almost feel . . . no, I don't feel anything. I'm numb to everything but my throbbing pain. Carina's harried face appears periodically, peeking over the edge of the ravine, urging me on.

The ravine's banks eventually slope downwards; the eight-foot banks become six feet, then four, then only one, low enough that Carina can wade into the ravine and grab my battered and exhausted body before I float away. She manages to drag me from the water and onto the bank where I lie on my back and let the rain shower my face. I stare into the churning, clouded sky; my body continues to feel as though it's floating, and I wonder if any of this is real, if I'm not actually still in the ravine, swept away by the current. Why else would the rain on my face taper in force, like a storm in its final throes?

Carina says we have to go. The rain may have weakened, but we're not safe. She helps me roll over, then get my knees under me. My joints are swollen and bruised, and even with her help standing seems impossible, but I'm able to move enough so that we can get out of the open. I still hear the howling wind, but it sounds farther away. Like distant thunder.

We take refuge in the fringes of the tree line, where Carina helps me splint my arm and wrap my wounds. I want to ask her about Jerry, but I know the answer. It's already written on her distraught face. But there's something else there, too, a perseverance that illuminates from beneath the scrapes and dirt and keeps me from losing hope. Once you lose hope, you're dead. I remember Kyle saying that, and it's never seemed truer. Once you lose hope, you're dead.

As soon as I'm able, Carina and I stumble through Iceteau Forest, taking care to study the trees, to listen to the winds, but the rain gently peters out and the wind dies down the farther we walk, which tells me we're moving in the right direction, away from this horrible nightmare. I don't know how far the road is from us. I just know it's somewhere ahead. I hope when we find it the car will be right there, right where Kyle, Jerry, and I left it, but it seems impossible. Iceteau Forest is so large, so deep, that the car could be anywhere along the road, or maybe even nowhere. Maybe Jerry and Kyle made it past the *Antripuu* and reached the car first. Maybe they're driving back and forth looking for Carina and me. Or maybe they've left to find help. Or maybe the car will be sitting behind a curve somewhere along the road, somewhere out of our sight, and will remain there until it eventually rusts away.

I don't know what we'll find when we get to the road. It could be anything, or it could be nothing. But the sun is already starting to peek through the drizzling clouds, and my banged-up knees are starting to hurt less. Carina has been telling me stories about the old country and what it was like for her grandmother there. She tells me she loved hearing those stories growing up, and I'm starting to understand why. A good story can make you forget about the bad stories, even if the bad stories are all you want to believe. All you've ever told yourself. And sometimes you have to choose to believe the good stories, even when it feels like there's no choice at all.

I've almost forgotten all the bad stories I know as Carina helps me limp through the trees. I think I hear the sound of a car engine somewhere in the distance. Or maybe it's the roar of wind echoing through the forest. It's difficult for me to be sure.

All I can do is hope.

Clay Pigeons

I

Reno broke the news to me once we hit Port Said.

"Liv, we're skint."

There were a few pounds left, but we'd apparently spent the rest. The north coast offered lots of opportunities and lots of marks, but as we made our way south those marks grew fewer and further between, and when the car finally broke down we didn't have much choice but to hitch a ride into the city and sit tight until something came up. At least there was enough to keep us drinking and smoking, and thankfully fucking still cost nothing, so we managed to have a lot of all three while we tried to find our next score.

I just wish I'd known before getting there how much I'd hate Port Said.

I'd met Reno at the start of the summer, back before the sun made Egypt a blast furnace for eight hours a day. I'd learned a long time ago that the hours between nine and five were not for me, so I'd spent most of my days holed up in cheap rooms sleeping off the night before, and most of my evenings in the local clubs with the local men, stoking their hopes that the drinks they were buying me might wet more than my whistle. It was into this world that Reno stepped, and I don't know if it was his trustworthy face or my need to have a conversation with someone who spoke my language, but I gravitated to him nearly as much as he gravitated to me. In any other place in the world we may have simply passed each other by; but there, without any other options, we clung together—less out of desperation and more to alleviate our shared boredom.

Port Said was the sort of between place that everybody without a home ends up in at one point or another. *An accidental experiment in multiculturalism,* Reno called it, since it took the refuse from everywhere and threw it all together at the entrance to the Suez Canal. There were just as many people running to get somewhere as there were people running to get away, and with me and Reno in the middle it should have been easy to fill our wallets with their money and slip out. Except we hadn't counted on so many other grifters doing the same, which meant the number of trusting worthwhile marks was low while the attention from local law enforcement was high. If we weren't careful, we'd end our mutual travels locked in a cell without hope of ever getting out. The Egyptian courts didn't mess around.

We'd been there for two weeks, and the lack of movement irked me and shortened my temper. Or maybe it was the sight of Reno sprawled across the furniture like a dead weight, eyes closed, shirt unbuttoned. It was grating, and if not for the way the sweat made his chest gleam I might have left. But it did gleam, and he presented himself with a laggardly confidence that suggested he cared about nothing; both those things turned me on from the first moment I saw him.

But even so, stretched out like that he seemed to fill all the space in the room, and there wasn't enough air left to breathe.

"We can't spend another evening in this fucking room. I'm going to rip out my hair if I don't get a break from looking at it."

"At it or at me?" he asked. That only irritated me more.

"Don't bother with that guilt shit. I'm not dumb enough to fall for it, and you're not dumb enough to think I might. We have to get out of this box as soon as possible. And I don't mean just the hotel room. I mean we have to get some money together and get the hell out of Port Said. You promised me we wouldn't end up stuck, and right now that's exactly how I feel. If I wanted to be in one place for the rest of my life, I'd have stayed home."

He took a long drag off the cigarette dangling from his lips.

"I'm having a hard time imagining you married to the star quarterback, nursing a couple of kids."

"That's why I ran. But you need to get off your ass and start running, too."

He scratched the contours of his chest.

"Trust me, I have no plans to get stuck here either."

That made me laugh.

"The way you're laid out there, you're all but glued down."

That's when he crushed out his cigarette between his fingers and bolted upright, all tanned legs and arms. He really was something to look at.

"I'll show you who's glued down," he said, reaching for the clasp of my shorts. With nothing better to do I turned around and let him.

It was as hot and sticky as the room, so afterward we went out. There were a lot of little places in Port Said to drink, each run by someone from a different place. There was Rifées run by a Kuwaiti, and Rick's run by an unimaginative American. We also had Lei's Dragon and the Tea Tree. They all offered their own experiences, all had their own back rooms where real experiences could be had for the right price, but Reno and I preferred the Kalai, because why not? It had everything we could want or need, plus the German woman who owned it kept her nose out of everybody's business. Or, at least, she normally did. That's what made it the perfect place for us, and made it so strange when we were approached by a short Frenchman holding a satchel and wearing a scarf around his face so only his puffy eyes peeked through. Eyes that lingered too long on our hands before making their way above our necks.

"Excuse, but the woman up front suggested I might introduce myself to the two of you. Do you mind if I sit?" His manners were so sharp you could cut yourself on them. I saw Reno shift in his seat as though he might make an allowance, but I wasn't ready to be so trusting.

"You know this guy?" I asked Reno while staring at the Frenchman.

"Never met him," he said. "And dressed like that I'm not sure I want to. Nice scarf, by the way."

"You should fuck off now," I said but the stranger didn't leave.

I looked at Reno, who just shrugged.

"Fine," I relented. "What do you want?"

"Pardonnez-moi, s'il vous plait," he said, before sliding into a chair. He unhooked the scarf from behind his ear, uncovering a sweating, unshaven, porcine face. My cigarette smoke appeared to bother him so I blew more his way. He waved his hand to dispel it, then gave up and opened his satchel. He pulled out a small brown leather roll and unfurled it across the table. Inside were a series of pockets, all holding various documents and drawings, haphazardly folded and scribbled over. Greedy excitement blossomed in Reno's eyes.

"What is it?" I asked, though the Frenchman was too focused on the presentation of his documents to notice. I blew more smoke at him until he finally looked up, eyes rheumy and streaked with red.

"I have come to talk to you about this. An opportunity. One that makes us all a good sum of money."

"Right," I said. "Such a great opportunity that you just need to share it with a couple of strangers."

"I would not say it so."

"Really? How would you say it?"

"I would say I am an investor, and I need the people to invest in. People willing to do what needs being done for everyone. I have been told this is you."

Told by who? We'd only been in town two weeks.

"Thanks," I said. "But we're not interested."

I stood up, but Reno didn't.

"Hang on, Liv," he said. "Let's hear him out first."

I shot down the rest of my drink. Dropped my cigarette in the empty glass.

"You can listen all you want. I've got better things to do."

I spent the next few hours at the bar, letting a group of young Australian travelers buy me drinks while Reno sat at the table with the Frenchman, deep in conversation. When the Aussies started to get stingier with their wallets than with their hands, I slipped away and back to the room. I lay down on the bed and watched the ceiling spin for a while until Reno came in.

I was still angry, and when he didn't notice I grew angrier. But he kept going, obliviously, dropping something off on the dresser by the door and then walking to the basin to wash his hands. He came back drying them on a towel and wearing a giant grin.

"You should have stuck around, Liv."

"Oh, should I?"

"Yeah, this guy's job sounds like no-risk easy money."

I had something cutting to say, but was too drunk and irritated to say it, so I kept my mouth shut. That didn't even slow Reno down. He sat on the edge of the bed and kicked off his boat shoes.

"You want to know what he needs us for if it's so easy, don't you? Well, that's the same thing I asked."

"I was going to ask something else," I lied, stifling a burp. "I don't trust him."

Not that trust was easy to find in Port Said.

Reno's smile widened as he pulled a folded piece of paper from his back pocket and handed it to me.

"This might change your mind."

The folded paper turned out to be a map covered in hand-drawn lines and hash marks, all in different colors. They showed the layout of a building and its entrances and exits, times and other numbers annotated beside each. If you didn't know what you were looking at, it would have looked like a confused mess.

And I had no idea what I was looking at.

"Maybe you better explain what you've gotten yourself into," I finally said.

"What I've gotten *us* into. It's easy, Liv. Look. All we have to do is get into this place, grab a box, and get out. That's it."

"Oh, that's it, huh? It sounds easy. Or like a setup."

"I know, I know, but it's not. It's real. Whatever is in the box is valuable, and Pequire said that he'll pay us well to get it for him."

"What's in this box, and why does this Pequire guy want it?"

Reno shrugged. I wasn't going to accept that answer, so I pressed him.

"Honestly, Liv, he doesn't know. He was hired by some guy to track it down and return it. It sounds like it was his client's, and this group of people called the Shaa' Kalyd took it. He hired Pequire to take it back by any means necessary."

"What the hell is a *Shaa' Kalyd?"*

"Fucked if I know. Does it even matter?"

I looked over the drawing again.

"I guess not."

Someone had definitely done their research on this job, and Reno and I did need the money so we could get out of Port Said. But on the other hand I was still seeing double and everything Reno said to me had that sloppiness that told me neither one of us was right enough to be making decisions about anything. Besides, with my anger ebbing, my exhaustion was catching up with me.

"So tell me again why exactly he needs us for this? If it's so simple, I mean."

"People know his face around here, apparently. He'd never get within ten feet of the place."

"I see," I said, and reviewed the drawing again. "And if it's so valuable, how does he know we won't just take whatever's in the box and sell it ourselves?"

"He told me it's only valuable to his client, and that client will only deal with him. I tried to get Pequire to tell me the guy's name, but he wouldn't do it. He just said the man was in Port Said, waiting. He also said that if we tried to sell it to anybody else, the Shaa' Kalyd would find out, and we'd be running from both them and him for the rest of our lives. He said we'd be idiots to try anything like that."

"I see," I said again. "So what did you do?"

Reno walked back to the door and picked up what he'd left there as he came in. He tossed it over to me.

"Don't worry about what I did. I did what I had to. Just worry about how we're going to get out of Port Said once we sell whatever this is."

For the first time in a while I was excited. We might get out. We might score big and actually get out. My hands shook as I unfurled the Frenchman's leather roll.

*

Studying was not something I was keen on—part of the reason I ran halfway around the world was to avoid becoming the kind of person who had to study—but if it meant getting out of Egypt I was willing to give it a shot. The biggest problem with Pequire's documents was he'd written his notes in French. That probably shouldn't have surprised me, but I was always an optimist and just assumed, naturally, everything would be easy. The amazing part was how often I was right. The whole trip down the coast had been that way—one trusting sap after another trying to help a down-on-her-luck foreigner; it was only when we hit Port Said that my luck turned. That change should have been a flashing red warning light, but being the optimist I just ignored it.

Since neither of us spoke French, and there was no one we trusted enough to ask for help, we had to figure something else out. Reno wasn't much help, so I cleared a space on the floor and laid out everything from the leather roll before me. I'd hoped seeing it all at once might spark an idea.

The thing about French is it overlaps a lot with English, so I was able to recognize more words than I expected. There was also the map, which was easier to decipher, and on which Pequire had helpfully drawn circles to highlight items of importance. What those circles represented wasn't always clear, but it was a start.

"Have you figured out how we're supposed to do this?" Reno asked. He'd already removed his shirt and was lying on the bed, watching the smoke from his cigarettes climb toward heaven where it belonged.

The sight stirred a couple of things in me, but I had to focus.

"I think a lot of these are notes he took casing out the place. There are times listed that look like shift changes or schedules, and a circled phone number beside what looks like a list of handguns. This will be more dangerous than anything we've done before."

"We're a little late to call it off."

"I'm not saying we shouldn't do it. I'm saying we need to be careful; it's dangerous."

"Does it say what we're supposed to be stealing?"

"Not as far as I can tell, but there's a shipping manifest in here, and one item is heavily circled. Whatever it is, it looks like it came from somewhere near the bottom of the continent." I tuned the page around so he could see for himself, but he didn't appear interested.

"And once we find this thing, what do we do with it?"

This time the shrug was mine.

"I have no idea yet."

"Well," he said, crushing out his cigarette, "not knowing what we're doing has never stopped us before."

Pequire's map was of a building fewer than three kilometers from the entrance to the canal. We crouched behind a pile of cardboard boxes along the side of the street, waiting to see if anybody came or left. The place didn't look like much—there was an arch over the doorway, but otherwise it was bland and beige, as though purpose-built to be unremarkable.

Both Reno and I were still buzzed from the night before, and we should have let another day pass before carrying out Pequire's plan, but the impulsivity was an aphrodisiac. If we'd waited, we might have done the smart thing and found the money to get out of Port Said some other way.

We watched the entrance of the building for an hour, waiting for somebody to appear. Then we waited another hour.

"I don't think anyone is coming," I said.

"Are we sure this is the right place?"

"You're the one who got the address out of him. Do you think he played us?"

Reno considered it.

"I'm not sure Pequire was capable of playing anyone. Most of what he said was in French, though, so I couldn't follow it all. But this is definitely the place he mapped, and this is definitely where they're keeping it. Whatever it is."

"And you're certain he isn't running off with our box right now?"

"Why would he have involved us in the first place if he was going to do that? There's no reason."

"Right. Of course," I said. "I'm just— We need to get out of Port Said before I kill somebody."

There was a quiet moment before he responded.

"Trust me. Once we get our money, we'll be gone."

I did trust him, so I kept watching the door. The street was emptier than I expected. Even in the heat, there should have been more people around. I didn't like it.

"It's our own fault," I said. "We should have taken better care of our money. At least, we should have held some back, just in case."

Reno didn't bother nodding. He knew I was right. I could tell just by the way his eyes were locked on the front of the building. Somewhere far off there was gunfire, but I put it out of my mind. The African and Asian sides of the canal were always at odds with each other; it was just more heated sometimes than others.

"This is ridiculous. I'm going over there," I finally said. "You coming?"

He started to answer, but I didn't wait around to hear it.

I hunched as I darted across the street, but it was a waste of energy; there was no one around. Even the windows in the other buildings facing us were dark, as though everyone in the area had cleared out, leaving me and Reno alone to deal with whatever was waiting for us. Something felt wrong.

"Try the door," I urged.

Reno looked askance at me.

"You try it."

"You got us into this. That makes this your problem."

"But you're the one who wants a big score before we leave Port Said."

"Yeah, but that's because you spent all our money."

He shut up after that one. Point for me.

"I'll try it, but if something goes wrong you're on your own."

"What else is new?"

He pretended not to hear me.

Reno checked the street behind us while I fretted, then he reached out for the door. I wished again there was light in at least one of the windows around us; just some indication the world had not stopped. But there was nothing. And when Reno finally tested the lock I knew it wasn't going to be good news.

"Liv, it's open."

Reno pushed the door slowly forward. We both waited. I was ready to bolt at the first noise, the first moving shadow, Reno or no. But there was nothing. The door merely hung open, exposing a cheaply and inexpertly tiled floor receding into the dark. We looked at each other and he swept his hand dramatically.

"After you," he said.

Pequire's map showed a long corridor lined with rooms, which looked a lot less creepy on paper than the string of doors confronting us. I'd assumed there would be people wandering through the building that we'd have to sneak past. The reality was much more baffling.

"Maybe we *are* in the wrong place," he suggested.

I shrugged.

"Too late now."

We traveled maybe another few feet before Reno stopped, suddenly looking back as though he'd heard something. I froze as well and waited for him to be confident it was nothing.

"What do you think this place is?" he asked.

"Why don't you open one of these doors and find out?"

I don't think he liked that answer, but nevertheless he started testing each knob. They were carved with a design I couldn't make out in the gloom. Like a lattice, or maybe vines. Or maybe a lattice with vines twisted through it. Each door was different, and each revealed something new: a small office with a narrow shelf of books and maps pinned to the wall; a half-kitchen with a plate of biscuits and tea pot; a room with a couch and a few folding chairs. One of the doors had light spilling out from the gap underneath, and I could hear voices behind it. I looked at Reno who was waving me on, trying to get me to forget about the Shaa' Kalyd, but I couldn't. Know thy enemy, as they say. I needed to put a face on what we were dealing with, even if it made the odds of us getting what we wanted worse. I lay my hand on the knob and tested it as slowly as I could. It turned, and when the bolt slipped back with a clunk I glanced up at Reno. There was a queer look on his face. I don't know how else to describe it. I carefully opened the door as little as possible—a sliver, really—and peered inside. Then I urgently beckoned Reno to join me. Reluctant and frustrated, he did, and the two of us put our good eyes to the crack I'd made.

What we saw wasn't what I expected. I might have been okay had it been a bunch of weirdos in hooded cloaks, each holding a lit candle, or whatever it was cultists did. Then again, it was Egypt, and that kind of stuff didn't happen in Egypt. Egypt was too busy with too many other things on its mind. So what we saw was what you'd see in any office in any country full of industrious people: a few desks with people working. There had to be about half a dozen of them, pecking at ancient typewriters or poring over folders filled with documents. A few smoked cigarettes and spoke a dialect of Arabic I barely recognized—it wasn't Masri, that much I knew. Everything was so normal and average that I didn't immediately notice why it all seemed so *off*, so fractionally out of sync. It took Reno to say it, and once he did I couldn't understand how I'd overlooked it.

"Are they all missing a hand?"

He was right: they were. I'd been so focused on them writing or typing or smoking that I hadn't noticed they all did so with only the one hand. On their opposite arms were the rosy stumps they used to hold down papers or push themselves up. The wounds looked old and healed, but I still got the impression their hands' absence was something recent, and not some defect at birth. Maybe it was in the way their arms moved, as though by habit trying to reach for something that couldn't be touched. Like at the end of each arm was a shadow, an intangible phantom.

"These are the Shaa' Kalyd?" I whispered. "They look more like an amputee support group."

"Can you understand what they're saying?"

I shook my head. Even the little Masri I knew barely lined up with what I heard. Whoever these people were, they didn't come from any part of Asia I was familiar with.

"Let's go," Reno said. "The longer we're here, the more danger we're in."

I nodded and closed the door. The only people in the building seemed to be in that one room, which meant the large room, the one at the end of the hallway, the one Pequire marked on the map, was unguarded. At least that's what I hoped, because the hallway was one long narrow passage leading to a set of double doors. It was where everything was corralling us, but there was no cover between where we were and where we were going. If anyone appeared on either end of the journey, we'd have nowhere to hide, so we sped toward the doors as quickly as possible.

But we didn't get far before Reno's face twisted.

"It smells in here," Reno whispered.

"Everything smells in Port Said. It's the canal."

"No, this is different. It's like old sayadeya or something? Maybe not as fishy?"

I sniffed. He wasn't wrong; there was definitely something rotten close by. All the weird things were starting to add up, and I didn't like the math. That should have been our cue to leave: we'd followed our guts before, usually to great success, and it's what got us all the way down the coast. And it probably would have got us out of that Shaa' Kalyd building too if it weren't for one simple thing: I needed to know what was in the box. I needed to know what it was and how much it was worth, and if it was finally going to get me out of Port Said.

At the end of the hallway were the double doors. The air was noticeably colder, and Reno guessed it was because we were too deep for hot air to circulate. It didn't make sense, but I was no scientist and I wasn't interested in arguing—not when we were at the proverbial X on

Pequire's map. I drew a deep breath and, looking at Reno, rubbed my hands together before exhaling. This was it. This was what we came for. I pushed on the doors and let them swing open.

The smell punched us hard in the face. I don't know if I'd ever experienced anything like it before. It was all I could do to keep from throwing up on myself. Reno was doubled over, covering his mouth and nose with his hands and moaning. I choked out a series of coughs. We were lucky no one heard us.

"What the fuck *is* that?" I asked. Reno was only able to shake his head.

It took me a minute to get over the shock, and when I did I slapped Reno hard on the chest so he'd catch up.

"We have to go in. If we keep standing here like idiots we're going to get caught."

He nodded, then reluctantly stumbled inside while I followed, closing the door behind me.

It wasn't so bad after a few minutes. By which I mean it was just as bad, maybe worse, but the initial shock had worn off and we could tough it out. I was amazed I was putting myself through the torture, but whenever I wavered I thought about life with that money and it got easier. I'd be able to leave Port Said and Egypt and go somewhere nice without worrying about being chased. Or chaste. That was worth stinking like garbage for a few days.

There was enough light in the room to get a sense of its size, which wasn't very large despite what Pequire had drawn. That cold we'd felt outside was double the intensity, which either meant the doors to the room were never opened or cool air was being piped in from somewhere. There were at least five metal carts, all stacked with boxes the size of small refrigerators, and a few were damp at the bottom. Whatever was inside had leaked through the paper, leaving a foul-smelling sticky residue I couldn't wipe off my hands. It was disgusting, but I wouldn't let myself think about it. Each had something in Arabic scribbled on its side using a heavy black marker. On the opposite side of the room, pressed up against the exterior wall, looked to be a large incinerator that wasn't giving off any heat.

The room was crazy with obscured shelves filled with smaller boxes. Reno and I started with those, hoping they'd be easier to carry and escape with.

"Do you have the manifest number from Pequire's notes?" I asked.

Reno nodded and read me what was written on the map.

"You start over there. It's got to be one of these."

The two of us worked quickly, methodically checking each box. Some were full of broken pottery, most unfired and fragile, but there were harder pieces mixed within. They didn't look like flatware: the pieces were twisted and grotesque, like multi-limbed creatures pulled from the deep ocean, and I shivered as I looked at them. One appeared more intact than the others, and I removed it from the box for a better look.

"What is that?" Reno asked.

"I have no fucking clue."

"It looks like a hand."

And it did, a little, if you squinted. But the texture was all wrong. The surface was rough and pebbly, and without sculpted joints.

I dropped it back into the box with the other broken pieces.

"Everything in here is garbage," I said. "You have any luck?"

Reno turned back to the shelves, running his fingers along the boxes. Almost immediately he turned to me with excited eyes.

"Bingo!"

"Are you sure?"

He nodded and struggled to pull the half-buried box free. It was no more than a foot square, but by the strain on Reno's face it was heavier than it looked.

All I saw, though, were visions of me leaving Egypt.

"Open it."

"Just about to," he said, lowering the box. He tore off the strip of packing tape in one movement, then bent back the flaps. He stared in the box, eyes wide and greedy before shifting to perplexed and unsure.

"What's wrong?" I asked.

"It's—" he started, then paused. I rushed over to him.

When I looked in the box, I was just as confused. The box was filled to the edges with what looked like a block of terracotta clay. Plastic lined the insides and was folded overtop to protect it. But protect it from what? It was *clay*.

"*This* is our big score?"

Reno shook his head.

"Pequire did say it wouldn't be valuable to anyone else."

Shouting in the hallway interrupted us. It was definitely not good.

"Just grab it, whatever it is," I said. "We have to go."

I sped to the door of the room. Reno was close behind, hauling the small box with both hands. We pressed ourselves against the wall and I turned the handle slowly. The young Egyptians were out of the office, buzzing in the hallway and arguing. Some rubbed their heads, others tried to calm the group. I couldn't tell what was happening, but they were nervous and I didn't like nervous people. Nervous people made unpredictable decisions. We had to get out of the place as fast as we could.

I scanned the room. No windows. Typical.

"This box is getting heavy," Reno whined.

"Don't you dare lose it after all this."

"What's going on?"

"They're fighting with each other. Don't know why."

"It can't be about us. This would have been the first place they looked."

"Maybe," I said. I was worried that even if it wasn't the first place, it might be the second.

"What's in those big boxes? Is it more pottery or is there something we can use as a weapon?"

I moved as quickly as I could without making noise. Reno stayed at the door, peeking through to make sure we weren't going to be surprised. I picked a large box from the nearest cart, hoping it would be something useful. It was heavy enough. I tore through the packing tape and opened up the flaps.

My stomach leapt as I covered my mouth to hold back my scream.

Inside the box was what looked at first like a disassembled mannequin, but by the smell clearly wasn't. It was a jumble of limbs and pieces I didn't recognize—a person taken apart and packed tightly. At the top of the pile was a human torso, its chest cracked open and its heart missing. At least, I thought it was the heart. I didn't know; I wasn't a doctor. But I was confident it was the most horrible thing I'd ever seen. I couldn't take my eyes off the old white scar that ran along the ribs to the torso's truncated neck. That puckered flesh curled like something written in cursive. And, of course, there was no head in the box, because why would there be?

"What the fuck is going on here?" I choked out under breath.

The seeping cardboard of the other boxes had the same rotting smell, and I knew there was nothing in the world I wanted less than to open any more of them.

"What's wrong?" Reno asked, still watching at the door for an opportunity to escape. I couldn't bring myself to tell him.

"Reno, are they gone? We have to get the fuck out of here."

He glanced at me.

"If we're going to go, we'd better now."

I folded the flaps down on the large box. I would just pretend I hadn't seen anything. That seemed best. Just pretend I hadn't seen a thing because there was nothing to see. It didn't matter what waited for me every time I closed my eyes, every time I blinked. It didn't matter what was seared into me memory. I saw nothing, because they was nothing to see.

"Let's go," I managed to say.

We rushed down the long hallway—me in front, Reno behind lugging the swinging box. I was sure we'd be caught, considering the struggling noises he made. But we made it to the row of offices and almost made it to the front door when the sound of voices erupted ahead. I literally had to pull Reno into one of the empty offices we'd seen earlier. The two of us ducked down and pressed ourselves against its door as the Shaa' Kalyd stormed by, arguing among themselves in their version of Arabic. Once they passed, I softly flipped the lock.

"What are we going to do?" I whispered. I was struggling to keep pretending I hadn't seen what I'd seen, but it was getting harder. The adrenaline from our escape only helped so much.

Reno put the small box down on the desk. He shook out his hands and looked around.

"There," he said. "A window."

"Can we fit through it?"

Reno tested the frame of the awning casement with the heel of his hand. It moved a fraction. He nodded, satisfied.

"I can open it. I'll need some leverage, though. Help me move the desk over."

He swept everything off the desk and onto the floor, then the two of us grabbed an end and lifted. The thing weighed more than I expected, and I couldn't move my side far. Reno ended up dragging the desk most of the way. It made a sudden shriek on the floorboards and we both froze, eyes glued to the door. But no one came in, so we kept going.

Reno leapt up once the desk was in place and fought to pry the window further. As he did so I kept watch, but my eye kept getting drawn to mess of papers and books he'd made. One book in particular caught my attention. It was bound in beaten-up leather and the cover bore a symbol like an upside down Q, but broken in two places. I picked it up and saw it was full of handwritten notes I couldn't read. I flipped through a few pages and wondered if it was valuable or not.

"Got it," Reno whispered. The window was open and he beckoned me forward. I shoved the book into the pocket of my pack.

"I'll boost you out, then pass you the box. I'll be out right after."

"Sounds good to me," I said.

First thing out was my pack, then Reno's. Each landed with a dull thud. Then Reno's interlaced fingers lifted me to the window. I swung my legs over and just as I was about to say something profound, the doorknob rattled fiercely, and Reno, without hesitation, shoved me the rest of the way out.

I stumbled when I hit the ground, pitching forward and landing on my hands. I was frightened and sore from impact, but nothing was broken. I heard Reno's voice through the window, first casual and gentle, trying to control the situation, while the other voice's Arabic grew louder and more insistent. Then there wasn't much talking at all, just the sound of things falling over and smashing.

My first instinct was to grab the bags and take off. But I didn't. I hesitated. Because if I ran, what did I have? Where was I going to go? There was nothing for me. The box was still in that office. Reno, too. So I picked up the bags and watched the window nervously, anxiously.

"Come on, Reno," I muttered.

There was a scream just as I was reconsidering my plan, and every inch of me leapt to attention. It was happening. Whatever it was, it was happening. I felt like my joints were frozen, but I managed to twist myself toward the window, terrified of what I might see looking down at me. The memory of that disassembled torso and its ghostly-white scar flashed across my thoughts. I couldn't swallow.

Worse was the window was empty, but it wouldn't be for long. It was as though I'd had a premonition, and had no choice but to watch the terrible things unfold. There would be the young crazed face of a Shaa' Kalyd as he pointed and screamed out my location. I'd run, but I wouldn't get far, not with two packs on my shoulder. It wouldn't take long before they had their hands on me.

Yet that didn't happen. It wasn't a Shaa' Kalyd I saw in the window. It was something else. Something I didn't expect, so I didn't immediately recognize it.

A brown cardboard box covered in bloody fingerprints being handed down to me.

"Grab it, Liv. Hurry!"

I lifted my hands, unprepared.

The box was heavier than I realized, and I had to set it on the ground so quickly I all but dropped it. When I looked up I saw Reno's bright red face beaming and out of breath. He leapt on the sill and pushed himself out, landing with awkward few steps beside me. He didn't say anything. He just picked up the box and ran as fast as he could. I scrambled after him.

I thought there would be more screaming. I thought there would be more people chasing us. I thought we would never escape in time, but none of that happened. We just kept running deeper into Port Said until Reno's arms gave out and he had to put the box down. We picked a doorway that looked as though it had never been crossed, one deep enough to hide us from the street. Reno's face looked redder and puffier than ever. His chest heaved in and out, and he was sweating like a motherfucker. He was the least attractive I'd ever seen him, which was still pretty attractive, and the sight of him cradling that box reminded me of why we'd stayed together so long, and of what we'd had to do to get there.

"We need to get off the street," he spit out between breaths. "We need some place safe to hide."

I was only able to nod, distracted by the state of his hands. His knuckles looked raw and swollen. Like fresh sausages. They had that newborn sheen to them, blood mixed with saliva. I didn't want them anywhere near me, but until we got out of sight I'd have to find a way to pretend nothing was wrong.

II

I didn't know what to expect, but I knew the box was radioactive with danger. It emanated like heat, and the longer we kept it with us, the more likely we'd be found.

I told Reno we should hide the box, but it was his idea to leave it in a rented locker. Even if someone stole the key, it would take them forever to track down where in the city it was hidden. That sounded safe enough to me, so I picked out the first nondescript place we saw and rented a small locker for a week. I figured we'd know what to do by then, and I couldn't afford to rent it much longer anyway. One week would have to do. The angry old man handed me a key and I put it in my pocket where it wouldn't get lost.

Ironic, since getting lost was exactly what Reno and I wanted to do. We had to cut ties with anyone in Port Said who had so far known or met us. It was too dangerous otherwise. Reno found us a small room above a fish market he said he had just enough to cover, a room far enough away from our last place that no one would find us if they came looking. The place didn't have running water, and the windows didn't shut completely so the stink of fish kept getting in, but it was better than the stench of the frigid Shaa' Kalyd temple, and the boxed body parts I was still trying to forget. The fishiness I could get used to; the memory of that torso was something else.

Getting hold of the box had only been the first step in our master plan to get Pequire's money and get out of Port Said. The next step was to sell it back to the man who'd hired him. That was where we hit our first snag.

"You never asked who it was?"

Reno alternated a towel full of ice against each set of knuckles, trying to stymie the swelling. His right hand barely closed properly, but it didn't seem to be broken.

"I meant to. But the evening didn't go that way."

"Oh, is that right? And it never occurred to you that might be important information to have?"

"Maybe if you'd stuck around you could have offered some of this invaluable insight. Maybe heard what he had to say for goddamn yourself."

We were both still pumped full of adrenaline and there was no outlet for it other than to fuck or attack one another, and I wasn't feeling especially amorous. We also tried to figure out how we'd let desperation lead us to a situation we had no control over. It was different from the minor scams and cons we'd been running, and no matter how easy it had first looked to us, the way it so quickly spiraled did not make me trust we'd ever get out of Port Said. At least, not in one piece.

As though reading my mind, Reno kept himself stationed by the window, obsessively checking to make sure no one had followed or was watching us. Or maybe he was looking for an excuse not to look at me. Whichever it was, when we weren't sniping he was somewhere else in his head.

And whatever he was thinking about clearly had nothing to do with me.

We sat in the room, not talking for a long time. He didn't utter a sound, no matter how heavily I sighed or often I cursed—triggers I'd hoped would spur him to at least acknowledge me. After a while, I was no longer sure if I was really mad or just thought I should be. And that confusion led me to wonder about our predicament. We had a box of clay worth nothing to anyone, yet a lot to someone; and we were hiding said box of clay from a large quantity of one-handed young men who were warehousing boxes filled with broken ceramics and body parts. If there was an award for being in over your head, I'd have to recuse myself, otherwise I'd win it every year for the rest of my life. And maybe for a short time after.

I needed an idea, anything to point us in the right direction. We still had Pequire's roll, so I leafed through it looking for information we might use. I tried to make more sense of the French without success, and the Masri was even more confusing. Nothing jumped out; not until I reached the manifest.

"Even though I'm holding the proof in my hands," I said, waving the manifest around, "I still find it hard to believe we took the right box."

"What else could it have been? The broken pottery?"

Or maybe the dead bodies?

"But who would want a box of clay?"

Reno shrugged.

"People want what they want."

I didn't like it. I knew life was arbitrary, but this added another level to it. Like a veneer of structure over the chaos, and that just made the chaos worse.

I looked at the crumpled manifest in my hand. There was the number of the box we'd found, right beside its weight and tariff code.

"Where did Pequire get this manifest, anyway? How did it end up in his stuff?"

"Who knows? Maybe he got it online."

"No," I said, drawing it out as I took a closer look. It wasn't an original; it was a copy that some unknown person had made and supplied to Pequire. "They don't just hand these things out. Not for all the shipments coming in during the day. Someone would have had to give Pequire this."

"Are you sure?"

I looked at the form again.

"Well, no," I said. "But it seems right. Seems logical. And who would be the most logical person to have this information?" I pointed to the page.

Reno leaned over me to look.

"It says 'Fathi Essam.'"

"It does, doesn't it. Do you think the guy who signed for the box into the country, who knew both the person it was addressed to and when it was going to be picked up, might also know its final destination? Do you think that's possible?"

"Possible, yes. I'm not sure how likely it is."

"Only one way to find out."

"So you're saying you think if we find the 'Essam' person, he'll tell us where to take the box to sell it."

"Sounds about right."

"And if things go sideways with him?"

"If they go sideways? When have things ever gone sideways for us?"

He gave me one of those looks that was supposed to appear incredulous but instead looked ridiculous.

"It'll work. Trust me."

"It better," he said. "And it better fast. The sun's already coming up, which means it's soon going to be too hot to do anything for the rest of the day but stay in here and choke on the smell of fish."

I added that to the list of incentives I didn't need.

But wanting to find someone and finding him were two different things, and I didn't know how we were going to do the latter. I tried looking through Pequire's roll for any information on his contact and came up with nothing. Whatever he knew, he didn't write it down. I grew more frustrated as the hours passed, and the rising heat and stench of fish didn't help my mood. It wasn't until late afternoon, the room a sweltering sauna, that Reno suggested we go to where Essam worked. "After all," he said, "we know the address. It's right there on the manifest."

It was so obvious I hated myself for not suggesting it first.

We waited until evening when it would be cooler and we'd be less likely to run into the Shaa' Kalyd. The shipping offices weren't far from the canal, and if Essam was like the millions of other dopes in the world with day jobs, someone in the stores around those offices was bound to recognize his name. No one was that invisible.

Once we left that rented room I didn't ever want to return to it; I couldn't bring myself to suffer through the heat and odor any longer. It was a one-two that dug itself into your reason to live and wouldn't let go. It was better that way, too: if we had everything with us, we'd be harder to find. Unless the Shaa' Kalyd had noses, because the stench of fish lingered in my clothes and hair long after it should have. Every time I managed to forget what I smelled like, a hot breeze off the Suez would change direction and remind me.

We were lucky to find someone working at a small tea shop near the canal who recognized Essam's name and was surprisingly eager to answer questions.

"Fathi, he comes here every morning to buy his tea. He sits outside in that corner and drinks it while reading his newspaper. He's very particular, this man, but he's a very good customer. Very good. Very loyal."

"Thank you," Reno said, pressing his hand on the counter. I noticed something peeking out from underneath it. Like a sliver of a hundred-pound note, but that couldn't be right. We had no money left—not enough to bribe anyone. Suddenly our spree through Egypt replayed in my head, and I saw me paying for things that we couldn't steal, and I saw him miraculously coming back with things we needed when I couldn't. It explained how we rented our fish room, too. The blood drained from my face before it boiled back up again.

I had a lot of questions, and he was lucky it wasn't the time to ask them. I didn't think he'd like my tone. Or the way my fists delivered it.

"Please be careful with him," the tea shop owner said as he discreetly slipped Reno's money into his pocket. "Please make sure he isn't hurt."

Oh, but I felt like hurting someone. I felt like hurting someone right then more than I could express. But instead I feigned being shocked.

"We don't want to hurt anybody. We just want to ask Fathi for help."

Then I laughed with as much innocence as I could muster. On cue, Reno joined me. We wanted the tea shop owner to believe he could trust us. Two funny people in over their heads.

I didn't get the feeling it worked, though.

I didn't get the feeling anyone in Port Said trusted us.

When we left the tea shop, I confronted Reno. I did that by shoving him so hard he stumbled over his feet. His face told me he had no idea what was happening.

"What the fuck, Reno? We've been stuck in Port Said for weeks, living like shit, barely eating anything, waiting until we had enough money saved to get out. But you've been holding out on me. You have a secret stash of money. Seriously, what the fuck?"

"It's not like that," Reno said.

"Oh, it's not? Then what's it like?"

"For starters, the money isn't mine. It's my sister's."

I literally couldn't speak.

"What are you talking about? What sister?"

"Is it so surprising I have a sister? She's back home. When I left . . . I'm not really proud of it, but when I left I broke into her bank account and transferred her half of our inheritance to me. I told you I had to get out in a hurry, and there was no other way. It was shitty but

I had no choice. Not if I wanted all my features to remain in the right order on my face. Still, I fucked her over even though she's the only family I have left. It's been haunting me forever; I need to get it off my back. So I'm trying to save enough to repay her. Selling this box might finally be enough."

"How much did you take?"

"More than enough to get me arrested if she could find me."

I really didn't know what to say. It was . . . *sweet?* Was that the word? I didn't know; sweet wasn't my thing. It's what they called it when you made moon-eyes at a guy, or hung onto his elbow, or whispered stupid things in his ear. Being sweet was talking in a baby voice to your partner, which is why I never had one. Boyfriends were a waste of time and got in the way. And family? Family wasn't much better. My own was a braided rope wrapped around my throat and knotted through an anchor. Even the thought of their cloying neediness dragged me down. I didn't care if I never saw any of them again. Escaping them was escaping insanity.

Reno knew all this. I'd told him repeatedly during our time together. Yet he also knew not to hold out on me, especially when it came to money, and that didn't stop him from stashing some away, so I no longer knew what to believe.

"Okay?" I said, unsure what more I could add.

Reno gave me a queer look, then he shook his head. When he was done, his features quivered and shifted, and his face became different, became the face I was used to.

I was relieved to see it back.

He wasn't very talkative after that, which was fine because I was tired and needed to lean up against him while we rested on a street bench. Once or twice, men watched us warily as they passed by, sizing us up as a predator would the competition. The fact that they didn't try anything was probably because they were smart enough to understand their place in the food chain and what might happen if they did something stupid.

By two A.M. I was drowsy, and my mind wandered in a semi-dreamlike state. I was back at the Shaa' Kalyd temple, opening box after box filled with body parts, all jiggling as though they were made of gelatine. But they weren't; they were excited, anxious to begin something I didn't understand. I started reading to them from a large book even though I didn't understand the words I was seeing. The oddity of my situation was enough to shake me out of my delirium. It also reminded me of what else I'd picked up at the temple.

"Shit!" I blurted as I sat up. Reno jumped, not prepared for the outburst.

"What's wrong?" he said.

"While we were at the temple and you were opening the window, I found a book. And I took it."

"Why?"

I shrugged.

"I don't know why I do anything." I picked up my pack and rifled through it while Reno watched groggily. My life was in there, but it didn't take me long to find the book, even in the dark. Reno motioned, but I wouldn't hand it over.

"If you wanted to see it so bad," I said, "you would have taken it first."

I opened the large book across my lap and found it filled again with writing nothing like the little Masri I knew. It figured: everything about this job was in a language I didn't speak or understand. I flipped through the pages and saw drawings of something that looked like a starfish, only misshapen and crooked. Maybe it was a hand. There were more drawings of similar hands, later, closer to medical diagrams than anything else, and I assumed they'd have to be related. But there wasn't much else I could glean from the book.

"Here," I said, surrendering it to Reno. "I can't make anything of it, other than the Shaa' Kalyd have a thing for hands. Obviously. Maybe you'll see something I'm missing."

He was irritated, but that vanished once he saw the symbol burned into the leather cover.

"This?" he said. "I've seen it before. It was on the wrist of the guy back at the temple. It must mean something."

I snatched the book back and looked at it.

"It means nothing to me. Do you think the book is valuable?"

"Maybe to the Shaa' Kalyd. I have no idea."

"When we sell the box, let's see if they want this, too. We need to buy our way out of this shithole. And you need to convince your sister to—what? Not put you in jail in a country you haven't visited in years?"

Reno didn't have much to say as I slid the book into my pack. He also didn't stop watching me, either. As though he was trying to work up the nerve to say something but couldn't, which sort of sickened me. I didn't have patience for games like that, so I ignored it because if I didn't things would have gotten messy and we couldn't afford messy. Not yet. Maybe when the deal was all over, but not until then, so I leaned back against him on the bench. There were still a few more hours to go before the tea shop opened, and nothing to do but sleep or talk, and I had run out of words.

The smell of Port Said was never great, but the morning stench carrying in off the Suez was particularly foul, and as soon as the sun hit the horizon the combination of the heat plus that odor was enough to wake me. My neck had a hard kink in it from using Reno's arm as a pillow, and no matter how much I stretched I couldn't undo the knot buried behind my shoulder.

The two of us watched the front of the tea shop, waiting for Essam to arrive. The proprietor had described him to us the night before, and offered to point him out for another five hundred pounds. It irritated me to see Reno hand over more of his hidden money, but I reminded myself it was an investment, and soon I would no longer have to deal with Reno's betrayal.

It still took time. First the owner arrived; awkward and stilted, probably because he knew we were watching. Thankfully, there was no one else around to notice. A few minutes later the first of the customers strolled in. Then more. One after the other streaming through, passing one another in the doorway. As we watched, the sun only got stronger.

"I'm not sure how long I'll be able to stay out here," I said. "I feel like a pot roast."

"Trust me," Reno said.

So we waited. We waited an hour, then two. During this time I stood, I paced, I grumbled. I did everything but talk through what we were going to do once we found Essam. I had some ideas, and for the first time I wondered if Reno had the same ones in mind.

"Look," Reno said, pointing across the street. "Is that him?"

The man matched how the tea shop owner described Essam. Lanky, dark-skinned with curling black hair, seated at a set of tables by himself. He wore a pair of thick glasses and was hunched over his tea as though he was trying to hide in the cup.

"Let's go," I said.

"Wait. If we ask him how to get rid of the box, he's going to know we have it."

"True, but what else are we going to do? Right now we have no idea what to do with it and we have no contacts. This is our only lead. Unless you got the information from Pequire and are keeping it from me like your stash of money . . ."

Reno ignored my jab, but still he hesitated.

"Tick tock, Reno."

"Okay, but play it cool. If you spook him, he'll make some phone calls and we'll have a whole platoon of people waiting for us."

"If I spook him that much," I said, "I'll owe you five hundred pounds."

Reno smirked. It didn't help me feel less prickly.

Essam looked up as we approached and attempted to stand when I took the seat across from him. Reno's presence stifled that urge.

"What do you want?" he asked. His voice was higher than I expected, and had a sing-song warble to it that made his thick hair seem less styled and more accidental. I supposed he might have been good-looking if he weighed another fifty pounds. And if his eyes didn't look like a couple of cue balls poking out of his face.

I took the manifest from my pocket and laid it down in front of him. He shifted in his seat; he knew where this was going.

"We picked up this box and need to know where to take it. Pequire said you could help."

"I do not know what you are talking about."

I folded the manifest and returned it to my pocket. "Your name's on the manifest, Fathi. It doesn't do any good to lie. And I know you know who Pequire is because he told us. He told us everything about you, and about the sideline you have helping boxes come in and out of Egypt. Pequire is an old friend of ours and he wants to make sure you help us out so you don't get in trouble."

I watched him as I spoke; watched beads of sweat coalesce beneath his thick hair. If he was going to lie to me, he couldn't have picked a better place to do it. In that heat everyone was sweating.

"Where is Mr. Pequire? I will only deal with him."

"Pequire couldn't make it. He's not feeling well."

"If you are friends, why did he not tell you where to take the box?"

"I don't know why. He's funny that way. Are you going to help us or are we going to have a problem?"

Essam looked up hopefully as a couple of men peeked their heads out of the tea shop. They looked at Reno, then at me. I glared right back. A moment later they were gone and Essam slumped.

"We don't have all day," I said. "It's already about a billion degrees out here and I'm getting crabby."

"I cannot help you."

"We aren't leaving, Fathi. Not after all the shit we've been through. Not until we get what we want."

"Please, I do not know what that is."

I looked over at Reno, who looked at me and shrugged. I laughed.

"You're braver than you look, Fathi, but a lot stupider if you think this act is going to work. Get up and let's go before I change my mind about how nice I'm going to be." To emphasize the point, Reno took a step forward and Essam cowered.

"Up," I ordered. He obeyed without more questions.

*

We led Essam to his home through the back streets of Port Said. The last thing any of us needed was to be spotted together, especially if the Shaa' Kalyd creeps were wandering around. Reno thought I was being overly paranoid, but I figured it was safest to assume the worst.

There were some nice homes in Port Said, but Essam's was not one of them. It had a door, which in hindsight was a surprise. I wondered if he was squatting, but it seemed unlikely; I didn't know much, but I knew a government job meant enough money to afford a house. It took some convincing to get him inside, and almost as much to take a seat on his old cloth couch, but once we did I regretted being there.

The house reeked of old sweat. It was worse than the fish market; worse than the canal. I wanted to congratulate him on his achievement, but instead I asked what he knew about the box.

Essam shook his head, bemoaning the trouble he was in or fighting to keep from telling me what I wanted to know. Reno, unsurprisingly, was no help. He just wandered, picking things up and setting them down. He moved like he was holding a grudge against me, but I was the one who was supposed to be mad. But maybe I was wrong; the dizzying heat muddled everything.

"I'm going to ask you again: what do you know about the box, and who are we supposed to give it to?"

"Where is Mr. Pequire?"

"Pequire isn't who you need to be worried about right now. He won't be coming by anytime soon, which is why we're here." I thought if I could keep reminding him of the story, he'd eventually buy into it. He didn't, but I don't think it mattered.

"Please listen to me: I do not care for you. I do not care for either of you, or Mr. Pequire for that matter. You may all die, if it is all the same. Port Said is not perfect, but it has been my home for many, many years. My brother and I lived here happily. Then this box you are looking to sell arrived and everything went bad. The things that make me happy disappeared, and people I do not like came instead. You know these people that call themselves Shaa' Kalyd? Have you heard this name before?"

I nodded. Reno touched his face absently.

"They want access to something and are not afraid to rise from the shadows to get it. They have already bribed many to get their hands on it, and it was only by luck they found out it was coming through my bin at the Port. That is when things turned bad."

He sank further into the couch, and I could see those golf balls start to wet. I almost felt sorry for him. I tried to head him off before he started wailing, but he waved me away. He was going to tell his story whether I wanted him to or not.

"First, they come to me politely and say the box is coming though Port Said, and I should ignore the address and give it to them. They say they will give me an identical box to replace it with so no one will find out. I know many people here do these things—I know it is everywhere in Egypt—but I am not these people. I believe if I do my job honestly I will be rewarded. So they leave. Then later they come back and ask me again. Only now they are no longer polite. I tell them again no and they leave again but they are not happy. I tell this to my brother, Botros, and he says I am a fool; do what they say. He says if I do not want the money, he will take it. He needs things too, and some extra money will help. I tell him it is not right and he tells me nothing is right. The days pass and I do not want to see these Shaa' Kalyd again, but I also cannot stop going to work, so I am there at work the day the box is coming through. I know the shipment it is on and what I must do. Only, before the box arrives, another smaller box is delivered to me. I don't see who leaves it, but it's covered in plain paper and has my name. The box is light, but I still worry. I know it is a mistake, but I open it and inside are four whole teeth in blood. And I have not seen Botros in days. That is why I agree to everything. Because it makes no difference now.

"A man comes by the office and delivers the replacement box. He has arranged for the cameras to be off while he and I make the exchange. I wonder why he has not bribed more people to make this easier, but he does not tell me. When the warehouse is going to close for the night, I sneak into the toilet and wait. My whole body shakes. I think about those teeth, and poor Botros. When the security guards have finished checking the building I leave the toilet and sneak into the warehouse. The box is easy to find on the shelf, and it is smaller and heavier than I expect. I look at my watch to make sure my time is right, and I wait.

"I wait for a long time, and my head fills with many thoughts that I am too afraid to understand. And when I think I have been waiting so long there must be something wrong, the light on the camera above the door blinks out, and I push the door open and find a tall man with little glasses holding a bicycle in one hand and a box that mirrors mine in the other. We trade them without speaking, and he straps the one I gave him to his bicycle and pedals away. It is so quiet I hear the gears of his bicycle change. I watch until I remember there is more I must do. I rush the door closed before the camera light returns and put the box he gave me in the place the first one was stored. When it is done I feel sick and I do not stop shaking. I never stop shaking.

"I go home sick; wait for Botros. My poor headstrong Botros. He doesn't return that night, so I do not go to work the next day. I want to wait for him, and I am too afraid of what I have done. If the exchange of boxes is discovered, things will be bad for me. Every time someone walks near the house I freeze in terror, listening. But it is not them and it is not the police and it is not Botros. It is no one. It is none of them. No one comes. My Botros never comes home. So why should I care anymore what happens to me?"

"We don't care what happens to you either, but we need to know what to do with the box. Who to give it to."

Essam shrugged.

"It does not matter. Botros is gone."

I looked at Reno, exasperated. I wasn't cut out for this feelings bullshit. I was good at faking emotions, not understanding them, and I didn't think this guy would fall for any of my tricks. He was broken. Reno picked up a framed photograph—it was the only thing sitting on a table and not lying on the floor—and walked toward us. He didn't have to say a word; I stepped back and let him work his magic.

"Is this him? Is this Botros?"

Essam nodded. Reno glanced at the photograph again, then handed it to me to hold. He seemed so genuinely concerned that I didn't look at what I was holding right away. When I did, I saw the two brothers shirtless with their arms around each other. Essam looked fit and filled with vigor, not the withered person sitting across from us now. But it was Botros that surprised me. Surprised, and horrified. At least I was smart enough to hide what I saw when I looked at him. No one seemed to notice the tremble in my hands as I put the photograph face down on the floor.

"I get it," Reno said. "I have a sister. Back home, I mean. I made some mistakes with her I wish I hadn't and it's probably too late to fix them."

"What happened with your sister?"

"I stole from her. Left her behind when she needed me. I think about her every day."

Essam wiped his face. Ran his hand through his thick hair.

"I too think about Botros every moment of every day."

"Sometimes you can't help but think about the people you hurt. It's even worse when times are good. When times are bad, it feels right, because you deserve it after everything you've done. When it's good, though? That's not fair. It's not fair to anyone because it means life isn't fair. That it's just random and nothing we do matters or makes sense. But, Fathi, you have to believe me: that's not true. What you do *does* matter. Who you help matters. Even if you mess up and let someone down or get them hurt, it doesn't mean you have to stop trying. It doesn't mean you're off the hook from helping the next person. It doesn't mean you give up, because giving up is the worst thing. Far worse than any mistake you've made or person you've hurt. You can't do that. If somebody is in need, sometimes you're the only one who can help them, and the only way to fix the things you've done wrong in the past is to do something right now. Does that make sense?"

Essam wiped his face again, then reluctantly shrugged. Nodded.

"Right now, she and I, we need to get rid of the box. We need to get it to its real owner. It's the only way I'll be able to see my sister again. It's the only way I'll be able to make all those wrong things right. I didn't know Botros, but I don't think he'd want you suffering like this. He'd want you to be happy, to be free, and the only way you're going to get there is to try to help people. All I'm asking is you start with us."

Essam shook his head and looked and Reno. Looked and me, too.

"The best help I could give you is to say you should leave Port Said. Go away as far as you can."

"That's what we're trying to do," I said. "That's all we want."

"Do you two know what this box is?"

I shrugged. "It's clay. It's a box of clay."

"It is more than clay," he said. "In the certain hands, it is much more. The Shaa' Kalyd call it Tinaldam, and it is used as a trap. To hold things."

"What? Like a bowl?"

"Maybe. They say a soul is poured into it, where it can be held forever. This is why the Shaa' Kalyd want it. They want a soul for something."

"They what?"

"A soul. The Tinaldam is for trapping souls."

What was this bullshit? I looked at Reno. I hoped he'd smack this guy for wasting our time, but Reno wasn't looking at me. He was watching Essam.

"There is a story the Shaa' Kalyd believe," Essam continued. "The story says that when Allah told the archangels He was going to create the Khalifa, He asked each to collect a handful of clay from the earth. They say this means the richest, rarest clay of the valley somewhere in the great deserts. This clay was red as blood and magical and had to be hidden from all and especially from the jin who inhabited the earth first; who Allah wished to destroy. With this clay Allah made all the men and women and He filled them with souls He pulled from the sky. Allah knew the souls would wish to stay only with Him, so He bound them to earth with the Tinaldam and promised they would only be released when the Tinaldam dried and cracked."

"And the Shaa' Kalyd?"

"They believe they have found this clay. This is why they want it."

"But what are they going to do with it?" Reno asked.

"I do not know," he said. "But it is important enough to steal, and to take Botros."

I swallowed, not wanting to think about what I knew.

"Can you translate something for us?" Reno asked.

"What is it?"

When it dawned on me what he was talking about, I shook my head.

"Come on, Liv. We should know what it is."

"I already know," I said. "And I don't want anybody else knowing."

I didn't want to share the book. It was ours; mine and Reno's. At least until we sold it. I was also worried what might happen if the Shaa' Kalyd found out we had it. I wasn't looking to have my body parts stored in a row of cardboard boxes.

"Don't be ridiculous. Let him look. Trust me."

Essam's wet bulging eyes stared at me as though he were a toad gazing unfocused into oblivion. I didn't like Reno's idea and told him so with a narrowed glare, but he was too busy watching my hands as they opened my pack.

"This better be worth it," I said, though nobody was listening.

I pulled out the leather-bound book and handed to Essam. He reached for it with trembling hands that didn't fill me with confidence, and gingerly placed it on his lap. Reno and I glanced at each other as Essam skimmed the pages.

Essam's brow wrinkled and he muttered to himself in Masri as he looked up at us, though I'm not sure he could tell we were still there. It took a moment before he remembered his English.

"Much of this is too. . . . It is not something I understand. It is very strange. Very strange."

"What's strange about it?"

"This?" he said, pointing to a diagram of a bisected circle with three marks near the bottom of the curve and a further two at the top. In the middle was a dotted spiral. Beneath, more writing. "This is hard because the Arabic is not one I can read. It is a different kind of Arabic. Some words I think I know, but not what they mean. And it is hard to say in English. Maybe it means 'the something that comes back' but it also may be 'the thing is refilled.' Maybe there is a cup mentioned? I think so. I think it says the cup is filled again, but maybe it is not the cup? I am sorry. I do not know what this all is."

"Thank you for trying, Essam," Reno said, carefully retrieving the closed book. Essam held on a fraction too long. Long enough that I was about to step forward.

"If you find my brother, Botros, you will help him come home, yes?"

"Of course," I lied. "But you still haven't told us where we're supposed to take this box of clay."

"Tinaldam," Reno corrected.

"Tinaldam," I repeated, more irritated than before.

III

I had the good manners to wait until we were out of earshot of Essam's house before I laughed.

"That was bonkers. I've got to hand it to you, though: you got him talking. I don't know how you did it, but you did."

Reno half smiled, but didn't say much or look at me. My amusement ebbed, leaving only irritation, but I didn't have the energy to fight about it. The heat wore on me, and even the scarf over my head didn't do much to stop it. No wonder everybody else wore something light and loose-fitting. I wish I'd thought to do the same. At least Reno was no better than me in his sweat-drenched clothes.

"What crawled up your ass?"

"Nothing."

"Then why are you so quiet?"

He shrugged. "Can't I be quiet? It's a million degrees out here. I'm not feeling all that talkative."

"Fine," I said. "At least this whole ordeal is nearly done."

I'm not sure if I meant dealing with the box or traveling with Reno. It had become tiresome either way, and I was itching to escape Port Said and all the people in it. Every goddamn one of them.

"Do you still have the name of the guy we have to see?"

He patted the front pocket of his shirt.

Essam had told us what little he knew. Not long after the Shaa' Kalyd took the box and Botros, Pequire showed up at Essam's house, asking after it. He was supposed to pick it up for his employers, and now that it was gone there were going to be problems.

So Essam told him what happened. Where the box had probably gone and with whom. Pequire knew who the Shaa' Kalyd were and promised he'd recover both the box and Botros. However, it would be dangerous for him in Port Said afterward, so if Pequire didn't come back Essam had to inform someone named Weldon Bush.

It got more complicated here, and I didn't think Essam truly understood the scope of what had been happening. All he knew was he was supposed to steal the box for Pequire, and if the Shaa' Kalyd had not taken it instead, Pequire would have delivered the box to Weldon Bush, and Bush would have subsequently delivered it to his employers.

But once Pequire failed to come back with the box, Essam didn't do what he was supposed to do. He didn't contact Bush. He didn't inform anybody. He kept to himself and prayed for it all to be over.

"The last thing I want," he told us over more tears, "is to be more involved."

Reno and I, though, had no such qualms.

For us, Weldon Bush was our salvation, the solution to all our problems. Meeting Bush would get us unstuck, and becoming unstuck was all I wanted at that point.

But meeting him wasn't easy. Bush didn't seem to have a phone, so the only option we had was to travel across town and face him in person. That was a lot to ask under a sun that couldn't have felt hotter if it were shooting microwaves at us. Actually, it was probably doing just that. So instead of going to see Bush we decided to spend the afternoon hiding from the Shaa' Kalyd in the back of a little bar.

Reno took the opportunity while we sat at the dark table to flip through Pequire's leather roll and inspect the documents again.

I asked what he was looking for.

"I'm trying to find out more about this Tinaldam stuff. Pequire said it wasn't valuable to anyone but the people who hired him, but then why steal it? Why all the effort to get it? Why hold onto Botros?"

"Christ, that reminds me," I said, emptying my kosna with a single throw. "They aren't holding Essam's brother. I mean, not anymore. I saw him. At least, I think I did."

"Where did you see him?"

"Do you remember the photo you handed me in Essam's house? The one of him and Botros? I don't know if you noticed, but there was a long twisting scar that ran from under his belt up to his neck. Well, I saw that scar at the Shaa' Kalyd temple. I saw it inside that box I opened. I saw it on the torso."

"What?"

"They took him apart, Reno. They took him apart and put him in a box. And there were more boxes just as big. Just as damp."

I felt ill. I felt so ill I needed to stand, to keep moving. The look on Reno's face twisted as he tried to process what I'd said.

"But . . . why?" he asked. There was no answer and he knew it. We both did. We'd never understand it; the best we could hope for was to forget. So I flagged the bartender for another shot glass full of tangy forgetfulness.

I wish telling Reno had alleviated my horror so I could put it behind me, but it was like I'd thrown a steak to a hungry dog. Reno wanted to know more. He wanted to know everything. And it didn't matter how I felt. It especially didn't matter if I had anything more to add.

"I told you all I know, Reno. I opened the one box and saw what was left of Botros. I don't know what was in those other boxes, but I can guess."

"But why? What were they trying to do?"

"How should I know? You're the one with Pequire's notes. Doesn't it say anything in there?"

He looked down at the table. It was covered in scraps he'd spread around.

"Why do you care so much anyway?" I asked. "I thought we agreed the plan was to get this box to Bush, get our money, and leave Port Said. Why are you messing with something that doesn't affect us?"

He looked at me for a minute, like he'd never seen me before and was trying to figure out who I was. I came close to punching him.

"I don't know," he finally admitted. "I guess . . . I guess I feel bad for Essam. His brother's gone and he feels like it's his fault."

"It *is* his fault. He should have just done what those Shaa' Kalyd goons wanted. His life would have been a lot easier."

"Would it have been?" He genuinely seemed to be asking. I tried to remember the Reno I used to know, the one who stole the wallet from a man looking for directions at a gas station, and who spent the money in it on getting us drunk for three days straight. The Reno who got into a fight for no reason with two rugby players just out to dinner and ended up putting one of them in the hospital. I tried to remember that Reno, because this one wasn't him. This one sounded like he was falling apart, and I wasn't interested in gluing him back together.

I finished the last of my drink and looked out through the filthy window. The sky was a burnt orange that reminded me of that goddamn clay, and of heat that wouldn't break. I wanted this done.

"It's time to visit Bush; find out he's offering."

A noise sparked at the front of the bar. Some sort of heated argument. I wasn't sure what the commotion was, but I didn't like the way it sounded. I glanced at Reno to be sure he was thinking what I was.

"Grab it all. Fast."

We snatched the pages spread across the table as the shouting intensified. Men at the other tables stood, shook their fists. It wasn't a good sign. Reno shoved everything into the roll and managed to fold it when the Shaa' Kalyd appeared. I recognized them and their stumps as they pushed their way through the irate crowd.

My mind raced. They hadn't seen us, so how did they know who we were? But who else could we have been? I caught Reno sliding the roll behind him. I kept my eye on it.

The men shouted, mostly in Masri. We returned the shouts in English. Everybody in the bar joined in, making it hard to track what was going on. One of the Shaa' Kalyd grabbed my arm, pulled me toward him. He was surprisingly strong for someone with only half the gripping power, and I wondered what he'd be capable of doing once he got his stumped arm around me. I wasn't sure I'd be able to break free, so I did the only sensible thing and punched him so hard in the mouth his teeth cut my knuckles.

He let me go after that.

The other two were stunned long enough for Reno to deliver a surprise haymaker right into the side of one of their heads. Then we were running, slipping through hands trying to stop us.

We hit the street hard. I didn't take time to look back, but I knew at least two Shaa' Kalyd were behind us. Maybe more. Probably more. Who knew how many? And all were looking to get even. Maybe cut us into pieces to do whatever they'd done to Essam's brother and that pottery.

Once we hit the marketplace there were enough people to get lost among. We took a few abrupt turns in the chaos before ducking behind a stall to see who might be following.

And sure enough I saw someone dressed in beggar's clothes and yelling into a cell phone as he paced through the market. He passed our hiding spot three times, then stopped, slipped his phone into his pocket, and picked up something from the ground. He slid it under his arm then looked quickly around before jogging out the way we'd come in.

When we were sure we were safe, Reno said, "We have to get as far away from here as possible right now."

"Well, I guess that means we're going to go see Weldon Bush with the Tinaldam earlier than we thought."

That's when Reno stood and checked his pockets. I saw his face pale.

"Oh no," he said. His voice sounded like his throat was closing in. "Oh no, oh no, oh no."

"What is it?"

He looked around where we'd been hiding, but it was no use.

"Goddamn it. I lost it. I lost everything."

"What? Pequire's notes? It's okay. It's fine. We already know where Bush is. We don't need them anymore."

"No, it's not his notes. It's everything. I had everything in there. *Everything.* All my money. All my sister's money. Everything I was saving. It was there. I had it there. Now it's gone. It's all gone!"

He collapsed to his knees, then fell onto his side. I thought he was going to start sobbing. He hid the money from me, now the money was gone; I didn't know if I should feel bad or smug. What I actually felt was disgusted.

"Good thing we still have the Tinaldam to sell. All we have to do is get to the locker and get the box without being seen by all the Shaa' Kalyd out to kill us. What could go wrong?"

*

Turns out, nothing. It was fairly easy. Reno and I were able to elude anyone following us, and reached the locker without incident. He sent me inside to buy time while he went looking for some way to get us and the Tinaldam away from the Shaa' Kalyd and into Bush's hands.

My knuckles had stopped bleeding by the time I entered the store, but they'd swollen enough that my fingers didn't bend easily, which made it impossible to carry the box. From behind the counter the stout middle-aged shop owner watched me from his plastic stool, a small black-and-white television perched on his lap. He eyed me as though I were up to something he either didn't want to be involved with or, worse, wanted a piece of. Either way, he was working up the nerve to become a problem, but before he could do more than take a breath Reno floated in. He didn't say anything, but he didn't have to; the shop owner took one look at him and knew better. Instead, he sat farther back on his stool and return to watching whatever he'd been watching. I wanted to say something cutting, but what would have been the point? It would have only caused us more problems.

"Did you get it?" Reno asked, the desperation warping his voice. "Please tell me you got it."

"Still in the locker," I said, then showed him my hand. "You're going to have to lift it out."

He grunted as he heaved the small block into his arms, clearly having forgotten how much it weighed. The owner stared as we walked out of his store, so I smiled and waved instead of following my instinct to flip him off. It was inevitable that he was going to call someone—possibly the police, but probably the Shaa' Kalyd—so we had to get moving fast and keep moving.

"This way," Reno said, and led me around the corner to where a moped waited.

"What's this?" I asked, unable to paper over my disdain. Reno loaded the box onto the carrier behind the seat and strapped it down.

"Trust me. There aren't a lot of options this time of night. Unless you want to walk."

"What I want is to not die before I get to leave Port Said."

Reno swung his leg over the moped and started it up. I didn't think it was possible, but the whine it made was more embarrassing than the way it looked.

"We don't have time for this, Liv. Get on and let's go."

I grumbled and I spat, but I got on the seat behind him and put my arms around his chest. Turns out, we never reached a fast enough speed for that to be necessary. I suggested it might have been faster if we'd walked after all, but Reno pretended he couldn't hear me.

We sputtered down the main roads for a while, then eventually crossed a bridge to the Asian side of the canal. It didn't look much different when you focused on particular buildings or people, but the atmosphere there wasn't the same: people slumped more, maybe moved slower. And there were fewer lights, if that makes any sense. Generally, it had the air of a city that had been worn down by the traffic it got. Reno and I cut through on our coughing moped and people stopped to watch us go, none surprised to see us. I wasn't sure if that should have worried me. It didn't seem to worry Reno.

Weldon Bush was staying in a motel that looked more like a boarding house. Even that description didn't do justice to how nondescript the place was. Whatever Bush was up to in Egypt couldn't have been lucrative. No one chooses to live like that.

By the time we arrived it was either too late in the night or early in the morning to knock. Reno developed cold feet, wanting to wait until sunrise before we did anything, but the Shaa' Kalyd had found us once, which meant the clock on getting out of Port Said had started—the longer we took the harder it would be. It didn't help that we were carrying around our only bargaining chip, or planning to get rid of it the first chance we got. This wasn't the movies; no one was going to care what our plans had been at the start or what they were by that point. All anyone cared about was who had the Tinaldam, and how they were going to get it back.

Frankly, I didn't care who ended up with it. All I wanted was my money and I'd be gone. Reno, though, was feeling more philosophical.

"Should we have played this different? From the beginning, I mean. Do you think we should have just worked with Pequire, done what he'd asked? Things would have been easier if we had."

I thought about it.

"Maybe," I said. "Or maybe he would have screwed us over. We don't know, and we never will. The only reason you and I have made it this far is because we're a team, and a team is built on trust. Everybody else is working a hidden angle. I mean, we're working angles, too, but we know what they are."

"Yeah? What are our angles?"

"We're both doing whatever it takes to get out of here, but also to avoid going back home because we both know there's nothing for us back there."

Reno grimaced.

"For you, maybe. But my sister—"

"Forget your sister, Reno. What did you do that was so wrong?

You took some money. Big deal. She's not dead. She can make more. Why does she deserve it any more that you? Any more than us?"

"I—" He started to say something but it never came. He was being an idiot. He could no more go back to his sister, to his old life, than I could my parents. Too many bridges burned. Too much blood spilled. There was no going back after that. Not if you didn't want what you deserved. And I sure as hell didn't want that.

"You're going to have to smarten the fuck up and decide what you want out of your life, because you can have this or have that. They don't work together. And I need you to be all in with me."

"Liv, you can't make me choose."

Actually, I could, but it was clear to me right then that I didn't have to because he'd already chosen. He'd chosen the first time he put money in his pocket where I couldn't find it. He'd chosen again when he let me go hungry for a night so he could make sure his nest egg was secure.

"It's okay," I said. "Don't worry about it. We're good." And we kind of were, because I knew once we got our money there wasn't going to be a "we" any longer. We'd split the bounty, then he'd step into the shower or go out to buy more cigarettes, and I'd pack up my things and leave. I could see it all happening right before my eyes.

Reno looked at me queerly, so I smiled. Everything was going to be fine.

"Come on," I said. "Let's get this over with."

Reno heaved the box from the carrier and we walked to the door through the midnight darkness.

He timidly knocked on the door, still uncomfortable about the early hour we were visiting. I could barely hear his rapping and I was standing right there. So I took over and pounded with my uninjured hand, loud enough to wake Bush's neighbours. After a moment, a light went on.

"See?" I said.

There was the sound of an automobile nearby. Both Reno and I turned toward the road to watch for lights. But as quickly as the rumble appeared it faded. We were still safe.

The sound of locks and bolts sliding recalled my attention. The door opened a few inches, but I didn't see anyone in the dark gap. I heard something, though. It was the clack of a magazine round being chambered.

"Mr. Bush—" Reno whispered, but we'd come too far for whispering.

"Pequire sent us," I interrupted. "We have the box of Tinaldam and he said you were paying to get it back."

There was no response, and I decided that bringing the box with us to the door had been a bad idea. We should have dropped the Tinaldam and run, but there was no way I was giving up on getting that money. Not after everything we'd gone through. Not when we were so close.

"If you're not interested any more, we'll go. I'm sure the Shaa' Kalyd would be willing to discuss getting their hands on it."

Another moment where no one spoke. We waited for someone to make a move, make a decision. I glanced at Reno, readying myself for anything. What I wasn't ready for was Bush closing the door.

Reno turned to me. I said nothing. Just reached out and tried the knob. It turned. The door swung open.

We entered cautiously. Reno was carrying the box of clay, and my hand was still a little stiff, so if Bush jumped us we would have been in trouble. But he didn't. What he did do was turn on a lamp just as we were walking in. I threw up my hands, blinded, but Reno didn't have that luxury.

The corona of light faded to reveal Bush sitting in a chair, pointing a pistol at us.

"Look at this. A couple of pigeons just flew in."

It was hard to be sure, but he appeared to be roughly as tall as Reno, though maybe not so broad. His beard was streaked with gray, and he wore only a pair of jogging pants. He was tanned, with the chest of someone not unfamiliar with heavy outside work, but who maybe had not done it in a while.

His eyes, though. Those are what got me. They were tiny—like a pair of opals—and they looked just as black and lifeless. Yeah, his eyes, and his stink. He obviously wasn't suited to the Egyptian heat.

"We're working with Pequire—" Reno started, but Bush wasn't having it.

"That's bullshit and we all know it. Pequire would be standing there if that were true. You two pigeons better start squawking if you want to make it out of here."

And I could tell he meant it.

"Pequire approached us," I said. "He gave us the information on the temple and asked us to get him the box."

"So where is he now?"

I shrugged, but that didn't appease him

"Really, I don't know." It was technically true. Reno and I had never discussed it. I just made my assumptions and he never corrected or confirmed them. It was easier that way. We had plausible deniability. "And, really, I don't really care."

He made a face, cocked his chin, and reached for the folded newspaper on the table beside him. He threw it toward me. It landed a few feet away. With a nod from his pistol, he suggested I pick it up.

The paper was in Masri, but the photo on the front was of something being pulled from the Suez, and beside it another photo of a man who looked a lot like a younger, less worn-down Pequire.

"They found him yesterday, bobbing in the canal face down. They find a lot of people in the canal like that, so they haven't ruled out suicide. Yet."

He looked at me, waiting for something to crack, but I knew the biggest mistake I could make was to look away. One glance at Reno would be the end of us both.

So I shrugged again.

"That's weird," I said as carefully as I could. "He seemed happy the last time I saw him."

Weldon Bush frowned, not wholly satisfied. But I didn't blink.

Eventually he decided my answer was good enough, and lowered the pistol. He placed it beside him where the newspaper had been.

"You have the Tinaldam?"

I nodded.

"Show me."

I looked over at Reno, who looked more than happy to put his burden down on a table. It landed with a thud that made the walls ring.

Bush and his pistol continued to face us as he stood. Then he waved us away while he approached the box.

He slid the barrel of his pistol beneath one of the flaps and lifted. Suddenly I worried we didn't grab the correct box at all. I started running through the scenarios in my head, looking for the right combination of words to prevent me and Reno from getting shot.

Bush lowered his pistol. Squinted his too-early-morning eyes and looked us up and down.

"You two pigeons realize I don't have the money with me, right? We're going to have to wait until morning so I can have it wired here."

That was indeed something I had not realized. I was used to quick cons for easy cash; this was outside my comfort zone. I wanted to dump Reno and get out of Port Said right away and thought Bush would be the ticket, but he just laughed at us.

"Maybe we should take the box back then," I said, irritated. "Maybe we'll bring it back later when it's not so inconvenient for you."

Bush stopped laughing and became deadly serious.

"You won't be taking that box anywhere, pigeon. It doesn't belong to you. If you want your money for bringing this back to my employers, you'll find a way of waiting until daylight. Otherwise, you're welcome to leave the box here and fuck right off."

The difference between his threat and mine was that he had a pistol. Which meant he had us. I took off my pack and sat down with a huff. Reno looked at us both, then took off his pack and placed it next to mine.

We all sat quietly for a few minutes, watching each other, waiting for the dawn to come. Finally, I couldn't stand it anymore.

"Can we at least have something to drink?"

Bush didn't bother replying.

There isn't much to do when you're stuck in a small Asian-

Egyptian motel room with a pistol trained on you. We had a television, but almost all the stations were off-air for the night. Not that I could have understood any of them. Bush wasn't set up for guests, and having both the box and the pistol in the room meant our movements were strictly limited: no one would let the others out of their sight. It made things incredibly complicated and boring.

I was often up late, but usually in a bar or on my hands and knees, not sitting around a depressing motel room, so after the stress of the preceding few days my exhaustion threatened to catch up with me. I had to pace the room regularly to keep from falling asleep in my chair. Reno didn't look any better.

Bush, on the other hand, was as sharp as I'd seen. He might have had cold water pumping through him. The way he watched us, I knew if Reno and I fell asleep, we'd wake to find both Bush and the Tinaldam long gone—and that was assuming we woke up at all. My only play was to start talking. Breaking the numbing silence might be enough to keep me connected.

"So who did you say this stuff is for, again?"

"This is my clients' property. I've been hired to do this."

"And that's your job? Finding lost property?"

He smiled a cruel little smile.

"Among other things."

"If it's your job, why send Pequire to hire us?"

"If he hired a couple of pigeons, that was his mistake. He's lucky they found him in the canal. If I'd learned what he did, he never would have surfaced."

"Without us, you wouldn't have the Tinaldam."

He shook his head.

"You two have bumbled deep into something you know nothing about."

"We know what the Shaa' Kalyd have boxed up in their backroom. Or maybe I should say who."

Bush laughed and it got my back up until I realized it wasn't me he was laughing at.

"Those idiots. It's never going to work."

"What isn't?"

He stopped laughing and looked straight at me. Two black pinholes fuming like coal.

He shook his head.

"It's a miracle you didn't follow Pequire into the water. I'll be amazed if you make it out of this alive."

"Why? Are you going to shoot us?"

He chuckled. Then shrugged.

I was tired, but not tired enough to put up with his bullshit.

"Can you quit posturing and talk like a normal person for a second? Why is this Tinaldam so goddamn important that people are dying over it?"

"You know the history of it? What Tinaldam is?"

"I've heard the story: Allah made us all from clay, blah blah blah."

"Suppose that clay is a real thing. That a god used it to bring life into the world. Imagine what you might be able to do with it. Imagine how far people might go to possess it, if they only knew what it was."

"But it's just a story. Make-believe. It didn't literally happen."

He sat back. "You're probably right. But ask yourself: what if? What if you're wrong? And what if it not only could hold a soul, but part of one, too? It sounds like the Shaa' Kalyd want to try. That would be why you found whoever you found in their back room. They're experimenting, hoping they'll get it to work."

"You're joking, right? This is the stupidest thing I've ever heard."

Bush grinned.

"I didn't say I believed it either, pigeon. But some do. The Shaa' Kalyd do. So do my employers. Enough that they're willing to steal for it. Or worse. Have you ever heard the name Hieronymus Slant? He was the head of a cult called the Order of Valzerial, and when he died some of those cultists couldn't accept he was gone and wanted to bring him back. That's why my employers got me involved. What better way to bring the dead back than with the true stuff of life?"

"And exactly how is that supposed to work? By speaking backwards Latin?"

He shrugged again.

"I couldn't say and I don't really care. I'm not paid to. I'm just supposed to get the clay and then find some book the Shaa' Kalyd stole. It outlines the process. Pequire had a line on it, he said. I assume he didn't tell you?"

"We didn't speak much."

He scrutinized my face, so I didn't react. Nor did I glance at my pack. I thought of blank paper, of white snow, until he seemed convinced I wasn't hiding what I was hiding. Then he turned his focus on Reno.

"Your friend looks as though he won't hang in much longer. Should I get him a blanket? It's going to be light soon, but there's still a few hours before the Western Union opens. Enough time for us all to get some rest."

Reno's eyes were wide but blank; his jaw slack. He was asleep but didn't know it. Looking at him, it amazed me I ever thought we were on the same page. I must have been mesmerized by his face, by his body, and not seen what should have been obvious. I hated him at that moment for tricking me, and hated myself more for letting Bush see that he had.

I nudged Reno harder than I needed to and he jolted, features tightening, lights coming back behind his eyes. He looked at me with a moment's annoyance, but it dissolved once he got his bearings. He wiped his mouth with the back of his hand and shook his arms.

"I think we're good," I said. "Some coffee or tea wouldn't hurt, though. If you have it."

I smiled, which no doubt looked as unnatural as it felt.

*

The three of us were in Bush's car a few hours later—Reno driving while Bush, now wearing a fresh white shirt under a tan linen suit, sat in the back with his pistol trained on us. We were heading back into

Port Said so Bush could have the money wired over for the box of clay sliding around in the trunk. I finally felt good about things; confident Reno and I were going to get paid, and pleased I had the book to sell for even more later. By the time I unloaded it, Reno would be gone and I wouldn't have to split all the money I got for it. I didn't know how much longer it would keep me going, but I was betting on forever.

I'd have settled, though, for enough to get me out of Port Said.

I watched the windows for any Shaa' Kalyd that might be following. I didn't think getting to the wire service would be problem, but waiting around for the money transfer would be painful. The longer it took, the more exposed we were, and the more likely the Shaa' Kalyd would find us. Port Said was big and multicultural, but Reno and I didn't quite fit in, and since Bush wouldn't leave the box with us and there was no way I trusted him enough to take it inside to get our money, our only option was to go in together—all three of us—and hope we weren't noticed.

I looked over at Reno and remembered how we'd met, and all the cons we'd pulled to get us to where we were. We really did make a good team for a while, and it was sad, in a way, that this would be the end of it, but despite his looks and everything else it was clear I could no longer trust him. He was more in love with his sister and fixing his past than he was grifting with me. Maybe these were things he could work out of his system in time, maybe he could go home and find some sort of closure, but if he did he wouldn't be the same Reno, and that Reno was the one I needed. The one that fit with me. It wasn't love—love is a word people made up to describe being too chickenshit to face the world alone—but it was nice to have someone on my page for a while. If only he'd stayed there. That's how it went, I supposed. And that was exactly how Reno would go.

We reached the Western Union just after it opened. I had on a hijab to disguise me from any stray Shaa' Kalyd while Reno just kept his hat pulled down and carried the Tinaldam inside. We were all too afraid to leave it in the trunk in the heat, even though it hadn't yet really warmed up. Plus we wanted to keep it in sight. Once we stepped through the glass door of the wire service, Reno put the box down and I handed him my pack. I couldn't afford to be encumbered, and with Bush carrying that pistol and the Shaa' Kalyd skulking around, the last thing I needed was to be off-balance. Reno hesitated a second, then took my pack before I followed Bush in to get out money.

The Western Union desk was the counter of a small shop in the middle of Port Said that sold everything from snacks to cheap electronics. There were handwritten signs everywhere. I couldn't read them, but knew from experience the sorts of things they were offering. Essentially, anything I wanted, all at a price higher than I'd pay elsewhere. It was a one-stop shop, its own mini-bazaar, and was the sort of place I tried to keep at a distance. The clientele were either people too poor to be a good score or were up to things that couldn't go through proper channels without flagging attention. Things like, say, wiring large sums of money to pay for an item stolen multiple times and involved in the death of at least two people. You don't handle that sort of thing through your corner bank.

The man behind the counter fit right in. He was dressed in a brown galabia and white headwrap. His eyes were red and moist, and the bags under them drooped down his tanned face far enough that they started to shift toward black. White stubble poked out of his jowls like tiny wires, and he stared at us as we approached the desk like the uninvited imposition we were.

He and Bush exchanged words in Masri. They sounded harsh, but I was no judge since everything anybody had said to me since arriving in Egypt sounded harsh. The man eventually threw up his arms and slammed an old rotary phone down on the counter before muttering and drifting to the back of the shop. I took a few steps sideways to watch him as he pulled aside the curtain there and stepped past. I glimpsed a thin mattress on the floor before the curtain closed again.

"How long is this going to take?" I asked, but Bush hushed me while he spoke into the phone. He didn't say much, choosing instead to do a lot of listening. Eventually he aggressively snapped his fingers at me and pointed to a ballpoint pen across the counter. I imagined for a moment jamming it through his hand but reminded myself I should get my money first. So instead I smiled insincerely and handed him the pen. He ordered the person on the other end to go ahead, then wrote down a long series of numbers.

"Hey!" he shouted, then again something in Masri, and the man returned from the back, only he acted differently, more uncomfortable with the two of us. Was it even the same person? Every idiot blends together after a while.

Bush pointed at his note and then said a few more words in Masri. The man shook his head, said in English "Go go go," and crossed his arms. Bush pointed at the car, then stabbed the note again with his finger. He followed that with a hard poke to the clerk's chest, hard enough that the old man stumbled. Bush said one more thing which turned the man red, but he snatched the note and started entering it into his machine.

"Not long," he said. "He won't be able to pay you in cash, obviously, but he'll give you a certified money order you can take to the bank."

"How much can you pay in cash?" I asked the man at the machine. He replied with more yelling, more hand waving. I turned to Bush.

"Can you ask this guy how much I can get in cash? Reno and I are going to need some to get out of Port Said before the Shaa' Kalyd find us."

"I don't think you need to worry about him, pigeon," Bush said. "That bird has flown."

I looked back at the door. I saw my pack there, and the Tinaldam, but Reno was gone.

"Oh, shit," I probably said.

I dashed over to my pack, not wanting to believe what I suspected. But when I got there and saw the contents rummaged through, I knew what I wouldn't find.

"No no no," I kept muttered.

"What's wrong?" Bush smirked, peering over my shoulder.

"It's gone. He took it. The book," I blurted. "He took the book."

"What book?"

"The book. *The* book."

"What? You had a copy of the book?"

But I wasn't listening to him. I was too busy running outside to scan the street for Reno. I didn't see him. I didn't see him anywhere.

"He took it. He took the goddamn book."

Behind me, the door burst open and Bush charged out, carrying the box of Tinaldam. He put it on the ground by the car and reached for his keys.

"I don't know which way he went," I said. "But he can't have gone far. We should be able to catch up with him."

"I'll find him," Bush said. "But you're not coming with me."

"What are you talking about? We had a deal."

"We had a deal for the Tinaldam, not for the book."

I glared at him.

"We had a deal," I said, clenching my fist.

That's when the pistol reappeared in his hand.

"Our deal is done, pigeon."

I looked at the barrel. Then at his eyes to be sure.

"What about my money?" I said.

He popped open the trunk.

"Money for what? You don't have anything my employers need. Which means you're of no use to them any longer."

That what I was afraid of hearing. I was too far to reach him and too close to run. I wouldn't have even made it back inside the shop.

"You don't have to do this. You can just leave with the Tinaldam. I don't need any money for it. I don't need the book."

"It's not that simple. I can already tell you're going to be trouble. And my employers don't like trouble."

"Right here? In the street?"

He didn't reply. He just pointed the pistol.

That's when I noticed someone madly sprinting toward us. He was lanky, dressed in a loose shirt and slacks, and I knew right away who it was before I even saw his missing hand. And once I saw him, I spotted his one-handed brothers also running toward us from opposite directions on the street. There were over a dozen of them, more than I'd seen in the temple, moving in waves from all directions to converge on us. There wasn't much time; I screamed and pointed.

"He's got it! He's got the Tinaldam! He's got it!"

Bush was confused, then turned and saw what I saw.

"Shit!" he said, and dropped the pistol in his pocket to free up his hands. Once he did so, I darted back inside the shop and ducked near the window. Bush heaved the box of clay into the trunk. The Shaa' Kalyd I'd first seen was practically on top of him, and as he leapt he threw something at Bush I couldn't immediately make sense of. Bush pivoted the last second before it struck, the cultist right behind. He fired the pistol from inside his pocket. The man's neck exploded.

I felt the sound through the window, not sure who I was rooting for. The clerk cowered behind the counter, and if it weren't for the gunfire I might have rushed over and strangled him for calling the Shaa' Kalyd. Or maybe I would have kissed him for saving me from Bush. It was complicated, and in the chaos I didn't have time to get my emotions sorted.

The Shaa' Kalyd spasmed on the ground as blood spurted from his neck, but Bush didn't notice. He was too busy struggling with the severed hand the dead man had thrown at him. It scrambled up Bush's chest like a huge pale spider, leaving behind a dark wet trail. I was petrified, but Bush never lost his calm. He grabbed the hand off his throat before it could get a hold and threw it to the ground. It landed on its back, fingers moving in a frenzy. Bush drove his heel into it before it could right itself.

More Shaa' Kalyd raced forward as Bush slammed his trunk shut and fired indiscriminately into the mob. I didn't see how many cultists he hit, but I expected it was one for each explosion. And there were a lot of explosions. It's why I kept my head down.

Bush cracked off a few more shots to keep the clustering Shaa' Kalyd from getting too close, then leapt into his car. I looked out the window at him, but he didn't look back. He'd forgotten about me, just as the Shaa' Kalyd had, as the engine revved to life. Before I could wonder if there were too many Shaa' Kalyd to get through, the car's wheels spun black and Bush peeled away as fast as the asphalt would let him. Hands and bodies bounced off the car as he plowed through the crowd of Shaa' Kalyd. When the smoke cleared I saw anyone still standing chase after Bush and the box of Tinaldam in his trunk—some on foot, some breaking the windows of old cars and hopping inside. Behind them a flock of disembodied hands followed, leaping across the hot asphalt like frogs in pursuit. I kept out of sight until the last of them had gone.

I decided I'd had enough. I grabbed my pack and shoveled all my stuff back inside. The clerk hesitantly peeked over the top of the counter looking frazzled and insecure. I stripped off my hijab and gave him a look intended to scare him as much as possible.

"I don't suppose the money came through?" I asked, and he started screaming and throwing anything within arm's reach at me. I managed to dodge most of it, but when I got winged by a steel wrench and my arm went numb I knew it was time to put as much distance between me and the shit show as possible.

"If I find out you said anything about me to anyone, I'm going to come back here and gut you!" I screamed, then ran out the door and in the opposite direction from the one Bush and the Shaa' Kalyd had gone in. I had no idea where I was going to go, just as long as I was as far away as possible from the police sirens I heard getting louder.

I ran and kept running until I couldn't anymore. When I finally reached the end of my strength I stumbled into a random alley and collapsed behind a bin of garbage. It smelled like shit, but I didn't care. I was struggling to block what I'd just escaped from my mind. But I couldn't. It kept replaying over and over. The adrenaline was burning away until only the shock was left. I shook uncontrollably and I burst into tears, heaving and sobbing and wishing I could forget everything I'd seen over the past few days. I should have stifled it, kept quiet and in control, but I couldn't. I couldn't do it. My body was betraying my trust just as everyone else had. Even under the baking Egyptian sun, I felt cold. Without anything. Alone.

The one person I'd trusted was Reno, and he was gone. He left without a word, without considering me or where I'd end up. He left as though he never cared about me at all. And, worse, he'd stolen the book. The chip I'd been hanging onto to get me out of trouble. He stole it from me after everything we'd done and gone through together, stole it and left me with nothing. He'd fucked me in so many ways I couldn't count them all, and my swelling anger was so great that I hoped Bush would find him and leave his bullet-ridden corpse on the side of the road to be devoured by vultures. Even that seemed too good for him, too good for the person who broke my trust and ruined my life. I hoped Reno got back home and found his sister dead. Brutally murdered. Maybe then the scales would start to even out.

My anger helped me calm down. I wiped my eyes on the tail of my shirt and my nose on the back of my hand. Fuck him. I'd been in worse straits and kept my head. Fuck him and his fucking sister. I wasn't going to let them stop me.

So what if I'd lost everything? So what if I had no big score, no Reno, no box of Tinaldam or rare book? So what if I had no money, or food, or change of clothes? And so what if it was only a matter of time before the Shaa' Kalyd realized they still wanted me dead? Why should I care? They were all just obstacles, and I could overcome obstacles. That's what I did. I overcame.

When my breath was finally under control and my arm no longer throbbing, I stood and slung my pack over my shoulders. There were still sirens but they were miles away, and if they were all over there, dealing with the dead Shaa' Kalyd and the escaping Weldon Bush and Reno, then no one would be over here keeping an eye on the cars parked haphazardly on the baking afternoon side streets of Port Said.

The Pontiac I found had to have been about thirty years old, and it coughed and it choked but it ran when I crossed its ignition wires the way Reno once taught me. With my pack in the passenger seat, I put all my weight on the gas pedal and aimed the car straight across the

Suez and as far away from the canal as I could get. Once the tank was empty, I'd find a way to get it refilled or get someone to drive me further away. The last thing I was going to do was get stuck. Not in Port Said. Not in any place ever again.

Acknowledgments

My thanks to John Joseph Adams, Sam Cowan, Ellen Datlow, Paul Finch, Stephen Jones, S. T. Joshi, Claude Lalumière, David Nickle, Jon Padgett, Brian J. Showers, Justin Steele, and to all the other editors who have bought my stories over the years and to all the readers who have enjoyed reading them.

SIMON STRANTZAS, Toronto, 2023

Publication History

"Antripuu" was first published in *Nightmare* No. 81 (July 2019); reprinted in *Best New Horror 31.*

"Black Bequeathments" was first published as a chapbook by Dim Shores, 2019.

"Circle of Blood" was first published in *Exile Book of New Canadian Noir,* ed. Claude Lalumière and David Nickle (Exile Press, 2015).

"Clay Pigeons" is original to this collection.

"Doused by Night" was first published in *Looming Low,* Volume I, ed. Justin Steele and Sam Cowan (Dim Shores, 2017).

"First Miranda" was first published in *Terror Tales of the Ocean,* ed. Paul Finch (Gray Friar Press, 2015).

"In the Event of Death" was first published in *Black Wings 4,* ed. S. T. Joshi (PS Publishing, 2015).

"The King of Stones" was first published in *Mammoth Book of Folk Horror,* ed. Stephen Jones (Skyhorse, 2021); reprinted in *Best Horror of the Year* 14.

"So Much Potential" was first published in *Uncertainties 5,* ed. Brian J. Showers (Swan River Press, 2021).

"Thea Was First" is original to this collection.

"Vertices" was first published in *Vastarien* 4, No. 1 (Spring 2021).

Printed in the USA
CPSIA information can be obtained
at www.ICGtesting.com
CBHW080945260324
5792CB00010B/71

9 781614 984214